ZOMBOSIS

S. G. BANSRAJ

~Accept full responsibility for leaving your fate up to anyone other than yourself~

Disclaimer:
This is a work of fiction. All characters, locations, and businesses are purely products of the author's imagination and are entirely fictitious. Any resemblance to actual people, living or dead, or to businesses, places, or events is completely coincidental.

Zombosis by S. G. Bansraj

ACT 1
DESPAIR

Survivor Group Nightmare

The world is a dark place, full of hate and greed
Humanity is cruel and vile
It is a pathogen to the Earth
Cleanse the host of the evil invaders
Their voices forever silenced
No longer would they be able to justify their sins
A fitting end to the human parasite

~Sometimes reality is worse than your nightmares~

1

BEGINNING OF THE NIGHTMARE

[Day 1]

~There is a right time for everything~

THE DOOR TO THE lecture room opened slowly, and all eyes gazed upon the student that entered. Dan was late for class again, but it didn't particularly bother him.

The lecturer paused his discussion and waited until Dan was seated before continuing. His eyes narrowed and remained fixed on the tardy student.

Dan stared at the almost illegible writing in his notebook, avoiding the lecturer's yellow eyes, which glared at the class like searchlights. He didn't like small lecture rooms, like this one, at all — it was a bit harder to avoid the attention of the lecturer here than in one of the large halls.

Scribbled names and graffiti covered the wooden finish on the desk. Dan had drawn a little owl to mark the spot he usually took when he attended class.

He began doodling something in his notebook, right next to the cartoon of himself driving a stake into the heart of a vampire. Only after five minutes did he realize that he had completely zoned out. He tried to focus.

He was seated next to Barry, who was busy watching videos on his computer and not paying the slightest attention to the lecture. The glowing yellow eyes had shifted their view to the first row of students, far away from Dan. He attempted to listen to what was being taught by the lecturer but eventually gave up, just as he always did.

"Why the hell do I come to this class?" whispered Dan.

"You say that every time," replied Barry, chuckling.

"What is he saying? How do you turn on the subtitles?"

The entire class looked completely attentive, but not a single person could decipher the lecturer's coded language. His words appeared to be made from a combination of languages, including one from a long-lost ancient civilization. His accent was likened to the infamous vampires of old, so the students had nicknamed him "the Count."

He looked like a vampire too, or at least like some beast from the underworld. Around his eyes were several dark, sunken rings, which made it look like he wore two pairs of spectacles. Deep creases locked his face in an eternal, menacing smile, and his skin was pale and wrinkly — obviously, his eternal life didn't mean eternal youth. He was even draped in a black cloak over his gothic suit. The only thing that was missing was a coffin to sleep in — it must have been in his castle or graveyard or wherever he lived. His eyes removed all doubt of his alignment with the forces of evil. Anyone unfortunate enough to make contact with those yellow eyes was cursed into a petrified state, at least temporarily.

Dan couldn't help but be distracted by Barry's

computer. A video was playing featuring a man with fruits for hands being chased by rabid (obviously fruit-loving) animals.

Barry trembled violently as he tried to restrain his laughter, and even though he thought no one noticed, everyone did. But not one person was prepared to tell the abnormally hairy and terrifyingly large Barry to shut up and be still. Even the Count knew that his death stare would have no effect on a magic-resistant giant.

Dan groaned and tried once more to focus on the lecture, but it quickly became obvious that he wasn't going to actually benefit from listening. He should have known this before he set foot in class. However, attending a lecture, even while learning nothing, made him feel a little less guilty after skipping as many classes as he did.

His degree was just another unplanned step in his life, which had neither goal nor direction. He lived in the moment and faced life as it came at him. *There's a right time for everything, and now isn't the time for this*, he would often say before tossing aside his reports and procrastinating until the very last day.

"Ah! Ah! Ah!" laughed the Count, in a tone that perfectly mimicked the old vampire stereotype. His teeth were bared, yellow and jagged, and his eyes opened wide with red capillaries branching through the curry-coloured sclera. The class immediately responded with their own laughter, which was cut short by the explosive sound of thunder.

The small, meat locker of a classroom had not a single window, but Dan knew there were no rain clouds in the sky. The thunder was suspiciously supernatural. Or perhaps it was nothing more than someone tumbling over furniture in an adjoining room.

"See me in the lab after class for the results of your assignment." The Count's final words of the class were the first Dan understood.

The students followed their lecturer out, excluding Barry, who hadn't realized the class was over, and Dan.

"What the hell are you watching?" Dan asked Barry, looking at the screen.

"My daily dose of essential viral videos," replied Barry in a voice that sounded too high-pitched for someone of his enormous size.

"Let's just go and get our assignments back." Dan slid his backpack onto his shoulder.

In his backpack was one book, a pen and a folded, white lab coat – simplicity was the most useful thing he'd learned in two years of tertiary education. He delighted in the suffering of the first-year students who had massive backpacks crammed with huge textbooks and neatly organized writing equipment.

Dan and the giant made their way up a flight of stairs and into a hallway on the upper floor. The hall was completely empty and quiet; very rarely did Dan see students here. The sharp disinfectant in the air shot up his nose and stung his brain.

Everything in this place was squeaky clean and blindingly bright. It was undoubtedly the cleanest place on campus, and perhaps, in the entire world. Grime from the bottom of shoes would just disintegrate to preserve the cleanliness. Dan used it to clean his shoes whenever he needed to.

At the far end of the hall was the principal's office, guarded by a black metal door. Dan was sure that he'd heard screams of torture coming from inside that dreaded room during one of his shoe-sanitizing visits.

Dan pushed open the doors at the other end of the hall and entered the lab. The smell was the same, only ten million times worse, but the view couldn't be more different. Where the walls should have been, thick barks of trees curled in all directions. The leaves that sprouted varied in sizes and shapes — most were green, with a few purple ones mixed in. A stone walkway and wooden tables interrupted the short green grass that covered the floor. From the ceiling hung flowers which produced the light that illuminated the entire room, and shimmering in the far corner, a small stream of water turned a little wooden waterwheel.

Most of the class had already gathered and were anxiously awaiting their results. Dan certainly didn't share their excitement. He wasn't too keen on studying this course. In fact, he downright hated it and was cross with his crew who had convinced him to do it.

"TWO?" someone shouted as he received his report. "I got two out of ten?"

Standing in front of the Count was a pear-shaped, bearded young man by the name of Omar. Omar swayed as if about to faint, his paper clutched in one hand and his hair in the other. His eyes looked like overripe berries about to explode from the stress of their own juices. Omar looked much paler than Dan thought possible, and his eyes and mouth were open wide in disbelief.

Classic Omar, Dan thought.

Dan's stomach churned as his anxiety over his own results spiked. He'd always been dreadfully afraid of failure — not just failing an exam but failing at anything. That's not to say he was successful at everything he attempted. In fact, he'd failed at a lot of things. Being the smallest, weakest kid in high school, he lost every sporting event he'd competed in, and his soccer team never scored a single goal. But even after he dusted himself off and kept on trying, he never grew to accept failure.

This course is for babies. There's no way I can get a...

Two — the same mark as Omar, who was in the foetal position on the grass floor with his thumb in his mouth. Dan looked down at Omar, whose tears were irrigating the grass. He gulped and his mouth went dry. He suddenly remembered that one time he had researched the name for the fear of failure — atychiphobia. He could practically feel it hovering over his head as he stared at the number "2" scribbled in red ink (or blood) at the top of his paper.

Barry had done one better, getting three marks. Steve, another member of Dan's crew, flipped back his dreadlocks and smiled in satisfaction as he received his paper. "Bless up!"

Steve had gotten the highest mark in class — eight out of ten.

"These answers are correct! There's no way I could get two marks!" blurted out Dan.

"What do you mean? These calculations are wrong! I did not teach you this," replied the Count.

Dan had gotten too close and could see the Count's face in extreme detail. The vampire-teacher's wrinkles looked like a badly misshapen puzzle and his yellow, jagged teeth were covered in plaque and beets.

"RAAAAAAAAAAAWWWR!" Dan completely lost his patience.

He lifted the Count up by his neck until the wrinkled bag of bones was completely overhead. He bawled again as he hurled the Count to the back of the room.

The little man, who was barely five feet tall, sailed through the air with bulging eyeballs and a shriek from his smelly oral orifice. He crashed into the waterwheel, sending it flying out a nearby window. The water was tainted with the vampire's blood, as he lay completely still. No one in the room spoke or budged an inch.

Dan spun on his heel and kicked open the lab doors. He stomped out without looking back. His crew followed him.

Actually, that didn't happen — he had only hurled the Count across the room in his own mind. Dan was angry, but not nearly enough to engage in combat with an alleged ancient vampire, at least not without a suitable weapon.

He crammed the paper into his backpack and left the room with all eyes on him, just the same as when he had arrived late to class. Barry, Omar, and Steve followed him into the hall and kept up with his brisk pace as he exited the building. Dan was annoyed that none of his friends had added their complaints but didn't dwell on it.

"The university really sank to a new low when they decided to hire a lecturer who was born before it was established," Dan added one more insult to meet his daily quota for the Count.

"Before the establishment of modern spoken language." Omar only decided to speak when he was far out of the vampire's earshot.

"Did you smell his breath? It's like he ate a cow pie before class," Dan added another pointless comment.

No one laughed at his crude humour and after a short awkward period of silence, Omar simply said, "Oh well, I am going back to my apartment then."

Fickle Omar was clearly not as bothered by his grades as Dan was. Apparently, he'd already come to terms with his failure and just wanted to get away from everyone. He skipped off gleefully, like a childish amnesiac.

For a moment, Dan was still fuming mad. Then his anger transferred to his stomach and it growled ferociously. There was no point in being both angry and hungry.

"Time to eat!" he declared as he stomped his way across the freshly cut grass.

Barry and Steve followed him quietly, as Omar headed the other way.

***

It was around noon and the sun shone brightly. Tiny white puffs of slowing moving clouds dotted the clear blue sky. Students had taken refuge under the trees and buildings, avoiding the burning rays. The tropical island was in the rainy season but with such sweltering heat, it could have easily been mistaken for the desert season.

Dan walked across the stone courtyard, with Barry to his left and Steve on his right. Other students scrambled to the shade as if the sun would melt their skin off. At the time, it didn't seem impossible for someone to spontaneously combust.

The sun didn't bother Dan very much. In fact, he actually liked the feeling of warmth on his skin. The glare was a problem though. His spectacles were no use in diminishing the sun's luminosity or the dazzle from the stones beneath his feet.

Barry's normally wild and dry matted mane was drenched and flat. His green plaid shirt was soaked with smelly sweat and his ginormous trousers looked as if two packs of rival wolves had taken turns urinating on them. His giant form dwarfed the other two in comparison, though Dan was a bit taller than average himself. Barry had an awkward walk — as if he were stumbling forward to help carry his massive weight. The soles of his shoes had been worn away on one side, making his flat feet collide with the ground at odd angles. Barry was essentially an anthropomorphic mammoth with shoes.

Steve advanced forward impatiently, grinding his teeth as they approached the entrance to the campus food court. Steve was the shortest of the three, and he hid his face from the sun with his black, knotted dreadlocks. Whether this improvised umbrella deflected the ultraviolet radiation or trapped it to cook Steve's head was up for debate.

Barry pushed open the double glass doors and twisted his enormous body so that he could fit between them. Dan and Steve walked in the wake he left as he parted the crowd of people inside the food court. It was much cooler than outside, and Barry's sweating immediately stopped. In fact, it was so cold that a group of students was building a snowman in the corner.

The rectangular tables normally seated three people — or one Barry — on either side. He displaced all those seated at the nearest table, like a whale pushing aside sardines. Dan threw himself onto a seat on the opposite side of Barry's table. Steve, who had almost died from heatstroke, just barely managed to crawl onto a seat.

The area was packed with students who had occupied all the benches. Barry was the only person capable of getting a table when the place was this full, as it always was around lunchtime.

On one side of the food court were five little restaurants all in a line. Each had one countertop, two grumpy workers, and no internal seating. At the opposite end were three large shops with four grumpy workers each and seating separate from the rest of the food court. They were all ordinary in appearance except for Pizza Dungeon, which was lined with grey bricks and guarded by suits of armour.

Steve volunteered to stand in the long line that stretched from one of the fast-food outlets. He stood behind a hungry man who held his round, growling belly as if to suppress the rumbling. At the front of the line was a petite girl with purple hair who had just ordered a bucket of chicken that weighed more than she did.

"Jah..." Steve whispered weakly to himself, his spirit broken by the thought of his long wait for nutrition.

Barry whipped out his computer and proceeded to watch his videos again. His giant fingertips were twice the size of the keys, but he somehow managed to type faster than he could talk. He cranked the volume up to the maximum, but the speakers produced mere squeaks amid the noisy conversations of rowdy, hungry students. Even the sounds from the jumbo wall-mounted screens were completely drowned out.

Dan was not the type of person who would openly talk about his feelings. His friends had no idea that he had the biggest crush on the girl who had just walked in with her clique of friends.

Her name was Kelly, and she was a pretty girl with perfect skin, raven hair and eyes always accented with thick, black eyeliner. She was guarded by a tall, slender girl and a stocky guy who looked like he spent three hours in the gym every day.

Dan's eyes were fixed upon her as she gracefully glided to a table that had been reserved for her by the rest of her entourage. Despite sharing half of their classes for almost a year, Dan was unsuccessful in penetrating the shield that was put up by Kelly's crew.

Still, he spent more time planning how he could ask her out than preparing for his classes, labs, and exams combined. He wrapped his fingers around the dog tag that dangled from his silver necklace.

She sat at the far end of the court, and her musclebound friend put his jacked arm around her. Her eyes strayed in Dan's direction. He immediately turned to Barry, who still hadn't shifted his view from the computer screen.

Dan spent almost as much time inside his own mind as he did in reality. In his dream world, he had destroyed thousands of evil dragons, rotting zombies, and abhorrent demons, perhaps even millions. Now he was saving Kelly from her wicked werewolf boyfriend.

As Dan delved deeper into his daydream, Barry finally spoke, "Interesting..."

"What is?" asked Dan.

"It has begun..." said Barry in the most ominous tone he could muster.

"What has?"

"The zombie apocalypse."

"What?"

"No more school."

Dan didn't bother to ask for Barry's explanation this time. He just sat quietly and stared.

"Look at this video." Barry pointed a gigantic, sausage-like finger at his computer screen.

If this video is anything like the fruit hands video, then it should be funny, at the very least, thought Dan, convincing himself to temporarily trade his view of Kelly for a look at Barry's computer. The video was dark and the sound was barely audible over the noise in the food court. Dan could only just make out a silhouette of a person tackling someone to the ground and violently clawing and biting the victim.

"Looks like a poor student film," said Dan.

"They say the infection can be transferred to humans and may possibly be airborne." Barry still didn't shift his eyes from the screen.

"Who filmed this?" asked Dan, unconvinced of the video's legitimacy.

Steve had arrived and placed three greasy boxes on the table when Dan asked, "So, do we have vampires or werewolves on campus now?"

"I just said 'the zombie apocalypse', man. How can you have vampires and werewolves in the zombie apocalypse?" said Barry, chewing on his enormous fingernails with coffee-stained incisors.

"Now that you mention it, the Count is clearly a vampire. Maybe that's him in the video! We can use it to get him fired! I also strongly suspect that dude over there is a werewolf." Dan pointed his nose at Kelly's burly friend whose body hair was as thick as a wolf's coat.

Dan opened his greasy box, trying not to get any oil on his fingers. It was like trying not to get wet while on a leaking pirogue about to go over a waterfall.

Steve squinted at the video with his mouth ajar. "What the ass? Dat is some kinda joke or what, bai?" He flipped back his dreadlocks and took a seat next to Dan.

"Barry is convinced that the zombie apocalypse has begun," said Dan with a grin. "But there's no way zombies could possibly destroy humanity before the machines do!"

"I like aliens, bai!" said Steve. "Alien apocalypse, bai!"

"There's no way an alien civilization would destroy us before we destroy ourselves!" argued Dan.

"Yes, bai!"

"I'd rank the machine apocalypse as most likely, followed by zombies, and aliens last."

"No, bai!"

"They're zombies!" Barry pounded the table with his mammoth fist.

"We woulda hear ah official announcement if the students was in danger, bai," Steve continued.

Steve was the type that scared easily, while Barry actually liked being scared. Dan was more skeptical about events that seemed supernatural, despite constantly comparing perfectly normal human beings to vampires, werewolves, giants and other mythical creatures.

"You know, a zombie apocalypse might actually be a nice change of pace," said Dan, with a mouthful of succulent chicken.

"Be careful what you wish for, bai!" said Steve, shuddering at the thought of his chicken coming back to life for revenge. He closed his eyes and took a huge bite of the juicy fried meat.

Steve's food was the greasiest of the three. The chicken was submerged in oil and the potato wedges were plump after having absorbed as much as they could. On top of that, he had put a thick layer of blood-red tomato ketchup and pepper sauce. Unable to quell his disturbing thoughts of zombies, Steve felt nauseous and lost his appetite. One bite was like stabbing a blood-filled balloon with six daggers simultaneously. From that moment, Steve became a vegetarian.

Engulfed and almost completely smothered by all the noise, was a faint ringing. It took a few seconds for Dan to realize he was receiving a phone call. He removed a small, rectangular slate from his pocket and pressed it against his ear.

"Hello, good day!" he answered politely.

The voice at the other end spoke quickly and excitedly, like a rat that had just found a mountain of cheese.

Meanwhile, Steve raised his head, opened his mouth and breathed red fire like a dragon. He had eaten too much super spicy pepper sauce and was now heating the air with his flames.

"PEPPAAAAAAAAAA!" cried Steve, emitting so much heat that the nearby snowman melted.

No one even looked his way. The world's hottest pepper sauce transformed at least ten people into fire-breathing dragons daily. The effects lasted no more than five minutes, but in that time, not even a torrent of tears could extinguish the burning tongue.

"ZOMBIES! GHE-HEHEHE!" shouted someone from behind Dan.

A chubby guy joined them, metal braces tightly grasping all of his teeth. He wore a t-shirt with the words "Bag yourself up! You dead!" printed above the image of a zombie being shot in the head.

"Do you have a minute to hear the good news?" He bounced on his toes and clapped his fingertips.

"And what news is that, Augie?" Dan said as he glanced over to the far side of the food court.

Dan almost suffered a concussion when Augie's bulky bottom violently forced him to the centre of the bench.

"I just told you! We're in the beginning stages of a zombie outbreak! Now I finally get to put my zombie apocalypse survival plan to good use!" replied Augie with a broad grin.

Augie's face was always locked in a smile, whether it be baring his braced teeth, or with closed, drool-pasted lips. Everything he said was delivered as a joke as if he were a clown by profession.

"We should take a bottle of pepper sauce and have Steve burn down all the zombies," suggested Dan.

"I've seen every zombie movie ever made and my plan is totally foolproof. We're definitely going to survive this!" Augie continued.

"I think you should consider the pepper sauce. I'm sure you didn't."

Augie unfolded a large piece of yellow, heavily curry-stained paper onto the table. The edges were frayed and torn, and the creases were uneven. Printed on the surface was an accurate map of the campus, which Augie had spent a great deal of time colouring with crayons. It looked like an old treasure map that had fallen into the hands of a child.

"Everything is colour-coded. The red areas are the zombie hotspots, which we have to avoid, and the green ones are supplies like food..."

Augie's drooling was all that interrupted his nonstop talking. His eyes were fixed on the oily food as if he were having a conversation with chickens instead of his friends. He only paused from talking to stop his saliva from leaking out of his mouth.

"Anyway, I have an entomology lab to get to this afternoon. Five hours long and it starts in ten minutes, so I guess I better head out," said Dan, interrupting Augie.

Dan did not enjoy sitting still for long, boring laboratory sessions. But he found entomology to be interesting for the most part, and the lab sessions were usually bearable.

After the food had been consumed, the oil remained in pools at the bottom of the boxes. Some of this oil had been used to fuel Steve's fire breath, which had ceased. Grey smoke still emanated from his mouth, and his eyes were red and puffy from crying.

The food court emptied as students rushed to their afternoon classes. Kelly had disappeared with them. Barry finally looked away from his computer as they all got up and marched off.

Augie explained the details of his plan along the way to the lab. Everyone ignored him and occasionally nodded to pretend that they were listening. Augie's excitement never once dwindled.

As they arrived at the doors to the laboratory, Steve and Barry bade farewell and headed up the staircase to their lecture, while Augie went across the paved walkway to a baby-blue building for his favourite mathematics class.

2

RIOT!

[Day 1]

~All human beings are vampires that leech from others~

DAN TOOK A SEAT on a wooden stool behind a large, white lab bench. This laboratory didn't have the pungent odour of the Count's and was twice as large — it easily held hundreds of students, with room to spare. There was no grassy floor or trees sprouting up from the ground. Almost everything in here was a clean, bright white. The walls, tables and even the stools looked like they had a fresh coat of glossy, white paint. Each of the two hundred students was cloaked in a lab coat as white as the walls, serving as a form of purposeless camouflage.

Against the walls stood animal skeletons — an elephant and rhinoceros flanked a human skeleton. In the centre of the room stood the bones of a Tyrannosaurus rex, its head just an inch from the ceiling. Out of all the skeletons and preserved organisms displayed along the walls, Dan always ignored the giant foot-long centipede (dead, of course), which, he had concluded, was by far the creepiest thing he had ever seen. With his over-vivid imagination, he could picture that abomination of nature wrapping its clawed legs and segmented body all the way around his neck. He would have taken his chances with a T. rex over a centipede any day.

Most of the class was already seated, with a few latecomers filtering in. Among them was Omar, who walked very lazily, almost zombie-like. He dragged his feet as he made his way to a vacant stool on Dan's bench. He yawned and scratched his butt. If he were an animal, he would have probably been a sloth.

Omar seemed to prefer spending all his time in his apartment, rather than on campus. Dan knew he enjoyed solitude and privacy, but, above all else, Omar loved video games. He spent more time playing games than everything else in his life combined. Labs and lectures only kept him away from his true passion.

Dan liked playing video games and skipping lectures almost as much as Omar, but he preferred to spend his time on campus. Dan fed off the positive energy that oozed from the young, enthusiastic student body, particularly the first-years.

The murmuring ceased immediately as a door burst open at the front of the lab. Out came a jade-green crocodile, apparently walking on its hind legs and muscular tail. Its voice rattled terrifyingly as it flailed its head from side to side.

Nestled between all the beast's armoured scales was a soft, underbelly that was being clutched by a pair of beefy, hairy arms.

"You're alright, mate! You're alright!" shouted the crocodile wrestler before suplexing the reptile over his head as if it were an inflated balloon animal.

The croc's head cracked the floor on impact, and it lay there, completely still. The class gasped in unison.

"Is it dead?" asked Omar, his eyes welling up.

"No, just knocked out," replied Dan.

"G'day, everyone! We have an exciting lab exercise today, as usual," said Dr. Graham. "The specimen you see behind me is commonly known as the 'dragon-head croc'. Its skin is so hard that it's virtually impervious, and it often uses its large head as a battering ram. Right now, it's just playing dead."

The beast was on its back and its soft belly slowly swelled and deflated as it breathed; it could have been confused for a dead animal if not for this giveaway sign.

One girl in the class, unsure if applause was appropriate, clapped her hands together lazily and stopped when no one joined in. Dr. Graham tipped his brown cowboy hat and nodded.

Edgar Graham was an academic adventurer who left his homeland to explore the tropical forests of Cupia, where he fell in love with the biodiversity — the wildlife and the even wilder women. He was utterly obsessed with his work and was fortunate enough to have married a woman who was equally as passionate about nature.

Dr. Graham was only five feet tall, maybe an inch or two more with his thick-soled boots. It was difficult to see him from where Dan and Omar sat until he jumped up onto a desk like a wild kangaroo. He wore a plaid shirt as green as the crocodile, tucked into a pair of faded blue jeans.

"Unfortunately, there'll be no silly crocs in this class." He spoke so loudly that the dragon-head croc twitched a little, while still lying on its back.

"Then why did he bring one to the class?" Dan whispered.

Omar shrugged and chuckled.

"Today we're observing arachnids. Some of the spiders you'll observe today are the deadliest things that you will ever come across!" continued Dr. Graham.

"Deadlier than the croc?" muttered someone in the front, close to Dr. Graham.

"This big baby won't hurt anyone," said Dr. Graham, pointing a short, stubby finger at the dragon-head croc. "It's often the small things that are the most dangerous!"

Dan glanced at Omar. Omar loved reptiles but absolutely dreaded insects and arachnids, especially spiders. His stories about all the times he had been attacked by spiders could have been made into an animated cartoon. Bathing, sleeping, driving, eating, playing video games — he was never safe. They were really out for him.

"The first part is simple. Just choose any three arachnid specimens, take notes of anatomical features, and suggest how they aid in their way of life. Oh, and please try not to get bitten because we don't have any antivenin," said Dr. Graham as he hopped off the desk.

Dan saved his laugher for the lecturer's punchline, but there was none. "Wait, what?"

Dr. Graham grabbed onto the dragon-head croc's tail and dragged it off into another room. His strength was remarkable for such a small man. It was rumoured that he had attained superhuman strength from a gem he found in the jungle.

On each of the long white benches were several

samples of arachnids to observe. The class had to work in pairs to quickly accomplish the assigned tasks in the allotted time. Dan didn't like random pairing because he always ended up with someone he had poor synergy with.

Omar, despite his laziness, was actually quite good at lab exercises and made an excellent lab partner. He wasn't a bad public speaker either — he had a lot of practice from addressing players in his favourite online video game.

Dan and Omar knew no one in this class other than each other, so they partnered up at the beginning of the semester like a pair of socially awkward penguins.

Dan retrieved the only notebook from his backpack and flipped to the section reserved for this class. While the Count's section was filled with drawings of vampires and vampire hunters, Dr. Graham's section had sketches of insects and arachnids. Even with all these drawings and scribbled notes, half of the pages in the book were still blank.

Omar, who was much less organized than Dan, pulled out a couple of random sheets of paper and an old, chewed-up yellow pencil. He held his backpack to his face, using it as a shield to hide from the spiders.

They secured some specimens to observe, none of which included a spider. In a glass box prison was a perfectly still, jet-black scorpion, which could have been mistaken for a statuette. Omar pressed his nose up against the glass to get a closer look. He cowered at even the tiniest spider, but this scorpion didn't seem to bother him in the slightest way, even with a tail as long as his forearm.

Dan's specimen was quite small and quite dead, so he placed it under a microscope to get a closer look. This device, in particular, had been fitted with a powerful but terribly energy-inefficient light bulb. Dan had ten minutes before it heated up like a miniature sun and incinerated the specimen.

"Small size, clawed feet, dorsoventral flattening..." he muttered as he took notes. "Obviously, the features of the tick are designed for its parasitic mode of life."

He didn't mention that it smelled horrible, only because the sharp scent was actually from the preservation concoction and not the tick itself. Still, he would have gladly included the odious odour in his report if he knew that it wouldn't affect his grade. Unfortunately for Dan, none of his lecturers shared his sense of humour — none of them seemed to have a sense of humour at all.

There was suspicion on campus (started by a cultish club called Students Against Artificial Intelligence — SAAI) that the lecturers were really lifeless robots who were activated just for work and nothing more. The basis for this preposterous presumption was in the lecturers' lack of empathy with struggling students along with completely unreliable anecdotal evidence of no lecturer having ever been seen outside the confines of the university. Robotics would certainly explain Dr. Graham's inhuman strength.

Omar looked through the microscope while Dan jotted down observations in his book.

"They are ectoparasitic, have mouthparts designed for withdrawing blood from a host, hemimetabolous development," said Dan to Omar as they began comparing notes. "Imagine how scary these would have been if they were the size of that scorpion. Humans would have gone extinct long ago!"

Ticks disgusted Dan — he hated all parasites. He also

hated people who acted like parasites, feeding off others while giving nothing in return. In his opinion, the worst human parasites were those who took credit for group projects after having contributed absolutely nothing.

***

Hours later, as the lab session was nearing its end, Dr. Graham addressed the class, "Okay, class, may I have your attention please, mates?"

The murmuring ceased as everyone faced their lecturer. He was just as calm as he usually was – he never appeared to be nervous about anything. Giant crocodile? More like playing with a baby! Speaking in front of hundreds of students? More like excitedly performing in front of an audience!

"Firstly, the lab report will be due one week from today," he said when there was absolute silence. "You can all finish up what you're doing right now, but no one is to leave early today. We have received information about some sort of rioting around the campus and have been asked to keep everyone inside until we have the all-clear. Just relax, you have an hour left in the session and I'm sure everything will be resolved by then."

"Did he say... rioting?" asked Omar, turning to Dan.

"Dieting, quieting, writing," replied Dan, trying to figure out if they misheard the words. "Yeah, definitely rioting."

Dan and Omar took their seats and began assembling their notes. Although Dr. Graham had tried to reassure the class that the situation was under control, it was obvious by the sudden shift from silent work to buzzing discussions that students were already concerned. Perhaps "rioting" was not an appropriate word to use in such an instance. The absence of empathy was more evidence to support SAAI's robot lecturers claim.

"Did he really expect to tell everyone that there is rioting going on right now and not have people panic?" asked Dan.

"They better not keep us here late!" said Omar. "I need to meet with my guild at quarter past six."

When Omar wasn't playing video games by himself, he was playing online with people from across the world, whom he had never met in person. He'd become quite the popular member of his gaming guild.

"Did you see that video about the infectious disease they say is on campus?" Dan asked Omar.

"No, what video?" replied Omar. "There are probably a lot of diseases on campus."

"Barry found a video about an infection on campus that turns people into zombies," Dan chuckled. "It would be really coincidental if this rioting was just a bunch of zombies killing everybody."

Dan didn't notice that everyone on the bench was listening in on the conversation until he was done speaking. The eavesdroppers all stared directly at him with dilated pupils and open jaws.

These people wouldn't really take a story about the walking dead on campus seriously, would they? Dan wondered.

They most definitely did! Omar sat slouched and sleepy-eyed, seemingly unconcerned, but everyone else began talking among themselves. Eventually, rumours had spread across the entire class, with each bench having a different version of the story. The bench closest to theirs was talking about mutants, and someone on a bench a bit further away was convincing everyone that hell was full and the dead had nowhere to go.

This lab had no windows except for little square glass panes in each door, so most students were unaware of the dying sunlight. Dan always stayed near doors to conveniently hurry in and sneak out. He glanced out the west-facing door window. The sun grew redder as it edged closer to the horizon. It had only half an hour before sleeping for the night.

With no official update on the situation and the rumours still circulating, the class was becoming panicked. Dan certainly didn't expect anyone to take a zombie hypothesis seriously. Perhaps the other students were bored and took the opportunity to exaggerate the situation. The ludicrous idea had spread like an easily communicable disease and the chief symptom began quickly manifesting throughout the class — fear.

Some of the students had started making phone calls when Dr. Graham spoke once again, "The rules of the lab still apply, mates! No communication devices allowed!"

All phones vanished from sight as he continued, "We still have no details about the riots, but for your own safety, please bear with us a while longer. It's getting late and most of you might want to leave before nightfall, so if we don't receive an all-clear in fifteen minutes, you will be required to leave anyway."

The university had made it mandatory to lock this lab at precisely 6:05 pm ever since someone tried to steal the T. rex.

Chattering began the instant Dr. Graham had spoken his last word. The fifteen-minute timeframe created a dense atmosphere of foreboding. Everyone scrambled to pack up their things.

"I think we would have been better off if he just lied," said Omar.

"Unless it's really serious," said Dan. "But if it's that bad, then the police should already be here."

The sun sank even lower in the orange sky and through the glass panes on the doors, the growing shadows outside were visible. The darkness itself was menacing, especially with the thought of the unknown chaos taking place outside. But they saw nothing unusual through the door — the tree that stood outside didn't move other than the occasional gentle rustle of its leaves. The riots could have been a joke if Dr. Graham had shown any trace of being a prankster.

Dan was becoming concerned as well, and many thoughts ran through his mind. He thought about what Augie had said about a zombie outbreak and while it sounded crazy earlier that day, it seemed somewhat plausible to him now.

"Did Augie ever tell you about his zombie apocalypse plan?" Dan asked Omar as soon as he was sure no one was listening.

"Oh yeah," said Omar. "I actually helped him come up with that. I was really bored that day."

Dan was not surprised. Omar had slain millions of virtual zombies throughout his gaming life.

"Well, if we assume that everybody outside is a zombie, then it may be possible to use that plan to get the hell out of here, right?" suggested Dan.

"I only saw his map once, but we basically just want to avoid the red zones and get to the meeting area at the library," explained Omar.

"What are the red zones?"

"The ones coloured red on the map."

Dan sighed. *Is he being serious? It almost makes me regret not listening to Augie's plan. Almost.*

"The library isn't that far. We can get there in under two minutes if we hurry," said Dan.

"You have your car, right? How 'bout we head to the parking lot and just drive out of here?" suggested Omar.

The parking lot was just as far away from their location as the library but in the opposite direction. It also happened to be closer to Omar's apartment. *This bum's priority is jumping online to play his video game!*

"Well, right now I expect that the roads are blocked with traffic and we don't want to get caught in that," said Dan, evaluating the situation. "The library is the safer route anyway, so we should be able to make it there without much trouble. From there, we can decide what we're gonna do."

Omar nodded in agreement as he rummaged through his beige messenger bag for his phone. The device was wedged between a bottle of soda and a large bag of cheese puffs. He kept it hidden and began typing a message. The crack that ran down the middle of the screen didn't affect its functionality.

"Dammit..." muttered Omar as his message failed to send.

"The network is probably overloaded right now. At least we know where to go from here." Dan glanced at the clock on the wall.

Seven more minutes.

"Overloaded? All the phones on campus couldn't possibly overload the network. The only way that could happen is if the entire country suddenly started making calls."

"Spooky."

By the final five minutes of the lab session, everyone was packed and engaged in nervous conversation. A group of students tried negotiating for more time, but Dr. Graham shook his head and pointed at the T. rex skeleton.

Nothing like this had ever happened before and no one was prepared (not counting two people with partial knowledge of a zombie apocalypse survival plan). The worst disaster to have devastated the campus was a sudden thunderstorm that eviscerated trees, drowned grass and sent rodents swimming; but this happened annually, so all but the first-year students were accustomed. There were no riots on the island, and no violent protests, except in Jumbieland, the controversially constructed prison colony. Things on campus were usually calm and quiet.

Dan and Omar discussed the route they would take to get to the meeting area, while everyone on the bench carried on their own conversations, too busy to eavesdrop.

Dr. Graham spoke once again, "Alrighty, mates, the lab time is at an end now. Goodbye!"

Everyone sat there quietly, staring at their lecturer, who just stared back at them coldly as if his battery had been discharged.

"What about the zombies?" shouted someone from the middle of the class.

"Zombies? In all my journeys to the thickest jungles

and hottest deserts, I have never encountered a zombie," Dr. Graham reassured the students.

Some of the fear melted away until he continued. "But perhaps I shall document them today."

With that, everyone went into full panic mode. Arms flew up in the air like tube men being suddenly inflated. One young fellow fainted, forcing tears to breach the eyelids of everyone around him in a chain reaction.

"Please be careful, mates. Take your usual mode of transport and head straight home. Travel in packs for safety."

Most of the students hurriedly made their way to the doors, like a herd of stampeding beasts. In the noise, only Dan heard him say, "We haven't seen or heard any sign of the riots in this area so we should be safe when vacating."

Graham doesn't appear to be worried at all. Perhaps the situation is not nearly as serious as it seems. Or maybe he doesn't actually know what's going on. Dan thought that the good doctor was just using the emotionless acting skills learned as a prerequisite for lecturing.

Through the lab doors that had been burst open, Dan saw that the sun had almost set. He and Omar waited until the frenzied egress ended. The doors swung back and forth, whining from the undeserved battering they had just been through.

"Let's leave now while we still have some sunlight. I don't think we want to be outside if the lights go out," said Dan.

Omar nodded in agreement and they headed to the door. Only one other student was left; she was speaking with the lecturer while twirling her bouncy locks. She bit her lip, which was as red as the blush on her cheeks, and giggled flirtatiously. However, Dr. Graham was only interested in locking up the lab.

Dan pushed the doors open and peered down the empty hall. There was no noise at all — even the footsteps of the student stampede had already faded. He and Omar went along the path they had planned. The building seemed almost completely empty as if it had been evacuated. Yellow light bulbs lit the path all the way through the building.

Dr. Graham exited the lab along with the seductress, who was now trying her best to expose some cleavage.

As Dan and Omar turned around the corner, there was the smash of breaking glass followed by a loud shout of "CRIKEY!" Then there was a scream of such high amplitude it stunned them both, as well as a nearby bird that plummeted to the ground and unintentionally buried its beak in the grass-covered soil.

Dan and Omar looked at each other, unsure if they should turn back or press forward. When they heard the fearless Dr. Graham holler, their legs automatically propelled them away. Even the fallen bird, who was pretending to look for worms after its embarrassing crash, wasted no time in darting off in an almost vertical ascent.

They continued with their initial plan to head to the library. Their footsteps echoed in the vacant building as they ran through. The lights in the hallway shone dimly and warded off the quickly approaching darkness.

As they exited the building, Dan looked back down the poorly lit corridor from which they had come. There was no one there — no Dr. Graham, no students, no angry mob, not even a single damn zombie. There was only an eerie shroud of darkness that was partially dispersed by the hall's lights. It was a bit disappointing, really. Dan expected something out of the ordinary but there was still nothing. His heart, disheartened by the deception of excitement, returned to its regular beat. There was no screaming, no shouting, no noise at all.

Dan and Omar stood on the paved open walkway and watched all around for any signs of the supposed rioting. The sun finally descended from view and only the light poles in the walkway provided illumination. The area still wasn't properly lit, as two of the light bulbs were blown, while another flickered dimly — cheap campus management.

Dan almost decided to turn around and walk back. *Maybe the dragon-head croc broke free and went after a distracted Dr. Graham for revenge.* He was beginning to convince himself that he'd been worried over nothing until some suspicious movement caught his attention.

In the distance, figures rushed about in the darkness. To their left, the black trees stood like titans, reaching up to the stars and groaning as the wind bent their ancient branches.

Beneath the trees, human-shaped figures moved energetically within the shadows, their identities concealed. *These must be the rioters*, he thought, jarred by the disorder. Dan noticed the dance of shadows from the corner of his eye as he began a sudden sprint across the walkway.

The people, who were nothing more than black silhouettes, darted about in the distance. Dan and Omar kept running, cries and screams just becoming audible; they sounded distant, but from all around. The sounds from the phantom figures travelled through open spaces, echoing off the walls, halls, and concrete floors. The more they pressed forward, the more plentiful the screams became.

They reached the end of the walkway, and Dan felt a small amount of relief that he was no longer in the open. The buildings on both sides narrowed the walkway into a corridor. If both ends of this corridor were blocked by rioters, they would have been trapped. They didn't stop to think of their next move. They darted down the short stretch, aware that any of the doors that lined the corridor could burst open at any time, engulfing them in angry rioters.

They made it to the final walkway on their route, which led directly to the library building. They slowed their pace and proceeded with caution. The courtyard was empty, but the food court on the opposite side had figures moving about inside. Dan remembered his suggestion about using the super spicy pepper sauce as flamethrower fuel. *Maybe it was the combination of the chicken's oil and the pepper sauce that gave Steve his fire breathing powers.* He suddenly had the urge for greasy fried chicken.

The library was by far the most noticeable building on campus. Not only did it tower above all the other buildings, but it also happened to be an ancient stone pyramid. It had been refurbished and upgraded with modern doors, plumbing and lighting.

They hurried along the wall of the library, crouching slightly to avoid being noticed. The library's main entrance was clear when they arrived, and the lights were off, making it impossible to see inside. Dan and Omar squatted at the glass front doors.

Dan pushed on the door, but it didn't swing open.

"It's locked..." he whispered to Omar.

As if in response to his words, something stirred inside and a small light came on. The light fell upon Dan and Omar before moving to reveal who was controlling it.

"It's about time you got here. I was beginning to think you weren't coming," said Augie quietly as he stood up and unlocked the door. "Get in, quickly!"

Dan and Omar squeezed through the narrowly opened door, and Augie immediately locked it again. For the brief moment Dan had his back to the door, he felt as if a mob of rioters would force their way in. He released his held breath when he looked back and saw no one except for the unknown figures in the distant food court.

"We need to move upstairs," said Augie before he ran across the room toward the staircase.

Dan and Omar followed him silently up the stairs and stopped at a locked door.

"It's Augie, open up," said Augie as he knocked on the modern, wooden door.

"What's the password?" asked someone from the other side.

"Aloo Himura," replied Augie.

There was some screeching as if something large was being dragged, and the door swung open. After they all passed through, it was locked again and a large table was pushed back in place to block it, serving as a makeshift barricade. It was the poorest fortification that Dan had ever seen but he chose not to say anything.

3

BOOK OF THE DEAD

[Day 1-2]
~Leave nothing to chance~

THE LIGHTS WERE LIT on this floor and a pair of persons stared at the three who had just entered. Dan could tell from their tense muscles that they were ready to run.

Dan and Omar followed Augie to a table in the corner of the large open room, which was partially obstructed by a tall, polished stone bookshelf. They each took a seat quietly and remained silent for a while.

Steve was already seated at the table. He was slouched over and looked like he had been vomiting. His shirt was wet and he smelled of something funky.

Omar trembled and appeared unnaturally pasty. The dark circles around his eyes made him look like a stressed-out panda. He had his face sandwiched between his shaking fingers.

Dan leaned forward with his elbow on the table and chin in his hand. His stubble was short and just barely noticeable, but rough enough to sound like sandpaper on wood as he rubbed his fingers across his jaw.

Augie spoke first. "Good to see that you paid attention to my survival plan earlier today. I was waiting for you for a while on the ground floor. That's *not* a place you want to be right now."

"Yeah... y-yeaaah," replied Dan, knowing very well that he hadn't heard a word of Augie's plan.

Augie loved superheroes and his main goal in life was to become one. He used every opportunity to wear full superhero attire – cape, mask, tights and all. Helping Dan and Omar made him feel heroic, but he still had to earn the title of "super". Dan tried to ignore that Augie had never outgrown his immature personality. Admittedly, Dan's imagination hadn't matured much either.

"I guess your zombie apocalypse survival plan does have some real-world uses. We managed to avoid those riots outside and we can probably hold out here 'til the police arrive," said Dan.

"Those are riots of the undead, man!" said Augie, in all seriousness.

"They're not zombies," said Dan abruptly.

Augie raised his eyebrows. "You've been trying to convince everyone all semester that one of your lecturers is a vampire!"

"First of all, you've never seen the Count. Secondly, that's a joke, Augie," Dan said in his defence. "The rioters aren't the undead."

"Well, we can't tell if they are undead yet, but they do display some zombie-like symptoms. Oh, and the police arrived a while ago but it didn't go too well," replied Augie.

"What symptoms? And what happened with the police?" asked Dan, his brow furrowed.

"The infected people are attacking and biting others. That's how they spread the infection, obviously. By the time the police arrived, late might I add, a lot of people were already infected. They were bitten too, so—" explained Augie.

"They should get back-up soon and clean this mess up in no time," interrupted Dan. "I don't think this is your zombie apocalypse, but I guess it's as close as it gets. Possibly some mass hysteria or psychogenic madness."

"Psychogenic madness?" Augie said with a chuckle. "Big words for 'zombies'!"

Dan's words seemed to calm Omar, who broke out of his dazed state and asked timidly, "Where's Barry?"

Augie sighed. "We were at the engineering block when the chaos started. A group of infected came from the north and began attacking everyone. We had to run, but Barry fell behind to get his computer and was bitten."

"So you left him behind?" asked Omar, his eyes widening.

"We had to because he became infected. Steve and I got to the library and managed to seal it off. That's why we only have a few people in here and none have been bitten," explained Augie.

Augie's eyes shifted between Dan and Omar. "You haven't been bitten, have you?"

"I... I was bitten by a dog once," said Omar.

"We came here directly from the lab," replied Dan.

"Actually, I was bitten like three times by that dog..."

"But were either of you bitten en route?" asked Augie, looking at Dan and Omar as if they had something worse than the plague.

"We didn't even run into anybody on the way here," said Dan.

Augie breathed a sigh of relief, seemingly content with that response.

Dan thought about what Augie had said about Barry: *Bitten? Infected? He can't be dead, can he? No, he must already be at home watching more shit on TV.*

Dan surveyed the room — he hadn't visited the library since he was a first-year student. The tall, yellowish stone bookshelves looked like they had been there for eons. They were, in fact, only a few centuries old, while the pyramid's original building blocks had been laid some millennia earlier. An open area with padded sofas and a few bean bag chairs, all faded yellow in colour and covered in hieroglyphs to match the pyramid's walls, had been positioned between the two rows of shelves that stretched from wall to wall. Like the Count's lab, the library had a unique smell — something like old musty books and air freshener.

Dan always disliked the extreme quiet in this place. It was too quiet to think, and the slightest noise echoed throughout the entire building. The many menacing statues of dead monarchs and mythological gods did little to encourage studying anything other than history.

At the very centre of the room was a hexagonal opening, which pierced its way vertically through the entire building. From there, it was possible to see straight down to the ground floor and all the way up to the enormous golden scarab beetle that hung from the ceiling above. A thin metal railing was all that prevented people from falling through the opening all the way to the modern marble floor below.

Dan turned his attention to the other people holed up

in the library, who had not spoken a word since his arrival. They all avoided the couches, which were close to the hexagonal centre. Instead, they had moved the bean bag chairs to a spot next to one of the walls, guarded by a life-sized statue of a mythological deity known as the Owl God.

Sitting atop the smallest bean bag, with her back resting against the granite statue, was a girl with long, dark, wavy hair. Dan filled his lungs with air and held his chest as if to stop his heart from jumping out. His fingers closed around his dog tag.

Kelly... How did I not notice her before? What are the odds that we both ended up here?

Over to her left sat a guy with a large, round afro. He had white earphones jammed into his ears and was nodding his head to music. His eyes were wide open and wildly darted between the two golden sarcophagi that stood nearby, watching him.

He looks like a Maurice. Yeah, I'll call him Maurice.

Next to him sat a blonde girl with straight shoulder-length hair, who had her face in her hands. She looked like the cheerleader type — thin and tall with golden hair, a short skirt and long, smooth legs that looked like they had just been waxed.

Every cheerleading squad must have a... Jessica.

"Did you consider all the mummies in the pyramid coming back to life? A mummy is just an ancient zombie, after all," said Dan to Augie just to break the silence and refocus his mind.

Augie bit his nails nervously and stared into open space as though contemplating the gap in his zombie apocalypse survival plan. The ancient pyramid may have been modernized and put to use as a library, but the historical artifacts remained. These included the statues and of course, the mummified remains of people long dead.

Dan got up and walked across the room toward the hexagonal opening, leaving behind a still stunned Augie. He peered down at the darkness on the ground floor. There was no movement below, but even if there was, he wouldn't have seen it. He leaned on the flimsy railing. If it broke, he was sure to die one way or the other — a broken body, or eaten alive by zombies who were yet to make an appearance.

Having seen no conclusive proof of zombies, Dan's logic eclipsed his fear. He felt safer now, and stupid to have even thought that zombies had overrun the campus.

"You shouldn't stand so close to the edge, Dan," said Kelly.

She knows my name?

Ever since he saw her sitting quietly by herself, Dan could not get her out of his head. Now her voice echoed in his mind. Her soft, sweet, angelic, delicate voice.

His mouth went dry and his fingers tensed around the cold metal railing. No other girl paralyzed his mind and body in this way. No matter how many times he had spoken to Kelly in his mental realm, he was still unprepared to do it now.

Just play it cool...

He looked in her direction and his eyes caught hers. In that moment, which was no more than two seconds, Dan felt like she could see into his soul. He would have gazed into her eyes for eternity had he not mustered the willpower to look away.

Say something... He opened his mouth, his lips just barely curling into a smile, but no words came out.

He slowly made his way back to Augie's table, trying to ignore that his legs had practically transformed into boneless tentacles. Suddenly, walking became the most difficult task in his life, but he managed not to stumble. He sat down once again with his chin in his hand and a dazed look in his eyes. He began imagining how things could have unfolded if he had gone over to her and conversed.

What should I have said to her? Should I go over and talk to her now? What do I say?

He checked the time on the digital watch strapped onto his left wrist — 7:30 pm. The sun had set completely and wouldn't rise again until 6:00 am the next day. *This is definitely not how I expected my first night with Kelly to go, but it'll have to do. It must be a sign, right?*

"We can probably get to the parking lot, but there are seven of us in the library. My car can only take five," said Dan when he was finally able to return to reality. "I guess we'll be here for a while."

He paused for a moment as he thought of a fix for their situation and then said, "The phone networks are down and we don't have access to a TV or radio, but did anyone check for online info? The power is still on so the internet should be fine."

"The library walls are too thick for the wireless internet, so our only option is the computer lab. The problem is that there's only one computer lab and it's on the ground floor," replied Augie.

"And d only way to get to d computa lab would be d stairs dat we jus' now block up or d elevator dat not wo'kin'," added Steve.

His accent was terribly difficult to understand

sometimes but Dan decoded what Steve had said. They didn't want to take the risk of moving to another floor.

Dan wasn't prepared to take that chance just yet, so he decided against it. Instead, his thoughts drifted back to Kelly and what his odds of success were with her. Surely, he had a better chance of having her fall in love with him than safely walking down the stairs.

The time flew quickly as Dan scripted cheesy pickup lines and scenarios in his head. He had forgotten about the riots and being trapped in the library all night. His anxiety hadn't disappeared though, only shifted to something else.

Augie had his large, round head resting upon the table and his right thumb in his mouth. He randomly twitched and muttered words like a baby, the most recurring being "zombie". Dan was sure that Augie would have enjoyed a nightmare about zombies ripping out guts and swallowing brains.

***

Dan awoke suddenly the next morning. Everyone was just as they were the night before. He looked across at Kelly — she was curled up on one of the bean bag chairs.

He washed his oily skin with cold tap water. It was a new day, and everything felt better. The events of the previous day felt like a strange dream. *We weren't attacked by zombies last night,* he smirked at his reflection in the washroom mirror. *We shouldn't have to worry about them devouring our brains anymore. As if that could have ever really happened.*

Dan's confidence grew and he decided to check the computer lab on the floor below for any news before anyone else had woken up.

He moved the barricade from behind the door with surprising ease. The table made only a tiny screech as he dragged it a little to the side, enabling the door to open slightly. Nothing was heard over Augie's snoring. Dan squeezed himself through and entered the dark stairwell.

It was a bit disturbing that he had managed to open the door without waking anyone. He reassured himself that it must have been significantly easier to open the door from the inside as he began his first steps down.

He could see some light below as the rising sun cast its rays through the glass. While the entire ground floor was largely blanketed in darkness, the faint light of the early morning sun made navigation simpler.

He stepped lightly onto the ground floor, peered around and saw no signs of movement. Even as he looked outside through the glass front door, he couldn't detect anyone. The food court, which had been a hotspot for activity the night before, was also completely vacant. He crept quietly on his toes toward the computer lab. It was much colder down here than on the floor above. Dan was almost tempted to warm up in the little stretch of sunlight that fell inside.

He entered a room lined with computer workstations; the black screens were all flooded with green encrypted computer code. The designers had made no attempt to blend this room into the ancient pyramid theme. Everything was made of black metal and plastic, with green glowing lights.

Dan sat by the computer closest to the entrance and activated it. The light from the monitor bathed the room in brilliant white illumination.

The university's website, which was displayed by default and was normally unchanged, had a new message that read:

"Notice: All students and staff are advised to evacuate the campus as soon as possible.

As of the 29th of October, there have been reports of rioting across campus. The actual cause of this event is still uncertain but the immediate threat to students and staff is quite real. It is for this reason that everyone on the campus is asked to calmly evacuate the grounds as soon as possible and avoid the premises until further notice. The police force is attempting to resolve the issue in a timely manner so that classes can resume shortly. Please check your student mail for further information regarding this situation and details on the resumption of lectures."

Office of the Campus Principal.

The message didn't provide much more information than he already knew. He searched a local news website that would have been hungry for a story other than the usual political propaganda. The page didn't load, nor did any other website he tried. He stared at the error message on the screen, trying to figure out how online communication could have failed.

The darkness faded, but the room's nebulosity was enough to conceal a stealthy adversary. Dan tilted his head, imagining the static shadows taking form and mobilizing. *Stop overthinking*, Dan chided himself, refocusing on the computer.

A heavy hand dropped onto Dan's shoulder, causing him to jump up from his seat. He spun around and struggled from the hand's grasp.

"What the hell? You almost gave me a heart attack!" gasped Dan when he recognized his assumed assassin to be Augie. "If you were a zombie, you'd have been eating a chokeslam!"

"I would have been eating your brains! You shouldn't try chokeslamming a zombie. What are you doing down here?" said Augie.

"I came to check online for any info on the situation," replied Dan. "They're suggesting we leave campus ASAP."

Augie rubbed his chin. "We have to get out of here anyway. We can scout the area to find a safe escape route. Did you try to contact anyone?"

"The internet is down."

"Classic zombie scenario."

"At least we have some sunlight now. I think things should be better today," said Dan as he looked out the glass front door to see the sun's rays starting to fill the courtyard. "It doesn't look so bad."

"Zombies always strike when you least expect them! And also, sometimes when you expect them but can't do anything about it!"

"Let's just wake the others and get out of here while it's still early. We'll get at least a day or two off from classes, so I can get some rest. I didn't sleep too well last night." Dan still wasn't convinced about the zombies, but it was too early to begin arguing with Augie.

"Me neither, man. I missed my transforming pillow!"

Augie had actually slept like a log, literally. He always kept his arms tucked close to his body and had his legs extended when he slept. Similar to sleepwalking, Augie rolled about in his sleep, like a tree trunk. He called it "cactus walking", for reasons difficult to explain.

Augie had a not-so-secret collection of stuffed toys that he was only too happy to talk about. His favourite was a green spongy cactus named Cacti, which he slept with every night since he was a baby. Cacti transformed into a blanket.

Dan and Augie proceeded back up the stairs to awaken everyone. The plan, for now, was simple — scout the area to see if it was safe enough for everyone to venture outside. If all was clear, then everyone could just go home, and things would return to normal soon after. They would have gotten an interesting story to tell, at the very least. Barry would possibly even find it funny that they thought he had died.

However, if the situation was still bad, they'd have to figure out the best course of action. Dan had no idea what Augie had planned from this point, but he didn't dare ask. The last thing he wanted to hear was more zombie folly.

Dan and Augie volunteered to be the scouts, while everyone else remained in the library. The doors were lightly barricaded in case they needed to get back in hurriedly. Those inside the building were unable to see outside since there were no windows on the second floor. They had to depend on the scouts to alert them if there was a sudden attack.

Dan stepped outside first, moving cautiously and scanning all around for anyone. Augie followed closely behind and was crouching slightly as if it made him harder to notice.

As far as they could tell, the courtyard was clear of people. There was no sign of what had happened the night before. No mangled bodies of beaten victims or bloodstains of any kind. Even the glass doors and windows in every surrounding building were fully intact.

The morning air was cool and refreshing. The crisp, clean wind blew gently, failing to waft a single strand of Dan's gel-hard hair as he walked across the courtyard. It was much more pleasant than the scorching midday sun. The air that deflected off Augie was far from pleasant though.

The place was eerily silent. The campus was normally quite empty and quiet early in the mornings, but it felt strange now. Perhaps it was because they expected some sign of activity. The only sounds Dan heard were the wind and their footsteps — things that normally went unnoticed.

Dan approached the glass doors of the food court and peered inside. Rubbish cluttered the tables — empty boxes, plates and cups. There were no people, living, dead or undead.

"I don't see anyone," said Dan as quietly as he could without whispering. "I wonder what happened here last night."

"There are probably zombies in there, man. We should head back to safety," said Augie in a low voice, biting his nails.

We couldn't have all been hallucinating last night. Something definitely happened here, thought Dan. He slowly pushed open the door and stepped inside. It was much colder in here than outside, as it always was.

Trash littered the tables and floor as if a blizzard had blown everything about, which sometimes happened because of the food court's microclimate. *Maybe it was just a wild party last night... or a blizzard... or both? No, it was zombies... I mean riots...*

The door creaked as it closed behind Augie and then slammed shut loudly, vibrating the glass almost to the point of shattering. *Great.* They had chosen the only one with squeaky hinges and a broken door closer.

The instant the reverberation of the noise ended, another sound started that froze the scouts in their tracks. It most closely resembled the whimper of a wounded animal. It was brief and just barely audible, but it definitely meant they were not alone.

The sound repeated, louder than before. Dan and Augie stared at each other, still not moving.

The whimper changed into crying.

"There's someone in here," whispered Dan to Augie as he slowly walked toward the origin of the sound.

Augie followed. "There can't be any survivors. We should go back."

Dan's gait revealed no fear of the potential threat. However, the dread inside him grew exponentially as they drew closer to the loudening sobbing. His cold fingertips trembled slightly, and he became aware of his very upright posture — a symptom of his tight muscles.

He tried to convince himself that the crying female voice did nothing to frighten him. He attempted to ignore the many horror movies where a similar situation would most certainly result in a sudden scare or death of the protagonist. Every single scary story defiled his mind, despite his efforts to suppress them.

At the same time, he had genuine concern for the girl and his bravery fought his apprehension. *Did this girl spend the entire night here? I hope she's okay.*

He moved between the tables until he got to a heavy

metal gate held up by a rusty old chain — Pizza Dungeon. He stared at the suit of black armour that stood inside the shop, piercing a faux pizza with the tip of its lance. The pizza knight had never seemed so intimidating. Dan crossed the threshold into the dungeon-themed pizza shop. It was darker in here and much warmer.

The crying had gotten louder — she was definitely in the dungeon. Fortunately, she wasn't inside the suit of armour.

Beneath an old, wooden table in the far corner of the room, someone lay curled up. Her dress was shredded into rags and her face remained hidden behind her dark hanging hair. On her arm, a wound trickled blood. There was no mistaking that she was the source of the crying. She made no response as Dan and Augie approached her.

Augie pointed to the red liquid that stained the floor beneath where she lay and upon her wounded arm. "B-blood! She's infected!"

The girl turned immediately to face them, giving Dan no time to respond to Augie's remark. Her crying suddenly ceased. Her skin was pallid and something red and viscous oozed from her mouth.

She crawled out from under the table like some wild quadrupedal animal. With a scream as loud as ten thousand crying babies, she lunged at Dan. He immediately knocked her back with a chest-crushing kick. Her body crashed into the table and then fell crumpled on the floor.

"Oh shit! We startled the witch! We startled the Bloody Witch!" shouted Augie as he ran out of the pizza shop. "Let's get the hell outta here!"

Dan wasted no time in exiting as well, just as the girl

was struggling to stand again. He had never seen Augie run so fast; he didn't think it was possible.

"Get back to the library!" ordered Dan as his panicked friend flung the food court doors wide open.

When Dan entered the courtyard, it was not as empty as before. To the right, a man staggered about and far to the left was an indistinct figure.

Augie sprinted as fast as he could across the courtyard toward the library, followed closely by Dan. The man to the right broke into a sprint as well, chasing after them. The Bloody Witch had also emerged from the food court and gave chase.

Dan felt like he was running in the open yard in slow motion. He saw Augie's body jiggle as he ran as fast as his legs would move; he saw the man approaching from the right side, much less jiggly than Augie, and the girl approaching from behind, jiggly in certain places. The person on the left had only noticed them by the time they were upon the library's front steps.

He thought about stopping. *Why are we being chased? They aren't zombies. They can't be.* But he didn't stop. They weren't running to hug him. He wouldn't have hugged them if they were. Stopping made no sense.

"Open the door! Open the door!" exclaimed Augie as he entered the library. He ran around to the stairs and dashed up.

"Aloo Kimura!" Dan had caught up to him and was closely being followed by the two chasers.

The door to the second floor opened at the very last moment. Dan and Augie dove inside as soon as the opening was wide enough.

"Close the door! Close the door!" shouted Augie as he struggled to his feet.

They could see the man running up the stairs just before they slammed the door shut. There was a loud banging as the man pounded on the door to get in. His snarls were clearly audible even as the barricade was put back in place. He continued slamming his fists with full force, clearly berserk.

Dan and Augie stood there with their eyes open wide and transfixed on the poorly barricaded, vibrating door. Perspiration leaked from their foreheads as they breathed heavily. Dan was concerned that the table was not going to stop the door from being broken down.

4

THE ENCOUNTER WITH THE DEAD!

[Day 2]

~Suffering makes your life a little bit more interesting~

EVERYONE'S LEGS WIGGLED LIKE spaghetti. Dan's thoughts drowned the screaming and panicked words that filled the room.

Is this a prank? It can't be... A dream? I'm definitely awake...

"Those were some... damn fast zombies," muttered Dan.

Augie opened his mouth as if to say, "I told you so," but nothing came out.

"Aww man, those zombies gonna rip my hair out! Nam sayin'?" shouted the afro man as he caressed his hair.

Maurice valued his hair above all else and with good reason. It was the roundest, neatest afro imaginable.

Dan couldn't help but smile at Maurice's inopportune, unintentional humour. No one else found anything comical about the situation. There was a clutch of crazy people trying to break down the door, which would not stand up against much more punishment. Every pound, bang, and vicious snarl sent a jolt through everyone in the room.

"We need to get the hell out of here!" said Dan as he walked away from the barricaded door. "There has to be another way out... an emergency exit."

Augie shook his head to break his dazed stare. "Uhh yeah, the b-building is designed in a w-way that we can climb d-down any side."

He pointed to a blue door at the far side of the room, directly opposite the barricaded exit route.

The banging on the door was persistent and it was clear by the distinctive screeching that the Bloody Witch was there as well.

All this noise would attract more attention, so we don't have much time to escape.

"I di'n' know zombies could climb stairs, or run dat fas'," said Steve in bewilderment.

"They are definitely berserk enough to be called zombies. Let's just say they are running, stair-climbing zombies. We can sort out what they really are when this is over," replied Dan, moving past the hexagonal opening.

Dan looked down through the opening and saw a person staggering on the ground floor of the library. The man below looked up when he noticed everyone moving above him. He snarled and then darted out of sight.

Dan pulled away from the railing as if expecting a deranged stranger from below to break the vertical jump world record.

Everyone followed Dan to the blue door. Augie fiddled with some keys he had extracted from his pocket. This door was undoubtedly the sturdiest on campus — it looked like it secured a vault rather than an exit route. They would have had an easier time forcing their way through the ten-thousand-year-old, solid rock wall than forcing this door open.

Why is the emergency exit door locked?

Fortunately, Augie had planned ahead.

The banging at the other door seemed to get louder and the barricade began moving out of place. Augie pulled out a single silver key and missed the keyhole nine times before opening the door. Everyone hastily exited the room and stepped out to the pyramid's exterior.

That barricade lasted much longer than I expected. Still, let's never use a table for fortification again.

Each block of the pyramid was the same size — about half Dan's height. They all fit together perfectly like a giant three-dimensional puzzle. The stepped slope was too high to comfortably walk down but short enough to descend with small jumps.

With haste, they made their way down the steps. Kelly, the shortest person present, had a difficult time going down, but she did it without the assistance of anyone. Maurice, with his terribly wild self, somersaulted down each step.

The last few steps on this side of the pyramid were broken, leaving them with two options: jump or go around to another side. With a loud snarl, the first attacker came through the open blue door, then another and another. The choice was clear.

"We all need to jump! Now!" shouted Dan.

Everyone pushed off simultaneously, posing in the air with the zombies approaching behind them. It would have made a terrific group photo.

Dan spread his arms like a bird of prey but instead of gracefully gliding, he fell with the elegance of a rock. The metal tag around his neck tried to hide in his mouth, then smacked his cheek. He rolled over his shoulder and stopped on one knee.

Maurice kicked madly, and his bellbottom jeans fluttered as he fell to the grass below. He landed with a crash and lay mangled and twitching. His hair was just fine though.

Augie fell flat on his belly and instantly sprang back up to his feet. Everyone else managed to land safely, with no broken bones or significant embarrassment.

"We gotta move, bai!" exclaimed Steve as he saw their rabid pursuers jump off the building without hesitation.

Everyone scattered, just as three pairs of feet landed heavily on the grass. The attackers were not fazed in the slightest by the fall.

Two of the attackers lunged at Dan while the female attacked Maurice. Dan twisted his body clockwise and smashed his right heel into the jaw of a moustachioed, bespectacled man.

The man's body twirled twice in the air like a spindle of unravelling yarn, before landing spread-eagle. Blood spewed from his broken jaw. Unbothered, he flipped back up to his feet. His glasses had flown off, and his moustache was strangely missing as well.

Augie leaned forward, stretched out his arms, and pulled his right leg back. For a second, he looked like a bigger version of the lab's scorpion. He fired his weaponized leg forward, eyes closed. His momentum was so great that his entire body moved, and his other leg slipped off the ground. His attacking foot sank deep into the belly of his target.

The second male attacker was knocked off his feet and flew back several paces. His ponytail loosened and greasy, black hair whipped about like windblown ribbons. He skidded on the grass, leaving stains all over his white t-shirt.

Maurice had, at some point in all the chaos, knocked down the female and was pounding on her with his feet. Steve and Omar looked on in disbelief, not sure whether to join in or just stand there. They opted for the latter — the Bloody Witch was scary.

"I think we have to go now... LOOK!" Omar pointed toward the pyramid.

More people streamed out the blue door and down the steps. They certainly didn't appear any friendlier than the three attackers.

Fighting was no longer a sensible option. Dan and the others ran off, followed closely by the people they had just beaten up. Not too far behind, a crowd of runners amassed.

Dan led the way as they sprinted across the grass toward Dr. Graham's laboratory. The titan trees, which towered high above, peacefully twirled their leaves in the playful morning breeze, mocking the chaotic scene unfolding.

Augie and Omar, who both had the unfortunate combination of slow speed and low endurance, should have made up the rear of the group, but instead, it was Maurice who was trailing behind with a limp. His ankle had been twisted either from the fall or from crushing the Bloody Witch's jaw.

When Dan made it onto the concrete walkway, he

looked back to see that the attackers had scattered the group. Some were running in any direction possible to avoid being caught, zigzagging, jumping, sidestepping, and rolling. All their years of playing tag were paying off.

The blonde girl was their primary target and most of the attackers chased her relentlessly. Then there was Maurice, being chased by no less than eight. Everyone else managed to shake off their attackers and regroup with Dan.

It was peculiar how the attackers divided their forces. *Are they picking off the most vulnerable ones?*

A sound came from behind the pyramid, like a stampede of rampaging animals. Dan and the others stood there, gripped by fear and curiosity, while Maurice and Jessica continued running for their lives.

From the right side of the library, one person ran out into the open, joined a moment later by another runner. Two seconds later, a person appeared from the left side. Then from both sides of the library streamed two enormous waves of people, which then joined together under the trees to form one massive zombie tsunami.

"I THINK WE DEFINITELY HAVE TO GO NOW!" Omar shouted even louder than before, with tears pouring like waterfalls.

Augie, Kelly, Omar and Steve imitated Dan as he spun on his heels and commanded his legs to get him to safety. Everyone's feet slipped on the concrete for a second, as if they stood upon polished ice, before they galloped away. They ran through Dr. Graham's building – a corridor with only two exits. If there were attackers at the far end, they would have been trapped.

They went straight through to the other side, passed the

lab, and continued without stopping or looking back. The noise from the angry mob slowly died down and fizzled out.

After running what felt like a marathon, the group slowed down, with Augie and Omar gasping for air and holding their waists. Dan scowled as they walked past the old, cream-coloured building that housed the Count's lab. They didn't encounter any other people along the way but could see a few scattered at the far end of the campus.

To avoid attracting any more attention, they passed through the greenhouse — a large white dome that housed exotic tropical plants. It was an experiment in a fully self-contained ecosystem. At the heart of the structure stood an enormous saman tree that spread its branches in all directions. In the shade of the tree's dense, green leaves, was a pond with colourful fish and cephalopods, and in an adjacent pond were giant crabs and shrimp. Strange plants and trees covered the entire land surface, except for the red brick walking paths.

The birds that roosted in the trees usually fed on the sweet nectar of the many flowers or the red and yellow fruits that were always in abundance. They hid in the highest branches and some squawked at their unscheduled visitors.

Yellow fireflies darted out of the way of the hurrying humans, then followed them as if curious about their guests' intentions. The greenhouse truly felt otherworldly, like a magical place long lost in time.

Dan felt an incredible temptation to stay in the greenhouse. The utopian garden made him feel safe, but its promise of protection was deceptive. The delicate skin of the dome could shelter them from the rain, but not the clawing hands of zombies.

As if passing through a portal back to their own world, Dan and the others came out the other side of the greenhouse. Just ahead stretched a large paved area surrounded by a wire fence – the parking lot. There were only two ways in and out — a small opening for pedestrians and at the far end, a large metal gate for vehicular traffic.

The university made sure that the tiny working staff had ninety percent of the parking spaces on campus, while the large student population had to share the remaining ten percent with visitors. This parking lot was usually packed beyond its recommended capacity but right now, it was only half full.

They saw no one inside the compound as they entered. Just beyond the fence stood new apartment towers and old, decrepit roads, usually bustling with students and traffic. There was no sound or sign of life there either.

Dan's car wasn't parked very far from the pedestrian entrance. They approached an old, pearl-white car with faded chrome rims and tinted windows. Dan's car was easily the most unique of all the vehicles in the lot — all the others were shiny, black and brand new. Dan's was built like a tank and could supposedly survive a nuclear blast.

For the first time since they were attacked by the mob, Dan inspected the group. Only five were left — Kelly, Augie, Omar, Steve, and himself.

"Shit... we lost Maurice and Jessica," said Dan, accidentally divulging his made-up names.

"Who?" Augie blinked and shook his head.

"I mean... you know who I mean."

No one suggested that they return to rescue the missing. For a fleeting moment, Dan wanted to, but he didn't know either of them — they could have been as bad as the Count, or at least those useless group project people. He made the choice to move forward. Going back would have been foolish.

"I call shotgun," said Augie as soon as the car's locks opened.

Interestingly enough, Dan's compact car would not have been able to comfortably hold more than five. Omar barely fit in the backseat and if Augie were back there as well, the two of them would have occupied the entire seat. But everyone managed to fit just fine. The car strained from the load as if about to break in half. It had never carried this much weight before, and its geriatric chassis creaked a little.

Dan drove off, surveying the campus' roadways. The engine sputtered as the vehicle picked up speed. They had only two routes from here. The first was shorter but ran dangerously close to the library. They had to take the long drive around the perimeter of campus to avoid running into the large mob they had just escaped.

He slowed down as he reached the giant bronze gate at the exit, which guarded the campus road network. The gate was twice as tall as the fence and crowned with sharp, rusty spikes. It was partially open but only wide enough for a person to squeeze through.

Dan brought the car to a halt. "Someone has to get out and open the gate."

They waited there for a while more, everyone reluctant to exit the car. Heads turned as everyone looked around, hoping that someone would volunteer.

"I go do it, bai," said Steve with a sigh.

He left the door open and jogged around the car to

slide the gate. His teeth chattered and his hands trembled madly as he grasped the metal bars. Even his dreadlocks looked like they were petrified and stiff.

The gate's wheels squeaked loudly as they turned and as they did, there was some movement in the guard booth to the left.

A security guard with a large potbelly emerged from the booth and groaned as he stretched his arms skyward. He looked like he had just woken up from a deep slumber.

Everyone in the car gasped and Steve was on the verge of soaking his pants. As soon as the guard laid his eyes on Steve, he ran awkwardly toward him with flailing arms and high-pitched wails. Steve stood there, transfixed. Tears flowed from his eyes and his muscles refused to move. His mouth looked ready to scream but only air came out in a wheeze.

Without taking the time to process the thought, Dan floored the accelerator as soon as the guard was in front of the car. The car jerked upward twice as if it had run over a speed bump, drowning the crunching sound with the roar of the engine. Steve still had not budged.

Steve stared, nose scrunched, at the crushed head of the bleeding corpse. The sight was quite gruesome, but he wasted no time in returning to the car as soon as it had stopped beyond the gate.

"He... he brains was splatta all ova d ground, bai!" cried Steve as they sped off.

Steve wiped his eyes dry and checked his crotch to make sure he hadn't peed his pants.

"He better bag himself up, 'cause you know he dead!" said Augie, in the most high-pitched voice he could muster.

Augie usually took every opportunity to use his favourite quote from his favourite movie — Body Bag Zombies. Feeling super sick? *"I better bag myself up, man. I'm dead."* Just had a really hard exam? *"Does anyone have a bag to lend me? I need to bag myself up, 'cause I am so dead."* Watching a nature documentary on lions? *"That gazelle needs a bag..."*

Dan drove toward the campus exit and was not hampered by any traffic. The roads were totally clear, and the campus remained silent. There was no sign of the crazy mob. All he could think about was the guard he had just flattened. He felt as if a murder of crows was trying to escape from inside his stomach. A murder.

He flicked a silver switch to his right and the radio turned on. There was no signal, so he adjusted the dial. No music played on any station, but he eventually focused on a news broadcast.

"This is a nationwide warning about the current crisis. There has been an outbreak of the highly contagious disease called 'Zombosis'. The infectious agent is a parasitic bug that infests human hosts. Once infected, the parasite travels to the brain, where it affects all bodily functions. When this stage is reached, the infected person is considered brain-dead, and the body would remain in what can only be described as a zombified state. The infected will move around just like regular people, but they are no longer those you know and love! Everyone is advised to avoid infected persons at all costs since infection occurs rapidly and is currently irreversible. You can identify the infected by the red blood-like excretion from their mouths, milky-white irises, and erratic or aggressive behaviour. The infected will attempt to bite victims in order to transmit

the disease to others. All citizens are advised to avoid contact if possible. If an encounter is unavoidable, target the heads of the infected to incapacitate them. Remain tuned in for further updates."

It sounded like a news bulletin that came straight from a horror movie. Brain controlling parasites, zombified people, aim for the head? It was all unbelievable. If only it were nothing more than an excerpt from a book.

The message looped over and over and was obviously a recording. It seemed to have been done in a hurry, but it gave some useful insight into what was going on. There was no other radio broadcast on any frequency.

"Yeah, dat guard had white devil eyes and blood leakin' from he mout'," said Steve, pointing back the way they had come.

"Good to know," said Dan, trying his best to seem nonchalant.

"Good t'ing you bus' he head, bai Dan bai," Steve continued, as he adjusted his colourful hat.

Dan was relieved to know that he wasn't a murderer, even though the thought of the dead walking was equally as terrifying. The idea that zombies now roamed the earth still felt unreal.

"Things must be really bad for them to actually use the word 'zombified' in an official news report," said Dan.

"Zombosis..." said Augie with a broad smile, overly proud that his zombie prediction was accurate. "They called it Zombosis!"

Steve and Omar shuddered twice.

"They're going to cause widespread panic with that broadcast," said Dan.

"That's the way the zombie apocalypse is meant to be!" said Augie, unable to contain his excitement.

As they approached the campus exit, they saw a few infected wandering about. The zombies could now be easily identified by their eyes and mouths, leaving no question about their infection status.

Dan slowed the car as they approached the pair of speed bumps by the exit. There was another guard booth here and everyone in the car stared nervously inside it as they passed by slowly. They leaned away as if expecting a zombie guard to leap out. Luckily for them, this one was empty. Dan eased his car over the speed bumps. The passengers caused the vehicle to sag and scrape the concrete humps.

"I think my brakes line just burst," said Dan as they crossed the second hump.

"What?!" said everyone in chorus.

"I'm kidding. It's fine."

Dan's jest elicited not a single chuckle, only simultaneous sighs.

They exited the campus and made it onto a roadway that branched off in three directions. Two of these branches led to the town and one led directly to the highway.

Dan turned right, onto the highway route. There were more speed bumps on this road, and it was necessary to slow down when crossing each one. He knew better than to put the car's old frame through unnecessary abuse.

Dan looked back in the rearview mirror to see if they were being followed — a single infected chased after the car. There were no other moving vehicles or people around. Still, one zombie was enough to fluster everyone in the car.

This zombie was remarkably obese; he looked bloated, in fact. If he managed to add his weight to the car, it would have been rendered immobile.

Dan increased the pace, causing the car to drag and bounce roughly at the last two bumps. The metal grazed loudly on the concrete, sending sparks flying in the zombie's swollen face.

As soon as he got flat road, Dan zoomed off, leaving the lone infected far behind. The zombie gave up the chase, leaned on his knees and vomited green sludge onto his own feet.

After a short, uneventful, wordless drive, they arrived at the highway. There was no flowing traffic here and some cars lay motionless in the middle of the road.

Dan filtered in and drove along the highway, heading away from the campus. His was the only moving vehicle and no other humans were visible. He carefully but quickly drove between the stationary vehicles.

Everyone in the car scanned the other vehicles for any sign of survivors or infected, but they were all abandoned. It was the strangest thing Dan had seen on the busiest roads on the island. Strange things were quickly becoming normal.

The windows of some of the cars were smashed, and their doors bloodied — possible signs of forced entry by the infected. Some appeared to be untouched — maybe abandoned to escape on foot during traffic. A few cars had crashed into one another. Some were parked awkwardly off the roadway.

"Now that we're out of campus," said Dan, passing his hand over the stubble on his chin, "where the hell do we go?"

"Well, the safest place would be some sort of military zone, but then again they won't have many supplies and I don't know of any real fort on the island," said Augie.

"Fire bun dem, bai!" exclaimed Steve.

"Is this as far as you planned? We can't drive forever..." replied Dan.

"Considering the crisis, the airport is either overloaded or in lockdown, or both," continued Augie. "I would say the safest place should be somewhere offshore, like on a boat. I've never heard of swimming zombies, except in that one movie, but it was really stupid."

"We dead, bai," interjected Steve.

"I could have used some help with the plan in the first place, Dan."

"You're the zombie expert, man."

"Ha! So you admit they're zombies!"

"Definitely zombies."

They continued driving but still encountered no other people, just more empty cars and silence.

"It looks like Zombosis spreads really quickly. The entire campus seems to have been wiped out and the surrounding areas must have been hit hard too. So either people are in hiding, or they're dead," said Dan, looking out the car as he crossed a bridge.

"Guys! We should go to the mall! Food, shelter, supplies! Everything we need!" said Augie with a sudden burst of enthusiasm.

"How 'bout the mountains?" suggested Kelly.

"That's too far away and we would have no supplies there," said Augie.

"The mall might be full of people," said Dan, siding with Kelly.

Omar raised his hand until it touched the roof of the car. "I agree with Augie."

"Oh, so it's down to a vote then?" asked Dan.

"I good with the mall, bai," said Steve. "Anyt'ing betta dan being on d road."

"We have the majority! Let's go to the mall!" said Augie with a big grin, celebrating his victory at the voting polls. "Too bad, little girl! GHE-HEHEHE!"

Dan didn't bother arguing with Augie and the others. He wasn't sure if going to the mountains was any better.

Dan stretched to get a view of Kelly in the backseat through the rearview mirror. She was in the middle of the seat, between Omar and Steve, and had her hands wrapped around her locket necklace. Her black wavy hair fell across her face as she stared downward. She brushed her hair to the side and raised her head. Dan, remembering that he was driving, swerved to avoid a car to the left and then another to the right.

In the chaos, he had forgotten she was there and now that he remembered, he forgot about the zombies. He planned out multiple conversations with her in his mind. None of them would be of any use to him — they only managed to make him anxious and nauseated.

"The malls always get busted down in the movies, but they do serve their purpose. The only problem would be the hundreds of zombies inside if Zombosis spread there already," said Augie. "But other than that, it sounds good to me."

The sun grew brighter and warmer and shone down through a cloudless sky. The light was very welcome but the heat in the car was becoming an annoyance. Even with the air conditioning turned on, it was quite hot.

"The mall is in this direction anyway, so I guess we could check it out. Our only other option right now would be to keep driving until we escape the infected area, but since we don't know how far the infection has spread, that may not be such a good idea," said Dan.

He checked the car's fuel levels – the tank was almost full. Dan never allowed the tank to drop below half. A full tank provided enough fuel to navigate the entire island. There was no immediate need to add transportation to their growing list of problems.

"The mountains are right there too," said Kelly, pointing out the northern mountain range.

"They're a lot further than they look," said Dan. "It'll take us about an hour to get there."

"Half that without traffic," she defended.

"True, but we don't know if the roads are blocked."

"Not to mention that you have to pass through the town to get to the mountains," Augie added. "I think it's best we avoid the populated areas."

"The mall always has more people than the town!" exaggerated Kelly.

The town, like every other on the island, was made of streets lined with buildings old and new, cramped shops, illegal vendors, and expensive parking lots. During daylight hours, the roadways competed with the sidewalks for the award of most congested. At night, robbers, killers, and prostitutes coexisted.

They continued driving and still saw no sign of anyone. Dan did not even bother to stop at any of the traffic lights — he didn't have to. Eventually, they approached the turnoff that led to the mall.

A lone structure stood in the middle of an open field of lush, green turf. The mall was a large, long building that had two hexagonal terminal ends and a slightly narrower middle bridging them. The roof of the bridge looked like the scarlet spine of a gargantuan beast and crowning each of the terminals was a crystal dome.

They were in luck — the mall appeared to be empty. On a normal morning, there would be hundreds of shoppers and, somehow, more parked cars than people. Now there was nothing but a lonely building. It was the perfect time to take refuge there.

5

THE DEAD RISE!

~Prolonged solitude tortures the sane mind~

THEY DROVE INTO THE mall's empty compound. The large parking lot, which could have held thousands of cars, was vacant, except for a small white car that chugged along steadily. Dan didn't bother following the neatly drawn driving paths. The car came to a halt at the spot closest to the main entrance.

"I never got this spot before," said Dan as he exited the vehicle.

"Zombie apocalypse benefits," said Augie.

The sun cast its scorching rays on Dan as he surveyed the area. He moved his hand over his brow to block off the blinding sunlight and squinted in the direction of the mall's entrance. He had been here many times before but never so early in the day.

The other doors of the car opened, and the passengers emerged cautiously. They all kept close to the vehicle as if expecting to make a hasty retreat.

There was a large chain strapped across the mall's door

handles, kept in place by the biggest padlock Dan had ever seen. No one had ever broken into this mall before. Dan's body tingled as he thought of breaking and entering — *laws can be broken during an apocalyptic event...*

"It looks like the mall wasn't opened today," said Dan as he walked toward the chained door. "I don't think it would be a good idea to break the glass."

The others were reluctant to move away from the car. It wasn't hard to imagine zombies running around the corner toward them, or even breaking through the glass doors and trampling them.

Augie leaned into the car while the others moved into the shade at the mall's front doors. He pulled out his bulky grey backpack and swung it over his shoulder. As he moved into the shade with the others, he unzipped the large compartment and pulled out a red bolt cutter.

Without saying a word, he clipped the chains, which fell to the floor with an unpleasantly loud, metallic thud. He then pulled out two small instruments from a leather pouch and began fiddling with the door's main lock.

"Where did you learn to pick locks?" Dan felt like this was the first time Augie was attempting to open a door with something other than a key.

"The internet, of course."

In under a minute, the door was unlocked, and Augie had an exceedingly smug smirk on his face.

"I dub thee the Master of Unlocking," said Dan.

"Lock picking is an essential skill for a post-apocalyptic world. I had a lot of practice with doors at home, but this was much easier than I expected." Augie returned the lock pick pouch to his backpack and rested the cutter on his shoulder.

"Why the hell do you carry that thing around in your backpack?" Dan just couldn't resist asking.

"I had my essential zombie apocalypse equipment stored in my locker," Augie replied casually as if everyone had the same. "I have another one in my room and one in my mom's car."

Augie had obviously planned for this meticulously. He may have been ridiculed for his eccentric behaviour all his life, but it was paying off right now.

Omar pushed the glass door open and they all filed inside the hexagonal structure that was called the Midnight Atrium. It was much cooler inside the mall and the air smelled quite pleasant – like popcorn, coffee, and cinnamon. There was no stench of death and no zombies in sight.

Everyone had been to the mall before but none of them had ever seen it so empty. It was a place that normally threw invasive advertising in the faces of thousands of shoppers daily, but now there were no customers or annoying ads. It felt like a desolate husk of its normal self.

They skirted around a knobby, orange pumpkin the size of a tractor tire. The mall had been decorated for Halloween — Dan's favourite time of the year. For now, there was no time to admire the seasonal occult ornaments and oddities.

"Wasn't that a little too easy to break into the mall?" said Kelly as the group rode the escalator up to the upper floor.

"A silent alarm must have been tripped. There are normally security guards around too," explained Augie.

At the top of the escalator was a high ceiling that always

looked as dark as night. The stars twinkled and the full moon glowed. Tiny orbs of light floated about like fireflies — some spiralled around the concrete mermaid fountain at the centre of the atrium. Around the fountain grew purple and pink mushrooms, which glowed via bioluminescence.

Beneath the artificial night sky and surrounding the fountain were numerous tables and chairs laid out very neatly. Hexagonal tiles formed a honeycomb beneath the six-sided tables.

They pushed together a few tables, interlocking them into a micro honeycomb, trying not to make noise as they did so. The large space in the atrium was normally packed with people, bustling about noisily. Now that the place was empty, any sound echoed throughout the mall.

"We need something to brace the door," said Dan as the group sat together, "and we need to search the area in case there is anyone here."

"Especially if they're of the undead variety," added Augie.

There were more than a few shudders at the thought that even the seemingly empty mall could be housing the infected.

Dan volunteered to get something to secure the door from which they had entered. This took their priority since it would take some time to search the mall for any infected, but only a moment to be swarmed by zombies via the unlocked door.

All the stores were locked, and there was no master control that opened them. That meant that they either had to cut chains and pick locks or break the glass doors. The latter was near impossible. Augie was only too happy to render his lock picking services.

Dan got some rope and a metal bar from a nearby sports store and headed back down to the entrance. Kelly followed him downstairs while the rest sat at the tables discussing their plans to search the area.

Her presence made him more nervous than a zombie could, but he was determined to play it cool. *Just say something to her,* was all that his mind could muster amidst his spiralling, muddied thoughts.

"Is this heavy enough?" Dan handed the metal bar to Kelly.

She held onto it with both hands, then using only her right hand she raised it above her head.

"It's okay," she said, balancing the bar that was nearly half her own bodyweight.

Dan was speechless. Kelly's strength was remarkable, especially for such a small, frail-looking girl.

He wanted to give his full attention to Kelly, but his brain and body weren't cooperating. His muscles worked on wrapping the rope around the door handles, while there were thunderstorms in his mind. He was not particularly good at tying knots and tied the rope the same way he would his shoelaces. Augie, a former boy scout, would probably have done a better job.

Dan stood back to admire his work. "That should be good... enough."

"So, what's this for?" Kelly pushed the large metal bar away from her dainty body.

"Oh yeah, that's a brace for—"

Kelly let out an ear-piercing scream. She slapped her hand onto her mouth, dropping the bar with a loud clang.

Dan spun to see what had startled her. An infected security guard had just come around the corner and was staring in their direction. His mouth was red and his eyes were milky, indicating full-blown infection. He snarled as he ran toward them, causing Kelly to flinch and trip over the giant pumpkin.

The guard wasn't very far from where they were standing and was upon them in an instant. Dan wasted no time in grabbing the bar from the ground and swinging it with all his might (though with great difficulty). It collided with the guard's left knee, which buckled against the natural bending motion of the joint.

The infected growled as he fell but showed no sign of pain. He appeared to be angrier and clawed the air, trying to reach the terrified Kelly, even in his crippled state.

Dan lifted the bar vertically, struggling to keep it balanced. He slammed his blunt, club-like weapon onto the fallen guard's head. With a loud crunching noise, the skull split down the middle. The body fell mangled on the floor, oozing blood from the fractured cranium.

Dan dropped the bloodied bar, and Kelly hopped back to her feet. The others gathered at the top of the escalator to see what had happened but didn't dare take one step down.

"The infected are already in here," said Dan, grabbing the bar once again and sliding it through the door's handles.

He rode the escalator back up with Kelly, staring down at the corpse below. He almost expected to see the zombie rise again and chase after them, even with a split skull and dangling eyeballs.

Kelly vomited over the railing and onto the doubly

dead zombie below. Dan, too, felt sick. His body was weak and his eyes saw everything as if covered in a grey veil.

"There are not that many guards in the mall. Only seven are on duty at a time," said Augie as the group gathered at the tables once again. "Actually, I guess you can say they're all off duty now."

"I don't think they're getting paid overtime," said Omar.

"Why do you know so much about the mall's security systems, Augie? Were you planning a heist?" asked Dan.

"Don't be daft, Dan. Why would I rob the mall? I was just very thorough in planning for the inevitable zombie apocalypse, obviously."

The fear of being attacked by zombies from outside the mall had subsided, but the internal threat was undeniably real. Everyone spoke in hushed voices, afraid of attracting the attention of any more zombies.

"If one infected, den dey all is d same, bai!" said Steve, leaning back in his chair and biting his nails.

"That means we have at least six infected on the inside. Our first priority is to get some weapons and take them out. Once the mall is secure, we should be able to hold out here for a while," said Dan to the attentive band of survivors.

Everyone nodded in agreement, but words were not spoken in response. The pressure was already starting to take its toll on them. Dan could tell the psychological effects were poisoning their minds, decaying reasoning and stability. One mental breakdown was all that was needed to break the squad.

Dan couldn't help but wonder how things could have turned out if he were alone. Certainly, it would have been more terrifying. He knew the importance of socialization, and with its prolonged absence, madness would surely set in, even in the most solitary of people. Dan could have tolerated loneliness to a degree, but would surviving be worth the trouble for the last man on the planet?

"If there were guns in the mall, I would say to shoot their brains out, but we'll be stuck with melee weapons," explained Augie, "in which case we should beat their brains out!"

Dan's stomach heaved, but it wasn't because of the living dead. On top of the stress of the recent skull crushing incident, he stacked something more worrisome — wooing Kelly. Ironically, the added troubles helped safeguard his sanity through distraction.

"We should split up—" said Omar.

"What?" spat Augie.

"We should go other—"

"Are you crazy? Do you know what happens when people split up?"

"I t'ink six guards and five ov we is not good odds, bai," said Steve.

"Someone always gets their guts ripped out when the survivors split up!" added Augie.

"Right, well, let's go get some weapons and we will have to stay together. We should cover the upper floor first since we will be able to see down below to the ground floor," said Dan, standing up.

The mall was one of the largest structures on the island, but it wasn't an overly grandiose labyrinth. One hour was all it took to be fully navigated by anyone other than a teenager with no spending limit. The spine of the mall, which connected the two atria, had an opening along its length, similar to the opening in the library. This meant that they were able to see down to the ground floor, while they were on the spine's upper floor.

They moved off through the spine, toward the Sunrise Atrium, keeping close to each other. They were totally unarmed, except for the bolt cutter, which could serve as a bludgeon.

They entered the sports store from which Dan had gotten the items to secure the door. The large red and white neon sign above the entrance was switched off but they were unofficially open for business, unbeknownst to the owners. Dotted across the floor were various exercise machines and weights, and in a lonesome corner rested a black lifting bench with a missing bar.

Along the walls were various sporting items. There were balls for almost every sport — soccer, tennis, and basketball were the most notable. The exercise machines and heavy weights on the floor made the store a maze.

Everyone walked about as if they were just casually browsing on a regular day at the mall. No one wanted to be the first to steal something. Dan's eyes met Kelly's and in a fraction of a second, his arm reached out to the nearest item within range. He slipped on the pair of black fingerless gloves, which he had locked on to like a vice-grip.

Be cool! She's just a girl. A pretty, smart girl who smells like a field of flowers...

Dan was the first to make his weapon selection too. He grasped the blood-red rubber grip of the wooden cricket bat and removed it from its display on the wall. He held it with his right arm outstretched, noting the bat's weight, balance, and range. It would do a better job beating zombies than hitting cricket balls — the handle would even match the blood.

He could see out the window straight into the parking lot. Everything was unchanged from when they had first arrived — his car was parked right at the entrance and no one was in the lot. He always worried about having his car stolen whenever he parked at the mall. He felt safe that there was no one to steal it now but worried about the damage zombies could pound into it.

After Dan had made his weapon selection, the others saw fit to steal their own. They were in an empty mall and could simply take anything they wanted. It was like a dream within a nightmare.

Kelly picked up a wooden hockey stick and grasped it tightly. It was the perfect weapon for her, though she was the strongest of the bunch and could fight with bowling balls if she so desired.

Augie selected a baseball bat, while Omar wielded a metal weight bar (smaller and lighter than the one Dan had used). Steve swung a titanium tennis racket as if it were a sword, to some doubtful stares. A racket wasn't the most durable object of those selected, but it seemed usable to the amateur zombie hunter.

"Okay, let's move out," said Dan when he noticed everyone standing at attention, awaiting instructions. "The guards won't be in any of the stores since they're all locked from the outside. We should be able to spot them fairly easily. Just pray that the lights don't go out when we find them."

Are any of them really prepared to beat the infected to death? He had already killed two of them, but he had doubts about his comrades. Augie seemed to be the only one eager to take on a zombie.

Dan took the first steps out of the store, staring to his left then the right. The others followed closely behind, with their weapons gripped firmly. Steve was the last to exit the store, and in addition to the racket in his right hand, he had a mop slung over his left shoulder. The fabric swayed at the end of the wooden pole, looking like white dreadlocks.

The place was quiet and there was no movement other than the band of survivors. However, they were fully aware that the silence was deceptive, and an attack was imminent. They stayed alert, holding their weapons at the ready.

Dan led the group, creeping forward. Every second that passed brought them closer to an encounter with the infected — it was inevitable.

He observed the mall with irrational attention to detail, like an overprotective parent scanning for hazards. He had never noticed all the jewellery stores or the tattoo parlour before. Despite having spent so much of his free time in the mall, he hadn't even visited half of the stores.

The mall's Halloween decorations were the best Dan had ever seen. There were cobwebs and skeletons, jack-o'-lanterns and rubber bats (the winged mammal, not the zombie-slaying weapon). One store had dressed all their mannequins as (sexy) witches. The zombies were an unintentional, but oddly fitting addition.

Dan's heart beat rapidly in his chest and a weak ringing in his ears whispered to him over the silence. He kept moving forward, peering into stores and over the railing to the ground floor below.

By the time they were almost at the end of the mall's

spine, Dan was no longer walking sneakily, and his pulse had just about returned to normal. His cricket bat was no longer raised above his head but hung lackadaisically at his side, although his trembling hand still shook his weapon. The fearfulness had implanted itself deep within his core.

He sighed as they reached the Sunrise Atrium, disappointed that they hadn't seen any zombies along the way. It meant that they had to wait even longer to clear the mall — the looming threat served only to exacerbate his anxiety. His left shoulder was stiff and tense. He massaged his knotted muscles as best he could without dropping his cricket bat.

The Sunrise Atrium was equally as large as the Midnight Atrium, but very different in design. Everything was bright-white and circular, from the tiles to the tables. The ceiling had fluffy white clouds slowly drifting across a digital blue sky.

Running across the floor was a virtual stream, with crystal clear water and vivid red fish. On the stream's bank were holograms of hopping green frogs and hovering above the flowing water were golden dragonflies. The simulated environment was designed to respond just as it would in real life, so they avoided splashing in the little river and scaring the animals. The only noise that could be heard was flowing water and the occasional croaking of frogs.

Like the Midnight Atrium, there was a physical statue here as well. This one was of a large ivory-coloured lion, whose majestic mane constantly fluttered in the artificial updraft. It stood upon its hind legs, clawing the air with its front limbs. Its jaws were open in an eternal roar, with large, sharp teeth bared.

Dan stood still and stared at the many tables and chairs neatly arranged in this space. There were no other people here, living or dead.

Bright white light from the artificial sun poured down upon the atrium. The walls were all covered in the whitest paint imaginable and had intricate circular patterns of silver and gold. The reflection of the light from the brilliantly white surfaces made the place glow. It was so bright that Dan had the urge to shield his already squinting eyes.

Dan's nervousness had diminished but the sick feeling in his stomach could only be cured by six dead zombies. The others seemed just as edgy, perhaps even more so.

No one spoke and they all tried to tread silently. The element of surprise was necessary in order to execute their plan. The last thing they wanted was to be ambushed.

The group spread out a bit, scanning the area for the guards. In the large atrium, they felt somewhat safe, since an attack would give them enough time to gather together. Omar checked beneath the tables while the others moved between them.

Dan snapped his palm to his chest and his muscles went as stiff as his unyielding hair, startled by a man inside the bookstore. However, it turned out to be nothing more than a cardboard cutout of a wizard holding a broomstick, standing right next to his collection of novels.

The group avoided touching any of the furniture and managed to make no noise until Omar crashed his head into a table when standing up. Everyone stood still, but there was no attack. Omar writhed like a befuddled earthworm, his large eyes all googly.

Everyone gathered together after, remaining

completely frozen for a full minute, and Dan whispered the plan, "Okay, the guards should be on the ground floor somewhere, so be ready. Let's go back this way."

Dan led the way once again, this time back to the Midnight Atrium. In the spine, the mall was less bright but still adequately lit. Dan stared at the mannequins in the windows, making sure that none of them moved.

Every single mannequin in the mall was incredibly realistic. They passed a little boy with a propeller hat, then a man in a three-piece suit worth more than Dan's car. There was even a sexy one in a short purple dress with breasts larger than a pregnant cow's udder.

Dan's anxiety grew the more he thought about the zombies. He became so stressed out that Kelly was no longer on his mind. He only cared about getting rid of the zombies so that he could relax. He thought about how he didn't appreciate the boring days of his life and wished for those days to return. *If things return to normal, I won't complain about being bored ever again. I'll enjoy my labs and lectures. I won't even mind seeing the Count again.*

The others wore masks of worry akin to the Count's grim face and looked about ready to flee at the first sight of the zombie guards. Steve's teeth chattered and everyone walked in a wobbly fashion as if on jelly legs.

They stepped into an area where a sports car was on display. Invisible strings of attraction tugged all eyeballs to the paint job. Red, green, and blue paints moved freely over white, like restless, liquid creatures moving around a canvas. They swirled and splashed together to form a cityscape painting, before separating again into colourful spirals.

This was the fastest and most expensive car on the island, with a security system so sophisticated it supposedly couldn't be stolen. Perhaps it was even magical because there was no discernible way to get such a large machine through the mall's human-sized doors.

"I have a toy replica of this car at home," said Augie, breaking the silence.

Augie slapped his hands so hard onto his mouth that everyone flinched simultaneously at the noise, even he himself. It was surprising he didn't knock himself unconscious with such a forceful open palm strike that would make any martial artist jealous. No one said a word in response, even after the echoing ended, but glared at Augie as if he had just committed a crime. Even so, the guards did not appear.

They all stood their ground, looking around as if expecting the infected to respond to the sound of Augie's voice or the sonic boom slap.

Dan suspected that the zombies were attracted to sound, but hadn't they made enough noise already? A pin drop would have sounded like an atomic explosion in the dead silent mall.

A loud ringing noise pierced the air, echoing in the empty mall. Omar clutched his chest and his knees buckled. Everyone's pigmentation temporarily warped to another dimension, and Steve's dreadlocks instantly bleached to the same colour as his mop.

Dan immediately planted his hand in his pocket and removed his phone. Without the fabric of his jeans to attenuate the noise, the phone rang even louder as Dan fumbled to answer it.

"Hello?" Dan answered, replacing the sound of ringing with his voice.

After exchanging puzzled expressions, everyone took out their own phones. They hadn't tried using the devices since they learned that the network was non-functional.

"The network must have been opened up recently. The phones weren't working earlier this morning," said Omar as he dialled a number.

The communications blackout had apparently been lifted, and the group's defences dropped. Weapons were lowered, stress temporarily melted away and fear was forgotten for a short moment. Smiles formed and chatting began.

6

THE DEAD ATTACK!

[Day 2]
~Similarities unite and divide~

SEVERAL JERKILY MOVING BODIES emerged from behind the nearby concrete pillars and kiosks. Blood-red saliva dripped from their mouths as they snarled at their unsuspecting prey.

Dan was alerted when a zombie stood up behind the car. All other uninfected eyes were focused on phones and ears were tuned in to their own chatter. They were completely oblivious to the impending threat.

"Oh sh—"

Before Dan could raise an alarm, the infected charged at the survivors, blocking all routes of escape. The attack was so sudden that the zombies were within attacking range before the survivors could reposition. They were surrounded. Phones dropped to the floor as chaos broke out.

The survivors instantly retaliated by swinging their weapons at the attackers. Having no real battle tactics, they just focused on immobilizing their enemies while avoiding their own infection — dodge, haymaker, breathe, repeat.

Screams came from every direction, echoing off the walls. Dan's eyes darted from one zombie to the next, until he had an idea of how many there were — four. He almost counted Omar as one, after he had turned a whiter shade of pale.

A uniformed zombie received a blow to the head from a cricket bat with such force that he was knocked down, leaving a crimson crescent of blood in the air as he fell. The crack was so loud that Dan thought the bat had split, but it was merely the sound of a splitting skull.

Steve's tennis racket proved just as useless as everyone had suspected. With two swift blows, the frame cracked and the strings became ensnared on a zombie's head. He quickly shifted to his mop, beating the zombies with the wooden pole. The white fabric whipped their faces as he jabbed them relentlessly. He did no damage to the infected with that mop at all, but he may have hurt their pride, if they had any.

Augie's weapon had fallen out of his hands and he resorted to wildly firing kicks. His eyes were shut tightly as he launched his meaty leg at a zombie. His pendulum kick, as he called it, was extremely powerful but also awfully slow, and missing the enemy meant that he was vulnerable in that instant.

A guard launched at Augie, opening his mouth as wide as it would go and extending his hands toward the uninfected skull. He grabbed hold of Augie's head and was about to bite when a hockey stick came crashing down on him. His grip slipped and Augie's leg swung forward again. The zombie flew back, knocking down another that was attacking Steve.

Omar had fallen and he struggled to get an infected guard off him. The end of his metal bar poked inside the guard's mouth, holding the zombie at bay.

The zombie struggled wildly, causing blood to leak down the shiny, silver-coloured bar. He clawed at Omar but was unable to reach.

Omar screamed louder than everyone else, much louder than Dan thought he was capable. His face was drenched in his own tears and his eyes were cartoonishly bulbous.

"Fireball! Fireball! METEOR STRIKE!" he yelled commands for magic spells, apparently forgetting he was Omar the lazy schoolboy and not Mango Meteor the mage — his online avatar.

Dan pounded on the back of the zombie's neck with his bat, causing Omar's bar to pierce through the undead skull. The body stopped struggling and slid down the bloody pole.

Omar rolled out from under the impaled zombie and scrambled to his feet. He looked like he was about to vomit, faint and wet his pants all at once; somehow, he managed to not do any.

Augie had recovered his baseball bat and pounded in the brains of the fallen infected. The others stood watching the corpses, utterly stupefied. While the brief, intense battle felt like it had gone on for an hour, the skirmish had lasted no more than two minutes and ended as abruptly as it had started.

Dan's heart raced, and his muscles burned as if highly corrosive acid coursed through his bloodstream. Judging by the heavy breathing, everyone else was equally as tired, if not more so. Just as important as being able to swing a weapon with force, was the stamina to keep doing it. Dan was pretty sure that none of these zombie-slaying warriors had sufficient training in combat endurance to outlast the tireless undead – not even Augie.

Dan wiped the sweat off his forehead and checked to make sure that there was no red mingled with the salty moisture. His cricket bat dripped blood as he walked past the bodies.

He counted the number of defeated infected. "So... four down."

Augie stood up when none of the bodies so much as twitched. His weapon was also coated in blood, but he had no problem with resting it on his shoulder — his clothes were just as drenched in blood, as were everyone else's.

The mall went silent again, and the survivors did not speak. They all knew that they had come extremely close to being overwhelmed, even when they had the advantage of numbers and preparation. If they had been attacked by all the infected guards at once, they surely would have lost the battle.

"Has... anyone been... bitten?" asked Augie, kneeling down to catch his breath.

Fortunately, no one had been infected and they all shook their heads. Physically, they were unharmed, but the distress from knowing there were still more infected guards was clear in their haggard faces. Steve had good reason to be more worried than the others since his racket had virtually vaporized and the mop was only good for wiping up the blood.

Dan kept his eyes on Kelly. She was breathing heavily

— hyperventilating almost — but she quickly recovered. Her athleticism was impressive, especially among the bumbling brigade.

"Apparently Ruby is with another group of survivors. I managed to tell her that we're at the mall, just before my phone went dead."

"No one is answering my calls," said Kelly as she dialled a number and pressed her phone against her ear.

"Me neither, bai!" added Steve.

Omar wept over his phone that had slipped out of his hand and shattered.

"Why is anyone surprised that phone calls aren't working? This is the zom-bie a-po-ca-lypse, people! Everybody's a zombie!" said Augie bluntly.

"Obviously Ruby isn't," said Dan.

"Not yet."

Everyone but Dan and Augie fidgeted — Omar tugged his beard, Steve's teeth chattered, and Kelly polished her locket with quivering fingers. They couldn't deny the possibility that everyone they knew had been zombified.

Sensing the building tension, Dan said, "The two attacks in the mall have something in common — the infected were attracted by sound. I think it should be possible to draw them to us instead of searching for them. All we need to do is make enough noise and be prepared."

"If dem eh hear we jus' now den dem zombies mus' be deaf, bai!" said Steve, through his chattering teeth.

Everyone followed Dan as he continued along their originally planned path. Their weapons were kept at the ready, gripped tightly but shaking slightly. The nervous trembling had heightened since the last intense encounter.

Dan stopped in front of a music store and peered through the window at the display. Every musical instrument ever invented by mankind sat inside this store. Surely music was the best way to attract the zombies. He swung his bat at the glass with enough force to eviscerate a zombie.

Upon impact, the glass flexed, and the bat rebounded, knocking Omar on his head. Omar sprawled on the ground like a starfish.

Augie calmly walked to the door and began opening the locks. Everyone made sure to stay out of Dan's striking distance as he continued beating the glass with his weapon. The race was on to see who would get in the store first. On Dan's ninth strike, the glass shattered, just as Augie pushed open the door.

Dan reached through the gaping hole and pulled out an instrument. In his right hand, he held his trusty cricket bat, and in his left, a shiny, black, electric guitar with a body shaped like a dragon's head. He slipped his cricket bat back into its case and slung the strap over his shoulder; the guitar strap went over the other shoulder.

Augie pressed a giant red button in the centre of the store, turning on all the speakers. Smooth jazz began playing, instantly causing everyone to bob their heads and tap their toes to the chill tunes — the relaxing music melted away everyone's stress.

Dan's dexterous fingers pressed down on the frets and plucked the strings perfectly. The hypnotic effect of the jazz was broken, replaced by a much louder, beautifully chaotic melody, which infused everyone with adrenaline – feet planted firmly, and eyes searched with the Count's vigilance.

He flicked a switch on the guitar's body, and from the head emerged a projection of a gigantic black dragon. It opened its armoured jaws, and breathed holographic fire, bathing the entire place in bright, red light. Through the speakers came a tremendous roar as the fire breath consumed everything.

"Maybe Steve was right," said Augie. "Maybe the remaining zombies *are* deaf."

Augie had spoken too soon, for through the flames, a lone zombie guard came running. The zombie clawed her way toward them head-on, with all her limbs digging into the solid floor like an animal ready to pounce. Her milky eyes scanned everyone before she dashed toward Kelly, who stood next to Dan, mouth agape in absolute shock.

The guard lunged forward but was stopped by a baseball bat bash on the head. Her neck made a cracking sound almost as loud as the collision of the bat and skull. She flipped over and fell onto her back, mangled and twitching. Augie, Omar and Steve wasted no time in clubbing her head to a bloody, unrecognizable pulp.

Dan didn't stop playing the guitar as he watched the zombie meet her demise. He did not even draw his own weapon to fight. Fortunately, they had been attacked by only a single zombie this time and each one they took out meant the mall had become a bit safer.

"One more down," said Dan, as the brain splattering ended. He continued strumming on the guitar strings.

"Nice, so that means just one more left," said a winded Augie.

The dragon glared at the survivors, growled, and shot fire in their direction. The monster's actions were wholly controlled by a malevolent artificial intelligence. Fortunately, the AI was trapped in the body of a ghost, which spat fire as cool as the surrounding air.

The guitar playing stopped as another sound entered the air — an unholy combination of snarling, scratching, and moaning. Everyone looked in the direction of the nearby elevator, which had started moving upward. Even the dragon stared with malicious intent. Through the glass frame a humanoid shape could be seen, wearing the uniform of a mall guard.

"Is that normal zombie behaviour, Augie?" asked Dan.

"What the hell?! Zombies can't use elevators!" said Augie, staring at the guard with his mouth open in disbelief.

Obviously, this was not something in his database of zombie knowledge. Zombies, with their destroyed, rotting brains, should not exhibit the same intelligence as when they were alive.

Maybe they can perform basic actions deeply encoded in the brain. Doesn't matter right now... Dan was more concerned with survival than troubling himself with zombie brain and motor functions.

This time, they could attack first. This time they were the predators, and the zombie was the prey. It didn't feel quite like that to Dan, though.

If I stand here any longer, I won't be able to move! Move!

Dan ran toward the elevator and pressed the call button several times. The transparent cylindrical tube slid down the shaft to the ground floor. The zombie guard stared through the slowly opening doors at Dan on the other side.

"Zoooombie, come out to plaaaaay," said Dan,

provoking his target in a manner easily misconstrued as a psychotic break.

Dan had not gone mad. He welcomed that which he feared to habituate to the zombie stimulus. He tricked his anxious mind into thinking that a zombie presented no more danger to him than a monster made entirely of marshmallow.

The guard's growls grew steadily louder with the taunts and the sight of a potential victim. He pounced as soon as the doors had opened just wide enough for him to exit.

Dan took a few steps back and everyone spread out as the guitar rose into the air. With a loud musical crash, the guitar smashed on the zombie's head. Holographic musical notes fell out of the broken, crying guitar. The dragon shrieked, breathed its final breath onto the ceiling, and disappeared.

The guard wobbled on the spot with the guitar wrapped around his head, covering his eyes. Dan drew the bat from its case and pounded on the exposed top of the zombie's head.

The beating was thorough and the zombie collapsed, his blood pooling inside the guitar's frame. With a sigh of relief, Dan turned to the group and forced his trembling lips into a crooked smile. Without looking back, he walked off toward the Midnight Atrium, shaking the blood off his cricket bat. The handle did indeed match the blood.

***

Finally, with the mall clear of infected, the survivors could take some time to rest their tired bodies and weary minds. They washed the blood off themselves as best they could and gathered again at the same tables from earlier. It was already afternoon when they settled down and it was imperative that they sort out their priorities before they lost the sunlight.

Dan sat at the table with his fingers interlocked and his chin resting on his hands. His mind wandered into thought as it so often did. In the midst of the zombie apocalypse, even after fighting for his life against the walking dead, Kelly once again became his primary focus. With every passing second, she grew more beautiful in Dan's eyes.

Dan was not particularly emotional by any means. His feelings were normally kept locked away, hidden behind a mask of indifference.

Thinking rationally is the only way to keep everyone safe, he thought, forcibly replacing emotion with logic. *Emotions can ruin us. Everyone wants to go home to their family and friends. We need food and security above all else. We need to prioritize needs over our wants for now, just so we can survive.*

His nerves had dispersed ever since annihilating the last zombie. However, the more he thought about Kelly, the more butterflies gathered and multiplied within his stomach. The gearwheels in his heart began turning, forcing his brain to release the key ingredients of a love potion. His stomach felt queasy and his face was sweaty, even in the cold, controlled atmosphere of the mall.

"We haven't eaten in a while and I'm starving," said Dan, leaning back in his chair and wiping the sweat off his nose.

"All the cooked food is spoiled by now." Omar looked woozy.

"Why would there be cooked food? There's no one here to cook," said Kelly.

"Zombie chefs, bai!"

"There are no zombie chefs, Steve," said Dan. "There are no zombie chefs, right, Augie?"

"Definitely no zombie chefs but I have heard that stale food is refrigerated at night and served in the morning. It would be an insult if I were to die of food poisoning during the zombie apocalypse. We can get stuff from the supermarket. That should last us a while," said survival expert Augie.

"I think I would vomit anything I eat right now," said Omar, grimacing and clutching his belly.

Blood and gore were not the perfect appetizers. Dan could see images of the infected when he closed his eyes (both with and without squashed skulls) and they made him sick. No number of violent movies or video games could truly prepare someone for the imagery of mutilated corpses, or walls, floors and clothing painted with blood.

"Eh, um, the news!" blurted out Augie after remembering the next step in the plan he had thought of in his head so many times. "There is probably a news report on TV!"

"It have ah electronics store right round d corna, bai!" mentioned Steve, pointing in the appropriate direction.

"Did anyone check to see if there's anything on the internet?" asked Kelly with a voice full of confidence.

"The internet is down. Nothing seems to be working right," said Augie. "But local TV stations use a different broadcast system, so we could try that."

"Okay, let's go," said Dan, getting up from his seat.

The group walked off together, making not a sound but that of their footsteps. Steve led the way to a store with many large televisions, computers and various electronic devices.

They stopped and stared at the unusual glass sign above the entrance to the Pork Chop Palace electronics store. The bizarre but captivating artwork depicted a chubby, pink, bipedal pig, toting a large bag of money, being chased by a fireman with an axe. Dan could not think of a reason why anyone would name an electronics store after meat, and the porker mascot made even less sense.

"Aloo Kimura," said Dan, with a small smile and the swish and flick of an invisible magic wand.

"It's actually 'Aloo Himura'," said Augie, whipping out the cutter from his backpack and immediately severing the chains that secured the doors.

The lock fell to the floor with a loud knock, followed by the clatter of the loose chains. But this store was more secure than the others. Obviously paranoid about having their overpriced merchandise stolen, the owners had placed no less than seventeen locks on the door.

"Let me see that for a second," said Kelly, grabbing the cutter as Augie searched his backpack for the lock pick.

Kelly took a close look at the door, stepped back and smashed the glass with the metal end of the cutter. One hit was all it took to puncture the glass, and a few more blows made an opening wide enough to fit through.

Kelly stepped inside the store, while everyone else stood and stared in astonishment.

Is Kelly really that strong or was that glass weaker than the one I broke?

"Are you secretly a superhero?" Omar's starry pupils quadrupled in size.

Augie folded his arms and twisted his face like a jealous toddler.

"It wouldn't be a secret if I told you," replied Kelly with a smile.

Everyone carefully entered through the opening, into the most expensive store in the galaxy. Dan had never purchased anything in Pork Chop Palace because of their ridiculous prices. Now that he could take anything he wanted, he didn't feel like it.

The large screen at the centre of the room immediately caught everyone's attention. It was twice as large as a king-sized bed and didn't look like it could fit through the average-sized door.

"Is this thing powered by magic?" Dan asked himself aloud, as he searched for a power button. "How the hell do you get the TV to turn on?"

The blackness on the screen slowly faded away, replaced by white light and colours.

"Magic indeed," said Kelly.

"If I knew it was this easy to steal a TV, I would have done this a long time ago," joked Augie.

"You woulda only need to kill a few security guards, bai!" said Steve, ruining Augie's daydream.

Projected in 3D from the TV screen was a female news reporter dressed in a black suit, with her cleavage exposed. She addressed them:

"...*Those infected by the Human Neural Parasite, HNP, suffer from extreme mental instability and become a threat to everyone around them. It is strongly advised that contact with the infected be avoided at all costs due to the highly contagious nature of this disease. Infection is irreversible...*"

"Come on, tell us something we don't know," interrupted Omar. He was immediately shushed.

"*...target appears to be the summit being held on the island. Leaders from around the world are now under threat of infection and becoming potential carriers as well. All means of exit from the island have been shut down. We are now in full quarantine. All citizens are required to stay indoors and should not attempt to reach anyone, for their own safety. Communications remain scrambled but rest assured that local forces are attempting to rectify the situation.*"

"So, whoever is behind this is trying to zombify world leaders? Looks like we got caught in a bioterrorism plot," commented Augie.

"Maybe it is just coincidence," suggested Kelly.

"Coincidence or not, it really doesn't matter. We're still trapped in this quagmire of shit either way," said Dan.

The news report went on for a short while, until they noticed a loop in the video. Just like the radio report from earlier that day, this was also recorded and set to play repeatedly.

Nothing else was being broadcast on the television. The news report was from a local source and very limited in content. They tried tuning in to international news for further updates, but to no avail.

"You don't think the disease spread so quickly that the entire country has completely shut down, do you?" asked Kelly. "I mean, there were no live news broadcasts, and this is the biggest story ever."

She shifted her weight to one side and fiddled with the smooth hair that fell next to her locket. Pearly front teeth nibbled her lower lip.

"And it's only the second day after the infection on campus," Dan added. "If it spread that fast, then things could be much grimmer than we thought."

"It's getting late, so we should get our barricades up before nightfall," said Augie, deep in thought, scratching his chin.

"I haven't eaten in a while and I think I'll die if I don't get something right now," said Dan, clutching his belly. "I'm heading over to the supermarket to grab something real quick. We will all need our energy to get those barriers up on time today."

Dan walked out of the store and headed toward the Sunrise Atrium. His cricket bat was fastened securely on his back. Everyone kept their selected weapons with them wherever they went, even though the mall was presumably safe — they really couldn't be *too* safe at a time like this.

Kelly followed Dan to the supermarket, while the others scattered. The walk to the other side of the mall was awkwardly quiet. Despite the threat of undead attacks behind them, they both remained silent.

So she decided to go with me. Does that mean she likes me or what? Dan wished now, more than ever before in his life, that he had the power to read minds.

7

NIGHT OF THE DEAD!

[Day 2]

~Consequence is a better teacher than reward~

DAN HEADED STRAIGHT FOR the snack aisle of the supermarket. He grabbed a golden sponge cake and devoured it like a greedy monster. His dry mouth made the mushy cake hard to swallow, but his burning, uneasy stomach finally felt relief.

Through the windows of the supermarket, the mall's parking lot was clearly visible. It was just as empty as when they had first arrived. However, the light and shadows were different — it was clearly getting late. The weather was the same — sunny with few clouds.

"So good..." Dan mumbled through a mouthful of sugary snacks.

"The mall isn't such a bad place to be stuck in, after all," said Kelly, ignoring Dan's poor etiquette.

"Well, there aren't any cakes on the mountains," said Dan, almost choking, while forcing down a couple peanut-butter-infused chocolates.

When she wasn't looking, Dan took the opportunity

to stare at Kelly. Her hair lay perfectly neat without a stray strand, her skin flawless, and she somehow smelled like a field of flowers.

Dan and Kelly were quite the opposites. Dan's naturally wild hair was only controlled by hair gel, his face glistened with a film of oil and his scent, at the moment, was far more similar to a zombie than a flower in bloom.

Kelly was very popular within her many social circles, including her school clique, tennis club, dance crew, a band where she was the lead singer, three charity organizations, and of course, her affluent family and their even richer friends. Dan was a poor bum with a group of nerd friends.

The list of differences went on, but essentially, Kelly was awesome, and Dan was pretty lame. Still, Dan embraced his lameness and liked being the underdog. He stubbornly held on to the belief that one day he would win a victory so monumental, it would make a lifetime of being a loser worth the trouble. But first, he would first have to overcome his atychiphobia.

Dan didn't want Kelly to be a failed attempt at love. His brain was busy running probability analyses.

Kelly walked over to a nearby shelf, swinging her hips. She bent over and began collecting edible items to take back for the others.

Dan was hypnotized by the way her jeans clung tightly to her body, revealing every curve. He quickly stuffed his open mouth with a cake when she turned around.

"Are you on a diet?" said Dan jokingly, noticing that Kelly had only eaten one chocolate-covered jellybean.

Kelly responded with an awkward smile, to which Dan returned an equally awkward chuckle.

Did I just imply that she's fat?

"Not that you're fat or anything..." he tried to recover but failed miserably. "Not that there's anything wrong with being fat if you want to be..."

Quick, change the subject!

"So..." Dan searched for something — anything — to talk about.

He was horrible at starting conversations. He was quite bad at maintaining them as well, if he ever got past the first sentence.

Think of a topic! Family? No, they could be dead. Friends? No, they could also be dead...

"What do you do for fun, Dan?" asked Kelly.

Perfect, she started the conversation. Wait... what do I do for fun? Dan's internal crisis escalated. *Quick, make a joke about killing zombies!*

"Other than killing zombies, I mean," she added.

Shit.

"I uhh... play the guitar." Dan was lucky enough to remember something interesting about himself without too much delay.

"Oh right, nice. Maybe you can teach me a bit. After the zombie apocalypse, of course," said Kelly with a smile.

This is it. It's happening!

Dan had bought a guitar for the sole purpose of picking up chicks. He could just barely string together a few chords and play a couple of songs. His investment was finally paying off.

"I can teach you what I know over lunch sometime... or dinner," replied Dan, while casting his most seductive look.

Smooth.

Kelly's eyes widened and she looked away for a moment, saying nothing.

"Did I tell you that I'm engaged?" Kelly had the perfect defence to Dan's weak pickup attempt.

"Engaged in what?"

"I'm getting married, Dan."

Dan's mouth fell open, and he was unable to mentally process such a sudden plot twist. He remained silent as the future he had fantasized about evaporated from his mind.

"It's scary actually, to feel like I'm giving up my freedom," said Kelly, the happiness leaving her face.

"Freedom might change but it shouldn't go away. Sounds like a fair trade for true love," said Dan. "At least you have a plan. I have only dreams."

"Dreams made real are the greatest adventures!" said Kelly, once again bubbling with optimism.

Dan let her wisdom sink in. The room fell silent for a moment and his precognitive senses tingled.

Here it comes.

"And what about you? Do you have a girlfriend, fiancée, wife?" asked Kelly.

Right on cue.

"No," he responded, simply.

"As free as a bird."

"Do you have a sexy sister you could hook me up with?" asked Dan with uncharacteristic charisma.

Kelly's eyelids fluttered and she stuttered, "Y-yes, I do, but she has always been the popular one who gets all the guys. So no, I won't hook up the two of you."

"Why not?"

"She's too wild for a nice boy like you."

"Nice boy?" said Dan, feeling insulted by both words.

"I guess I can forget about those guitar lessons."

Dan glanced down at his wristwatch.

"We really need to get the barricades up before sundown," said Dan, changing the subject. "This time, they need to be useful, unlike the one in the library. Seriously, whose idea was it to use a table?"

"There's not much else in the library except books."

It was risky to have gone as long as they did without fortifying the mall, and Augie had been constantly reminding them about how important the barricades were. Dan stuffed Kelly's shopping bag with cakes, chocolates and canned meat for the others.

I'll still teach you, but you have to bring your sister along. That's what I should have said!

Dan looked back at the shelves once more to see if he had missed any snack that he wanted to try. He saw none, but even if he did, he couldn't swallow another morsel. He turned on his heel, with Kelly at his side.

As they began the journey back toward the Midnight Atrium, Dan noticed something in the corner of his eye. He slowly rotated his head to the left and stared out into the parking lot. A sudden jolt of terror zapped his heart. A sole figure stood in place, swaying slightly as if drunk, in the middle of the open lot.

Dan cursed the zombie in a hushed tone, as he ducked behind a shelf.

Kelly immediately mimicked his actions with a squeak. She was very careful not to spill the contents of her bag. They stayed there for a moment.

Dan peeked his head out from cover. The zombie had its back to them, so they took the opportunity to sneak away.

They sprinted across the mall, finding the others along the way, and urged the importance of an immediate meeting. Augie was picking the lock to the toy store when they passed him. He stared longingly at the stuffed toy giraffe on the other side of the glass before joining them.

Within minutes, the entire group sat at their meeting spot in the Midnight Atrium. Everyone was extremely tense — it was clearly visible on their faces, which appeared to have aged ten years. Dan and Kelly spread out the snacks they had collected onto the table, but no one took any.

"Couldn't this wait a bit longer?" pleaded Augie. "I was just about to hit the mother lode."

"There's a zombie in the parking lot," said Dan, getting straight to the point. "We need to get our barricades up right now and clear him out before he attracts more of them. The last thing we want is a large horde in the middle of the night."

"Doesn't the mall have too many glass windows and doors to barricade?" asked Omar.

"No rotting zombies can break through the glass," Augie immediately replied.

"But the zombies aren't rotting..." said Dan.

"Ent Kelly break d glass like non, bai?" whimpered Steve, chewing on his fingers.

"Zombies won't be strong enough to break the glass unless they come in huge numbers," argued Augie.

"I hope you're not delaying our fortification so that you can go play with toys, Augie!" snapped Dan.

"...No," replied a shifty-eyed Augie.

"We just need to make sure that the doors are securely locked and that the inside of the mall isn't visible from the outside. They won't break in unless they know we're here," said Kelly.

Dan stood up. "Okay, so you can start with that. Just be sure not to make too much noise. I'll take care of the zombie outside."

"Are you insane?" Kelly fired at Dan. "That's just being reckless and selfish!"

"How am I being selfish?"

"We need each other here. This lone wolf attitude of yours will get us all killed!" Kelly quarrelled, springing to her feet like a wild rabbit.

"Lone wolf? Really?"

"You wandered off to the supermarket earlier and now you want to go out there by yourself!"

"Is that why you went with me?"

Kelly puffed out her cheeks.

"Perhaps you would like to accompany me on this zombie hunt?"

"Stop being such an ass!" Kelly pouted, with her arms akimbo.

"If I'm not back in ten minutes, then I'm probably dead."

"Ugh, you're impossible! If you want to die then fine, but I hope your ghost feels guilty!"

"Why would my ghost feel guilty?"

"For being such a huge ass!"

"Guys, help me out here..."

"I not getting myself involved in this husband and wife

t'ing, nah!" said Steve, with folded arms.

"Is anyone else willing to go out there and get rid of a zombie?" asked Dan, calmly.

No one responded.

"Maybe that zombie out there is like a scout. Maybe more will come if it stays around. All I know for sure is that I feel really uncomfortable with it being there."

Dan hadn't given his plan much thought. He knew that the more he thought about his decision, the more hesitant he would be to execute it. He walked to the exit with the desire to complete his task quickly, trying not to think about what awaited him.

"It's dangerous to go alone. Take me," said Augie, posing with his baseball bat.

Dan nodded. *Now we have the advantage of numbers, but zombies aren't usually alone. We need to be prepared for a drastic change for the worse.*

Dan took the first step outside into the parking lot. His car was right there, casting a long shadow in the afternoon sun. The outside air was warm, and Augie began perspiring profusely almost immediately.

The lone zombie couldn't be seen from their location. Dan surveyed the area, making sure no other infected were around before heading off in the direction of their target. The place was quiet and empty and appeared to be safe. The danger was looming just beyond their view.

They moved at a brisk pace, hoping to accomplish their mission quickly and without any mishaps. They were sure to check every corner in which a zombie could hide so that they could avoid being pounced upon.

They neared the Sunrise Atrium, where the zombie

had been spotted. Dan scanned the area but saw no sign of the infected.

"Dammit, he's gone!" said Dan in an undertone to his fellow zombie hunter.

"Are you sure..."

"Yes, I'm sure he was there! Let's move around to the front."

They pressed forward, planning to circle the Sunrise Atrium in search of the zombie. Dan knew that their target was around somewhere, but being unable to locate the threat felt worse than just facing it head-on. It was like seeing an aggressive, deadly centipede and taking his eyes off it for one second, allowing the creature to scuttle away and come back later to kill him in his sleep.

"Maybe it was a reflection of a mannequin in the glass or YEAAAAAAARGHH!" Augie shot into the air like a decompressing spring.

A zombie ran out from a spot nestled at the entrance to the Sunrise Atrium. It was the same one Dan had seen, and no longer appeared to be drunk.

"I told you so!" said Dan, feeling both relief and a hint of fear. "At least now we don't have to walk all the way around the mall."

"Indeed."

It could be worse. At least he didn't bring his friends. He felt confident that they could bring down this zombie without much difficulty.

Dan readied his bat, and Augie collected himself and did the same.

"Holy guano! It's the Count!" exclaimed Dan.

Augie had never seen the legendary vampire lecturer

known as the Count. The zombie's face was even more wrinkled than before — his sunken eyes and bloody, sharp teeth made him look even more vampiric. If Dan thought that he smelled bad when alive, his infected corpse was far worse.

"You were right," said Augie. "He really does look like a vampire."

The zombie snarled as he lunged forward to attack Dan. His teeth were bared, and the bloody secretion from his mouth leaked low and stained his suit. The infected was not going to allow himself to be an easy target.

Dan wasted no time in crashing his cricket bat into the skull of the undead fiend. Zombie Count stumbled back, clutching his head. He was counting stars now.

In an instant, the zombie continued his attempt to infect Dan, charging forward like a gaunt goat. Augie struck him at the side of his knee, causing it to twist. The zombie fell, but stood again quickly, despite his mangled leg. A barrage of attacks on his head then followed and he fell again. The attacks didn't cease even as he touched the ground.

"Bloody hell!" said Dan, short of breath, as he finally stopped crushing the zombie's brain.

"Well, that was... easier than I expected," said Augie, panting.

Dan might have had daydreams about slaying the evil vampire, but never did he expect to actually do it. He felt a bit psychopathic, having just bludgeoned the zombie to a second death. At least his bad score wasn't going to affect his grade point average anymore. Of course, his grades were among the least of his worries at the moment.

"Let's get back inside quick! This empty lot is creepy,"

said Augie, as he turned and began walking back.

"Wait, we should hide the body so that it doesn't attract more."

"What? I'm not touching that thing. I could get infected... or worse!"

"The infection zombifies you. What's worse than that?"

"Getting expelled. Zombies can't go to school! I love school, Dan!"

"Just help me drag him into that ditch," said Dan, grabbing onto the zombie's heel.

Augie reluctantly held on to the zombie's broken leg — it felt bony and very loose as if only a few strands of muscle fibres and tendons held it together. They shielded their noses as they got a whiff of his ghastly scent — a mixture of manure, a sweaty body odour, and death.

They dragged him a short distance, just out of the mall's compound and left him inside a drainage ditch at the side of the road. They kept looking over their shoulders and at distant buildings where they thought the infected may have been hiding in wait. The blood and brains they had trailed all the way to the ditch stayed in the parking lot — Steve's mop would have been useful.

As they headed back to the entrance, Dan took a look around. *The highway is still deserted and this place is barren. I wonder if we are the only survivors. No, Ruby called earlier so she must be alright. Maybe there are more survivors on their way here.*

As if reading Dan's thoughts, Augie then asked, "So what about Ruby? Do you think she is coming here?"

"She should be okay if she's with a group of survivors like us," replied Dan.

"Another group, huh? You know that can be both good and bad. More people means a larger fighting force, but at the same time, it means a struggle for resources and power. I saw a movie where..."

Dan tuned off Augie's voice as his mind swam in thoughts. *How did the Count get all the way here? Where are the other zombies? If we survived and so did Ruby, then there must be others holding out as well. Where are the other survivors?* Only when he was almost back by the mall's entrance did he realize that he hadn't heard a word of Augie's story. Dan just nodded at everything Augie said, without even looking at him.

As they re-entered the mall, Augie immediately locked the doors. Everyone was relieved to see that they had returned unscathed.

"It also means that we will have to remove our barricades if they arrive here," Augie continued.

"You haven't been bitten, have you, Augie?" asked Omar, mockingly.

"Zombie experts like me never get bitten!"

"Happy to see that I'm still alive?" Dan asked Kelly.

She simply puffed up her cheeks, folded her arms and turned away with a "Humph!"

"Were you all just waiting here the entire time? Let's set up the defences!" Dan instructed.

Everyone immediately got busy blocking the glass doors and windows with whatever they could find. They dragged shelves from nearby stores and plastered the glass with posters. At the main entrance was a poster for Body Bag Zombies.

Augie had gotten frustrated with opening locks and

tried smashing the glass, to no effect. Kelly laughed at him every time.

By the time the sun was about to set, all the barricades were up. They had no idea how effective their makeshift defences were; no one wanted to go outside to test them. As the darkness crept up on them, the outside seemed increasingly menacing. The exit at the Midnight Atrium was chosen for emergency evacuation — should the need arise, they could easily and quickly remove the barricades there.

When their task was done, and they had the time to rest for a while, Dan took a new phone from Pork Chop Palace. With the communications blackout, it was only good for playing games. Dan's eyes locked on to the screen for two hours straight, as he directed an owl to shoot down evil llama enemies. He only stopped when Omar slipped and fell in front of him with a loud thud and a groan.

Even as the sky darkened, there were no phone calls. There was just a ghostly calm and fearful dread of the impending darkness.

***

The night was upon them and Dan stared through an uncovered window on the upper floor, right into the parking lot below. The lights were off in this store, so he was cloaked in the darkness. On the nearby mountains, there were scattered dots of light where houses were seen at daytime. His car was illuminated by photosensitive lights down below, with an engine as cold as the night air.

Logically, he should have been pondering on the distant lights and wondering if there were any survivors on the mountains. Logic was fading, quickly being replaced by emotion.

She's too young to get married. I should advise her to wait. No, I can't interfere in her happiness... she can't marry a zombie anyway...

"Are you expecting another phone call?" asked Kelly, entering the room.

Not anticipating any visitors, Dan jumped in surprise and his heartrate soared. He could just make out Kelly's figure, glowing almost, in the darkness. His stomach lurched. *I am not prepared!*

He waited until she moved closer before replying, "I wasn't expecting the first one."

She stood beside him and looked out to the mountains which she seemed to long for so much. Her body melded with the shadows but upon her chest was a glint of green and gold that could not be hidden.

"I like your locket," said Dan, mesmerized by the pendant that Kelly always wore around her neck.

The green emerald embedded within the golden heart locket glowed as Kelly held it between her fingers. "It was a gift from my father. He told me to find whatever I love the most in this world and keep it inside."

Dan's eyes remained fixed on the locket, expecting Kelly to open it without being asked.

"And what's inside it?"

As if attempting to immediately appease Dan's curiosity, the golden heart split open like a clamshell. The inside didn't shine like the outer surface.

"It's dark in here, Kelly. I can't see anything!"

"That's because there is nothing inside."

"Who carries around an empty locket?"

"I love many things, so it is difficult to select just one

that is above all others. But I feel like this unexpected adventure of ours will help in my decision. It's in the darkest times that we see what is most important."

Dan had not known love as Kelly did. He liked many things but never loved anything or anyone in particular. His affection for Kelly grew unopposed and so, he found no conflict in himself when deciding what was most important.

"Wisdom from someone so young feels unnatural," said Dan.

Kelly's pink cheeks glowed as much as the emerald.

"Aren't lockets for lovers?" asked Dan.

"I guess."

"Then why not keep your fiancé in it?"

"I love him, but I don't see him in that way."

"In what way? Like a lover?"

"I've known him since we were kids and I've always seen him as my brother."

"You don't see your fiancé as being your lover? How does that work?"

"It's complicated, especially now."

"What makes it so complicated?" asked Dan.

Kelly hesitated for a moment, before finally responding, "You."

Well, this was certainly unexpected. Don't mess this up!

"I... I..." Dan stammered like a malfunctioning robot.

"I know we haven't spent a lot of time with each other, but I feel like we're connected in a way. I want to say something but I'm not sure how you'd react..."

Say it!

The stars had finally aligned and Dan had to act within

this infinitesimal window of opportunity. The conditions were right and his probability of success was astronomically high. Dan's doubts dropped to zero.

Dan mustered all his courage, reached out and held Kelly's hand, "I love you."

The heart locket snapped shut with a click.

"I don't wish to give you hope where there is none," said Kelly, slowly releasing her hand from Dan's gentle grip.

The perfect future was merely an illusion. Dan was devastated. Fortunately, his glistening eyes were invisible.

"Hope..." Dan scoffed. "Hope can destroy you from the inside, like a parasite."

Dan turned to face the window again and tried to hold back the tears that wanted to trickle down his cheeks.

The gold and green locket silently went out the door.

What just happened?

***

Half an hour had passed since the brutal rejection and Dan still stood there in shock, trying to crush his dog tag with a clenched fist. His head was flooded with thoughts. He couldn't stop thinking about Kelly.

He leaned against the window, staring into the nothingness. The shadows were still and no living thing budged at all. Even the trees dared not move a leaf.

I was sure it was the right moment. Was it too soon? Of course it was too soon! We've barely spent a day together! People can fall in love in a day, especially after what we've been through...

The doldrums of peace and quiet came to an end as a faint wailing sound cut through the silence in the mall. It was coming from outside, but its origin wasn't clear. It steadily grew louder, loud enough that everyone was alerted and had gathered in the room.

"What the heck is that?" asked Augie, pressing against the glass and trying to see if anything was moving below.

Another noise became audible — this one sounded like rapid pounding. The beat was regular and familiar.

"LOOK! What is that?" Omar pressed his nose against the glass and looked up at the starry sky.

"It sounds like a helicopter," said Dan.

The noise kept getting louder.

"There it is!" said Kelly, pointing at the only moving object in the night sky.

Then everything came into view in a rush. Two bright lights came speeding along the pitch-black road. A large, yellow SUV sped onto the mall's parking lot and a black helicopter followed. The chopper hovered over the road, facing the direction from which the SUV had come.

A wave of shapes flowed over the road. The yellow glow of the streetlights revealed the infected spreading like a shadow, growing larger as their wails became louder. The waves from the ocean of death flowed turbulently as if being forced forward by a powerful, otherworldly storm.

Everyone stared, held by either fear or intrigue. A bright light burst from the helicopter, accompanied by a noise that could only be the firing of an automatic machine gun. The infected toppled and the incoming wave slowed down.

The bullets glowed white as they rapidly cut through the darkness and planted themselves in the infected flesh.

"They're trying to get inside!" shouted Augie over all the noise.

He pointed down to the parking lot, at the group of survivors approaching the entrance. Everyone rushed downstairs to clear the barricades.

Didn't Augie say that other survivors can mean trouble? Why is he so eager to let them in?

Just like they had planned, the barricades were cleared away and they could see the other survivors through the glass door — normal eyes and no bloody mouths. The rope slid off and the door opened. The air that rushed in was even colder than inside the mall. Augie looked about, ready to bash the skulls of their surprise guests.

The new survivors rushed into the mall as if the undead were snapping at their heels and clawing at their backs. Dan saw the helicopter fly low above the road as the horde of infected was eradicated by the heavy gunfire.

"Dan, it's so good to see you!" exclaimed one of the new survivors as she threw her arms around him.

"Ruby!" said Dan, short of words as he always was for a proper conversation. "I knew you'd be alright."

Ruby was taller than Kelly and her red hair looked like she ironed it twice daily. She released Dan and flashed a broad, forced smile.

Augie stayed far away and kept looking at the new guests as if he would have to crush their skulls at any moment.

"This is Zoe," said Ruby, pointing to a girl who was wearing a white t-shirt with a red cross on the back and had her hair tied up in a ponytail.

At the very moment Zoe saw Dan for the first time, an invisible arrow of lust struck her in the bum. Her eyes were replaced by pink pulsating hearts, matching the colour of her blushing cheeks.

"And Rock," continued Ruby, patting the shoulder of a guy with a beautiful afro and a bird's nest for a hat.

It was the very same afro from the library. Maurice was really named Rock. Shocking. *Maurice suits him better.* Dan was amazed and impressed that Rock had survived the chaos on campus.

"Is that a military helicopter outside?" asked Dan.

"Yeah, apparently they have a large force posted where the summit is being held. Lucky for us, this squad found us on campus," explained Ruby.

"So there are more survivors from campus?" asked Kelly.

"We were the only ones those guys got out. We didn't see anyone else around except for the infected. Zoe was in the apartment building with me and Rock was running like hell around campus."

"Cardio, bitches! Nam sayin'?" said Rock with a pose.

After several more rounds of gunfire, the helicopter set down in the parking lot and soldiers approached the mall. Not a single zombie stirred — their bodies remained piled up on the road.

Two soldiers entered the mall, with war-worn faces, which told more about their experiences than the weapons they carried. They looked as if they were completely unfazed by the walking dead.

"Now that you're safe, we need to get some info from you," said one, who appeared to be the commanding officer.

"You doh t'ink we should close the door first, bai?" asked Steve in a trembling voice.

"Let's have a little chat, kids," said the soldier.

Everyone stood quietly beside the giant pumpkin, with

wide eyes and trembling fingers. The wind blew inside and it was as cold as ice. Augie kept shifting his eyes from one soldier to the next, and to the parking lot outside as if expecting more zombies to rush in at any moment.

"My name is Captain Stone. I'm sure that you are all aware of the situation the country is in at the moment — the military has been mobilized to restore order. My squad was sent to recon and it's extremely important that you tell me all you know about the infection," said the captain.

Captain Stone was taller than Dan and clearly muscular despite being covered from the neck down in heavy protective equipment. His jaw was sharp, eyes stern and hair short.

"Well, the mass zombie infestation began sometime yesterday in the afternoon, but the first infection might have been earlier that day or maybe the night before," explained Augie.

"We moved from campus to here and that's basically it," said Dan. "These things, what are they? What's Zombosis?"

"And what about you, fire head?" asked Stone, with Ruby in his gaze.

"Zoe and I were right where you found us all along. Rock was the only person we saw who wasn't infected."

Zoe had been staring at Dan all the while with her hands clasped together and fingers interlaced.

"These bitches here left me running for my life! You should arrest them for abandonment or something! Nam sayin'?" said Rock, pointing straight at Dan.

"Some info is being released about Zombosis via local media. It's essentially a disease that forces aggressive behaviour and once you're infected, there's no cure. It basically turns you into a zombie, as fat boy said," explained Captain Stone.

"Ha! He said zombies! I was right!" Augie smiled broadly, proud that his theory was acknowledged while ignoring the insult.

"But you killed those zombies out there like they were nothing but a mild nuisance. So things should be back to normal in no time!" said Omar enthusiastically.

"They become more dangerous with greater numbers. We can handle them as long as we have ammo, but the infection spreads easily, which leads to my next question. Has anyone been bitten by the infected?"

"No," said everyone simultaneously.

There was a brief pause and their eyes darted across to each other.

"Are there any infected corpses around? I mean, those that aren't moving," continued Captain Stone.

"Umm, well..." Dan began.

The survivors stepped aside to reveal the first zombie guard that had been dispatched by Dan. The body was stiff and the blood dry.

"Some zombie guards attacked us, so we had to defend ourselves," said Kelly quickly.

"Well, we might have a problem here," said Stone.

"Dem was goin' to kill we, bai!" cried Steve.

A distorted noise then came from Captain Stone's walkie-talkie.

"Hellfire 1, send," he spoke into the black box.

The voice came from the walkie-talkie again and this time Dan tried his best to understand the message: *"Your squad is to return to Hellfire immediately, over."*

"Roger that," said Captain Stone as he turned on his heel.

He walked straight through the door and continued his conversation over the walkie-talkie. Everyone shared a puzzled look before Dan followed him.

"Are we leaving?" he asked Captain Stone as the survivors stood behind him.

"No, *we're* leaving. We can't take civilians to Hellfire, it's a hotspot right now."

"What's Hellfire?" asked Augie.

"Why can't we go with you? It's not like we're any safer here!" argued Kelly.

"Hellfire is the summit site and it's flooded with infected right now. You'll have to stay in the mall for a while and we'll send transport for you tomorrow," explained Stone. "Just block all entry points and keep the noise levels down. You seem to have done a good job of staying alive so far."

"Give us some guns at least," pleaded Omar, his eyes like ping pong balls.

"We don't give guns to civilians, son. Oh, and stay away from the corpses, they might have crawlers that will infect you if you get too close," said Captain Stone as both soldiers entered the helicopter.

The flying machine's blades began turning and the noise steadily rose. The survivors watched the helicopter hover before locking the mall's doors and putting the barricades back into place.

"I can't believe this!" screamed Dan, as he moved further into the mall.

"Fire bun dem, bai!" said Steve, shaking his fist.

"We are going to get dead for sure now. This stress isn't too good for my hair..." muttered Omar, slumping onto the thick pumpkin and rubbing the thinning areas that marked his receding hairline.

"What I would like to know is, what the fock are crawlers?" said Rock, in his fast, high-pitched voice.

8

DEAD INSIDE

[Day 3]

~The one good thing that can come from suffering alone
is an interesting story to tell~

NO ONE DARED VENTURE out of the Midnight Atrium that night. They stayed close to the exit, just in case their transport came early. The night passed quietly; not a screech or moan of a zombie, or the rhythmic beat of a helicopter.

Dan managed to get some sleep, though he wasn't sure for exactly how long. He awoke early in the morning when the sun had just started its daily duty. The cold hard floor was his bed — definitely not comfortable but at least it was safe.

It was the third day since the spread of the infection — a long time to go without a good, proper washing. The only things that smelled worse were putrid, rotting, walking corpses. Augie did not think to pack any soap or deodorant in his backpack.

Fortunately, they were in a mall and could get almost anything they needed. The taps still had running water and all the stores were open for business (sort of).

Dan picked out a toothbrush that looked like a blue dinosaur and spread colourful toothpaste all over it. He had never gotten anything as useless and expensive as a fancy toothbrush when he was a child, but it just wasn't as fun for an adult to brush his teeth with a dinosaur.

By the time Dan started having breakfast (chocolate chip cookies and milk), everyone had changed their clothes and the place smelled like air freshener and perfume. Dan gobbled down the cookies instead of pecking away at the sandwiches he normally had every morning. He tried not to spill anything on his new, clean, expensive shirt, as he drank the milk straight from the carton.

Augie had advised everyone on how to dress — "fitted clothes so that the zombies have nothing to grab on to!" He looked chunky in his own selection, but he was very content.

Dan just made sure he had a pair of jeans that wouldn't fall to his ankles if the belt ever broke.

"Dude, that shirt is awesome. Where'd you get it?" Augie asked Dan. "And those shoes, too!"

Dan just scratched his head. His scalp was itchy even after washing off the gel, and his hair was wild as if he had just gotten out of bed.

"Well, my shoes are steel-tipped and rubberized so that I can never slip!" said Augie in a know-it-all tone.

"Don't worry, I'll run slow enough for you to keep up," said Dan, with a small smile. "Did you have breakfast already?"

"Yeah, I had some protein combined with vitamins and minerals. Everything the body needs."

"Is that right?"

"Yeah, I call it tasty wheat."

"Sounds delicious."

"Tasted like chicken."

"I'm going to get some more carbohydrates. Got to keep the energy up," said Dan as he walked off.

"Carbohydrates! I knew I was missing something..." Augie mumbled to himself.

Dan flung his cricket bat (already in its sheath) across his shoulder and headed away from everyone else, toward the Sunrise Atrium. Having fended off so many zombies with his bat, Dan was convinced that it was the best anti-undead weapon ever.

The sun shone brightly, and the light could be seen entering along the edges of the barricades. But the warmth had not penetrated, and the mall was still freezing cold on the inside.

Dan entered a candy store and grabbed a fist-sized chocolate ball wrapped in orange foil like a little jack-o'-lantern. The brown chocolate was carved like a Halloween pumpkin and had a centre full of cream so orange that it looked as if it fluoresced. It was certainly the sweetest breakfast Dan had ever had.

He added an oatmeal cookie and a caffeine-filled beverage to his order. Dan was impervious to the dreaded sugar crash that came after the energy rush, so he could eat as he pleased without worrying about the potential consequences.

For the moment, Dan was alone, and he felt some comfort in being so. He was not unaccustomed to doing things solo — it gave him time to think.

He thought about how they were trapped by death, only just managing to keep it at bay. And of course, he thought about Kelly. He was devastated after his last conversation with her, but deep within his sore heart, he didn't want an end to the zombie apocalypse until he had won Kelly's affection. He tried to forget what had happened.

He tried to imagine being the only survivor in the mall. Assuming he somehow survived the zombies, what were the benefits of being alone? He could scream his favourite songs without judgment. He could run around naked, not that he wanted to. He realized that as much as he disliked people sometimes, life was better with them.

He shook his head to awaken from his dreamlike state. Everything that was happening was unmistakably real. It was terrible, but he was glad that he didn't have to face the adversity by himself. Being with the other survivors preserved his sanity, at least.

He finished off his cookie and was about to head back to the others when he heard footsteps approaching. The crunching cookie had hidden the noise until the footsteps were just outside the candy store. Dan immediately spun around to face the entrance and grabbed the hilt of his weapon.

"Whoa there, Dante, it's just me!" said Ruby as she entered the store with her arms raised. "Is that a cricket bat? I didn't know you played sports."

Dan and Ruby had been friends since the first day they started attending university. Ruby was the pretty girl who needed help in her labs, and Dan was with the nerds who provided that assistance. Ever since then, they were at each other's throats with petty insults. Now that she wasn't immediately threatened by the walking dead, she initiated smack talk.

"Cookies for breakfast?" She was just getting warmed up to have a war of words with Dan. "You need to eat some man food and fatten yourself up!"

Ruby had sexy hips, which swung with every step, and a narrow waist always exposed in a crop top. She was beautiful and she knew it. Dan had a hard time coming up with quips.

"You would know about fattening up."

"Yeah, I should have some for breakfast. I need to gain a few pounds."

"That's not what your jeans say."

Ruby believed that her flawless face and enticing eyes controlled the weak minds of the lustful. It was, in fact, her plump, round booty which had the hypnotic effect.

Dan was constantly irritated by Ruby's bloated aura of arrogance. Finding no other physical flaw upon which to draw, he often teased Ruby about her curvy bottom — the literal butt of his every joke. However, it was a time when buttock size was directly correlated with attractiveness; his insults were not only absurdly ineffective, they were actually unintended compliments.

"I meant to ask you something," said Dan, becoming serious for a moment. "Where's Donald?"

"I think he's dead," she replied bluntly.

"And Charlie?"

"Same, I think."

"Jeff?"

"No idea."

"How about Robert?"

"Dunno."

"Johnny?"

"Gone, I suspect."

"Who's the one with the pink hair again?"

"Jess?"

"Yeah, Jess. Is Jess okay?"

"Don't know, don't care. It's a good thing I got the hell out of there or I might have ended up like them," said Ruby, without a modicum of remorse.

The names Dan had called formed a fraction of Ruby's seduces — victims of her supposed succubus powers. Of course, she held no emotional attachment to them, as she was indubitably loyal to her long-time partner.

"So who's that girl with you, Danny boy? Finally found yourself a girlfriend?" asked Ruby, changing the subject and grabbing a cookie.

Ruby's stare went straight through Dan's glasses, directly into his eyes, up his optic nerves and into his brain — he felt as if she were probing his mind. His eyes were fixed onto hers, which were outlined with heavy, black eyeliner.

"Kelly isn't my girlfriend. She just..." Dan's voice had changed from the scolding, confident tone, to a nervous one.

"Oh my God! You like her!" squealed Ruby, delightfully clapping her hands.

"Shhh!"

"I'm going to tell her!"

"No, you're not!"

"Ha! Yes, I am!"

"You better not say anything!"

"Consider it payback for..." Ruby paused for a second before dramatically completing her sentence, "...zombie girl!"

"W-what?! That's not fair! It doesn't even compare with zombie girl!"

"You had your friends call me 'zombie girl' for two semesters!"

"Okay, so it might be fair, but it still isn't right! Besides, I didn't make them call you that! They did it out of their own free will!"

"Sorry, Danny boy, but it's going to happen! It's going to happen when you least expect it!"

"It's not my fault you looked like a zombie in your school ID!" said Dan, mounting a terrible defence. "Besides, I already told her."

"You told her that you like her?"

"Kinda..."

"Kinda? What did you tell her, Dan?"

"I might have said I..."

"No..."

"Loved her..."

"No, Danny, no!"

"It felt like the right time."

"This isn't a fairy tale, Dan. She's not gonna fall in love with you at first sight."

Dan remained silent as he revisited his traumatic conversation with Kelly in his mind.

"So, did you cry?"

"No."

"I bet you cried."

"I did not cry!"

Dan dusted the crumbs off his shirt, finished his milk and exited the candy store. He walked with large, quick strides, leaving Ruby behind, gobbling down her cookie.

"Aww, you mad at me?" teased Ruby, as she hurried to catch up.

"No, I'm not mad at you."

"Why you mad?"

"I'm not..." Dan stopped in his tracks. "Shit, we should have gone upstairs..."

The corpses of the infected guards lay right where they had been left. Only after seeing them did Dan remember why they had avoided the ground floor all along. Dan kept moving forward.

Ruby gasped at the stiff bodies on the ground. The stench was horrible but far outmatched by the gruesome appearance. She covered her mouth with both hands and looked like she was about to vomit all over the corpses.

They moved closer to the bodies as they headed on their way. Ruby kept as far away as possible and hid behind Dan in an attempt to block her view.

When at the closest point, Dan could no longer avert his eyes from the carcasses. He glanced down at the one nearest to him — it looked worse than before. The guard's uniform was dotted with spots of red and the face was completely obscured by a rough, red, meaty mat. All the other guards had a similar appearance — as if their skin had developed swollen lesions.

Dan carefully dropped to one knee to get a closer look but was sure to keep a safe distance. He held his breath as his face slowly moved closer to inspect the strange sight.

The red lesions on the face of the infected looked like hundreds of tiny bumps on the surface of the skin. Dan could feel the horrid image being carved into his mind. He was transfixed by the disgusting sight — his eyes narrowed and his mouth was ajar. He instantly closed his mouth when he realized it had been open, feeling as if he could catch the zombie's disease by swallowing the infected air.

Ruby nervously moved forward with one hand over her mouth and the other shielding her eyes from the corpses.

"Dan, let's go please," she pleaded as she continued walking.

"Wait!" said Dan, holding up his hand and motioning for her to stand still.

The zombie's skin twitched and rippled and then Dan realized what he had been looking at. What he thought was a red mat of sores was actually a large group of tiny insect-like creatures, which appeared to be attached to the deceased human host. The red scales on the corpse wriggled and dislodged themselves from the host's skin. Dan backed off.

On the floor scuttled hundreds of these microscopic monsters, all moving together. It looked as if the floor itself was melting and flowing, red as a river of blood.

"Okay, don't wait!" said Dan as he stood up and rushed to Ruby's side.

She grabbed hold of his hand and the lights went out immediately after. Some daylight filtered in between the barriers they had erected, providing just enough illumination for them to see their way.

The mall was dark, but it wasn't like the total blackness

of night. The loss of natural light was an unforeseen consequence of blocking all the glass windows and doors. They manoeuvred their way carefully back to the others. Dan's body sped forward automatically, as his brain tried to understand what he had just seen. *Those things were going after Ruby, I'm sure of it.*

As they neared their regular meeting place, the artificial lights returned. Everyone scrambled for their seats.

"Current gone bai!" cried Steve.

"The power is out. I think the lights are running on the backup generator now," said Augie.

Without power, survival would be significantly more difficult, especially at night.

"And now, we're dead," said Omar, in a dull, somewhat sarcastic tone.

Heat seeped into the mall and the cool air slowly warmed.

"On the bright side, I figured out what crawlers are," said Dan as he took a seat. "On the not so bright side, they happen to be bugs coming out from the infected corpses. There are hundreds of them on each zombie, and they look infectious."

"Awww, hell naw!" shouted Rock.

"Zombies that can actively infect you even after they are put down... fascinating!" Augie was impressed.

"How long can we actually stay here with the power out?" asked Kelly, with distinct nervousness in her voice.

"We definitely need to move to another safe house," suggested Zoe.

"I'm sure Danny boy will come up with a plan," said Ruby.

Ruby's chair was directly adjacent to Dan's, and she kept so close to him that their shoulders jammed together. Ruby was as extroverted as they came and loved human contact. If she was the only survivor in the zombie apocalypse, she surely would have died from loneliness. Ruby's need for human energy was ten times that of Dan's.

Zoe stared at Dan and Ruby with puffed up cheeks and folded arms.

"Remember, Stone said they'll be sending us transport today. We can hold out till then, as long as those crawlers don't get here," said Dan. "There's a problem though. The bugs seem to be able to sense humans somehow. I think they may be selective."

"You mean like choosing victims?" interrupted Kelly.

Zoe's eyes narrowed and her lips tightened when she saw how Dan looked at Kelly.

"Yeah, exactly," continued Dan. "Remember the blonde girl we met in the library?

"You mean Jessica? Yeah, I remember Jessica." Augie tried to poke fun at the nickname Dan had invented for the girl.

"The zombies seemed to target her for some reason. And just now, the crawlers didn't respond to me at all, but they went crazy for Ruby." Dan ignored Augie's attempt to derail a serious conversation with ill-timed humour.

Ruby shuddered upon hearing Dan's words.

"I'm guessing that they either choose a victim based on vulnerability or maybe some characteristic like scent or blood type," lectured Dan. "I think as long as we keep our distance from them, we should be okay. We just have to hold on for a little while until we get our transport."

"Right, so everyone just has to stay on this side of the mall," said Omar, biting his fingernails.

"Just make sure you're all ready to leave as soon as it's time," said Dan, concluding his speech and standing up to stretch his tense muscles.

***

The time crawled by, and everyone took turns staring out the window, hoping to see a car, truck or even a helicopter. As it crossed into the afternoon, Dan was beginning to have doubts.

The mall had gotten significantly warmer and there was no sign of rain or cloud cover that may have lowered the ambient temperature.

Dan sat alone at a table, with his chin resting on his knuckles and his eyes staring aimlessly.

"I know what you're thinking," said Kelly as she took a seat on the only other chair at the table.

"And what is that?" asked Dan, straightening his posture.

Dan had mixed feelings about speaking with her. The crawlers were disturbing but insignificant when compared with the rejection of his affection.

"Hope can destroy you from the inside," she said jokingly, deepening her voice, "like a parasite!"

Is she mocking me? Dan took no offence and forced a weak laugh. Kelly's aura soothed him and began healing his fractured heart. The tension and fear dissipated a little.

"I know what it's like to wait for something that will never come," said Dan.

Kelly gulped as if nervously expecting Dan to discuss their last awkward encounter.

"I'm worried that Captain Stone's transport is one of those things," continued Dan.

Kelly sighed in relief.

"Have some faith," she said.

"You know, hope really can be a parasite that robs you of your expectations."

Dan held the silver dog tag that hung around his neck and showed the single engraved word to Kelly.

"Hope..." read Kelly.

"But I like to think of it as a symbiote – something that helps me endure. See, I do have faith. Faith in myself."

Kelly paused for a moment with her mouth open, before curling her lips into a pleasant smile.

"Every time I hold on to this tag, I hold on to hope," said Dan, wrapping his fingers around the dog tag.

"That's the cheesiest thing I've ever heard," giggled Kelly.

I... I thought it was cool... Dan stared down at the table, embarrassed.

"But still, let's hope together," said Kelly, placing her tiny hand over Dan's larger one. Her fingers moved to the spaces between his.

What the hell? Did she have a change of heart so quickly?

Dan felt as if the world had all its colour muted and Kelly just radiated a spectrum of light. Kelly's pale cheeks turned pink, and Dan felt as if his were red as the fire that blazed within his chest. Her eyes were big and bright and glistened in the light. Her luxuriant hair lay perfectly on her shoulders and her rose-red lips formed the most angelic smile.

They stared into each other's eyes; her pupils dilated.

His heart pounded so hard that he worried it could be seen through his clothes. Dan held onto her other hand with his free one. Her skin was so soft and enchantingly warm.

Dan had more adrenaline in his veins now than when he had been fighting and vanquishing zombies. *Is this really happening right now? Are we going to... kiss?*

"After we survive this, I want you to be my bridesmaid!"

"Wha...?"

The lights suddenly went out again and sunlight poured in through a nearby uncovered window. Everyone grouped together quickly and once again, the tension rose rapidly.

Bridesmaid? Is that code for something? She can't mean an actual bridesmaid, can she?

"I'ma put this under the category of not fockin' good! Nam sayin'?" screamed Rock as he stared at everyone with his wild, wide eyes. "Where the fock is our focking transport, man?"

"They'll get here, Rock... calm down," said Zoe with her arms folded while leaning against a concrete pillar.

"I say we take the fockin' SUV and drive to the fockin' Hellfire or whatever the fock he said! Nam sayin'?" yelled Rock, flailing his arms.

The afternoon sky outside was orange — it was already late. Dan glanced down at his wristwatch — 5:07 pm.

"We probably have around an hour before sunset," said Dan.

"How long will it take to get to Hellfire if we leave now and drive?" asked Omar.

"Ten minutes tops, bitches!" bawled Rock.

"Think fast, guys! We can either wait for Stone, which may mean spending another night here, or we can leave now!" said Dan, awaiting a democratic decision.

Dan, himself, wasn't sure what was best. *With no lights, we won't have a chance of seeing the crawlers or any infected. But leaving now could possibly result in being on the roads at night, if we don't meet up with the military.*

"I say we—" Augie started but was interrupted by an ear-piercing scream.

The scream was mixed with wailing and a violent struggle in the darkening room. Ruby had sunk her teeth into Steve's neck and blood gushed from the open wound. In the dim light, her zombie-like characteristics were disguised.

Dan stood transfixed, with his cricket bat already in hand but unable to use it. Everyone scattered.

Ruby focused her eyes on Dan; the sclera seemed to glow in the dark, and the pupils dilated. She threw Steve onto the ground and lunged at Dan. Her arms were outstretched and her bloodied jaws opened wide.

To Dan, she seemed to be moving toward him in slow motion. His brain flooded with thoughts, images, memories and words that felt out of context. He had to hit her, or he would die, but it wasn't that simple. In that moment, he understood how easily the infection could spread if people were reluctant to harm their friends or family. He understood that he wasn't nearly as emotionally detached as he thought he was.

A hockey stick broke on Ruby's head, stopping her in her tracks. Kelly backed off, staring at her destroyed weapon and then at Ruby who had turned to face her.

Dan then fully understood that there was no hope for the undead, but there was for the living. With a loud cracking noise, the trusty cricket bat crashed into the side of the zombie's head, sending her flying over the railing. Ruby landed on her head on the tiled ground below, painting the floor red.

Kelly ran to Dan with tears in her eyes and threw her arms around him. Dan was still stiff, except for his heart, which beat like a tassa drum.

All eyes then focused on the bleeding person slouched against the wall — was he alive, dead, or undead?

"Steve's been bitten, so you know what that means..." said Augie.

Steve was sobbing and clutched his wound, which bled profusely.

"It means we have to put him out of his misery," said Zoe.

"It's not as easy as that. He's still human, so that would be—" Dan stopped as Steve rose up.

Steve's dreadlocks hung down, obscuring his face, and the weeping had stopped. When he looked forward, it was with eyes like Ruby's — milky-white with dots for pupils. The two dots were dark as the blackest night, like black holes sucking in light and life.

Dan brought his cricket bat down on the zombie's head, splitting the bone. Steve wobbled and then everyone proceeded to crush his head with whatever weapon they possessed.

"Now let's get the FOCK out of here!" shouted Rock as he ran for the stationary escalator.

Everyone hurried downstairs and kept a close eye on

Ruby's corpse while the barricades were removed.

Dan had just had to kill two of his closest friends. *Have I become a monster worse than the undead? Ruby and Steve are gone forever by my own doing. No, they were infected with the HNP and already dead!*

Two vehicles awaited them outside — Dan's old car and the SUV.

9

THE NIGHTMARE IN HELL

[Day 3]

~Having everything means nothing if you are alone~

"SHOTGUN!" SHOUTED AUGIE AS he made a beeline for the passenger seat of the yellow SUV.

Rock climbed into the driver's seat of the SUV and started it up. The headlights came on and cut through the growing veil of darkness. Omar plopped himself onto the roomy back seat and flopped like a fish for a second before settling his curves into the cushion.

The distance between the mall and the car was short, but Dan felt vulnerable being there. His trembling hands struggled to insert the key and open the doors. Kelly took the passenger seat, while Zoe settled in the back. Dan turned the key in the ignition and the old car coughed itself to life.

"She takes a while to warm up," said Dan, when the engine sounded like it was just about to fail.

Dan revved up the engine as Rock began to move to the exit. The SUV waited at the end of the parking lot as the engine of the white car sputtered and then roared. Dan could tell everyone was getting increasingly nervous the longer it took them to leave — they expected that the noise would attract any nearby infected.

That minute of waiting felt like a zillion years, but they were off without alerting any infected. The SUV sped onto the highway, followed closely by Dan's old clunker.

The roads were just like they had been before — abandoned and quiet. The stillness of the environment was eerie, especially with darkness creeping in.

The sun was directly ahead of them, a perfect red circle. Dan had never seen the sun that red before, or perhaps he never took the time to appreciate the sunset; he considered that this could be his last. But even if it were his final view of the sun, he was sharing it with Kelly. She had chosen to go with him instead of in the armoured SUV, which was undeniably faster and more reliable.

As he drove along the straight road, his mind was far from the physical realm.

Should I ask her about the bridesmaid thing? Maybe I can go undercover as her bridesmaid and get close to her. Then I can interrupt her vows on the wedding day, sweep her off her feet and ride off into the sunset. No! That's stupid... and wrong... and it won't even work!

"I like your car, Dan," said Zoe, obliterating Dan's ridiculous fantasy.

"Huh? Uh, oh yeah. Thanks."

"I like older things."

"Nice."

"Think we can get some music?"

Before Dan could respond, Zoe leaned between the front seats. She took a quick, discreet whiff of Dan's scent, powered on the car radio and jacked in her phone with a white cable. She began playing some retro tunes and dancing in the back seat.

Dan smiled and his anxiety faded. Zoe's aura radiated good vibes.

They drove beneath the large concrete overpass, which was only partially constructed. Its unpaved road stopped abruptly in the air. It would have been completed in a few more months but work was unexpectedly halted. A red flag stood at the unfinished end of the bridge and flapped hauntingly in the weak wind.

As they got closer to the city, and the overpass faded from sight, the highway became an obstacle course. This was the busiest roadway on the island and was normally congested with traffic, especially during rush hour. Many abandoned cars blocked the path, even on the emergency shoulder lane.

The abandoned vehicles all faced the same direction in every lane — the opposite direction from which the survivors were heading. Everyone had been trying to get out of the city – the same city the two vehicles were about to enter.

Dan and Rock were forced to slow down significantly, and it was clear by the semicircle sun that night would befall them. They weaved between the stationary cars as they pressed on toward their goal.

Shadows filled the motionless cars, making it difficult to see if anyone was inside. They all appeared to be abandoned; nothing stirred or made any attempts to devour human brains. Most of the cars looked brand new, and their shiny coats of paint glistened in the final rays of the sun.

Dan, attempting to get Kelly off his mind, tried to imagine scenarios that would force people to abandon their vehicles. *Maybe the only way to escape the infected was on foot, because of the traffic,* he thought. *Or maybe they became infected in the cars, killed and infected everyone in the vehicle and then moved on to find other victims.* Whatever happened, Dan was glad that he wasn't in traffic when the infection reached the area. Normally, with his terrible luck, he would have been in the wrong place at the wrong time.

They approached another overpass, this one much older and clearly neglected. Upon the worn, grey, concrete surface "Welcome to Jumbieland" was spray-painted in luminous red.

To their right, on the very edge of the highway, rose a huge wall made of the strongest construction materials known to humanity. At the top of the wall, rusty razor wire and broken glass shards were fused into the solid concrete. Jumbieland was a city of its own, made of dilapidated houses, drains that coursed with sewage, and no supply of electricity or water.

Despite the best efforts of the snipers housed in towers around the perimeter and the soldiers who regularly patrolled the area, the inhabitants of Jumbieland (known as jumbies) had managed to break free on one occasion. Some were quick to attack the drivers on the highway and other peripheral roadways. Most just ran, trying to escape their oppressive detention.

Dan was sure that Kelly and Zoe were wondering the same thing he was — did the jumbies break free again? Even if they did, their threat would have been insignificant when compared to the zombies.

The sun hid completely now but there was not total darkness. The headlights of the vehicles illuminated the roadway, which appeared orange as it was bathed in the glow of the streetlamps.

"Maybe there are others in all those buildings," said Kelly.

From afar, the city looked unchanged from the usual — the lights were on and the structures were undamaged. But Dan was pretty sure zombies preferred living prey over inanimate buildings. As much as he would have liked to be carelessly optimistic, he remained wary that they were possibly driving into something worse.

As they entered the city, the large highway narrowed. There were signs on the streets indicating that the main roadway was closed for the summit. Detour signs pointed traffic into the bowels of the city. They ignored the signage and pressed forward. There was no indication of life, not even a police officer to enforce the traffic signs.

To their left was the ocean, black and calm like a giant paved abyss. It was littered with old, abandoned ships, unmoving and partially submerged. On the waterfront were twin towers — the tallest skyscrapers on the island. Red and white lights lit up the towers like giant lighthouses on the port. To their right was the heart of the city, which was well lit but empty.

The vehicles slowed to a halt as they neared an obstacle — a burnt helicopter wreck blocked the roadway. The engines hummed as the vehicles approached the pile of crumpled metal.

To their left was an unblocked road that led to the waterfront. Dan expected to have met some military force by now since they were at the most critical location in the country at the time. He turned onto the waterfront road and drove into the towers' courtyard.

Just like the city, it was well lit but empty. Dan stopped next to the fountain at the foot of the giant buildings — the dancing water changed colours every few seconds. The SUV pulled up to the side of Dan's car and Augie rolled down the window.

"Where the hell is the military?" asked Dan, trying to keep his tone calm.

"This place is dead! Do you think we should go back?" replied Augie, partially hanging out the window.

"We can't go back there now. Maybe we could try these buildings, but we can't be sure if they are safe," suggested Dan.

Augie then retreated into the SUV and quietly spoke with everyone inside, gathering their opinions. Dan consulted with himself. *This is a difficult decision. As long as we have the vehicles, we could move to a new area, but there's no way to be sure that the infected won't be there already.* The military was completely absent, and the survivors were in a state of confusion.

"We could try the hotel across the road. It might be empty," suggested Kelly.

"They probably served brains for dinner today," said Zoe, with a forced laugh and a sigh.

Why would the hotel be empty? Besides, we're looking for the military, not a place to hide. Aren't we? "I think we should—"

"Hey! We're in here!" said a man in a hushed voice, standing at the entrance to the nearby tower.

He appeared to be uninfected and was waving his hand to grab their attention. In his other arm, he cradled an assault rifle, ready to fire at a moment's notice.

Dan took the lead, choosing to act before he had the chance to overthink. He turned off his car, got out, and headed toward the stranger. *They have weapons*, he thought, *so this could either be a godsend, or another problem.* He grabbed his dog tag and assumed the former. *Perhaps there is a military force in this tower or a resistance at least. What the hell am I doing?*

Everyone followed him without saying a word; Augie looked extremely nervous though. They walked briskly, keeping an eye on the surroundings in case a sudden rush of infected approached.

When they had all entered the building, the man scanned them with his eyes, "Have any of you been bitten?"

They were able to reply honestly but dreaded that the man would be more skeptical. Fortunately for them, he wasn't, and he led them directly to the elevators.

Ah shit, this guy can't be a soldier, given that his zombie screening test was literally just one totally subjective question.

He dialled in "12" on the large silver keypad, and a door to the left opened immediately. They all got in and fit quite comfortably in the expansive elevator. It flew up so quickly, that the elevator music consisted of only two seconds of saxophone.

The doors slid open and the man walked out first. He looked to his right where three people hid behind a desk, which was blocked by a glass door. He then swiped his access card for the door on his left and opened it for everyone to enter.

"We were actually expecting the army, not more civilians," he said, as he took a seat by a long wooden table.

Behind the table, a large glass window wrapped around the building. From there stretched a clear view of the city, as well as the roadways below.

"I'm Zack, by the way," said the man.

The sound of approaching footsteps put Dan and his group in a state of alertness.

"Relax," said Zack, "they're with me."

The three persons who were at the front desk revealed themselves.

Both groups stood still for a moment before Zack broke the silence, "I believe introductions are in order."

Dan introduced himself first, followed by everyone else. There was no physical contact in the introductions – not so much as a handshake. Both groups knew very well how easily the infection could spread.

Among the new group of survivors was Jill, a slender girl in office attire; Ash, a very tall man with pointy shoes; Pixonov (also known as "Pixie"), a shirtless man with bulging muscles; and Zack, a man dressed in a white shirt with a tie. They had all been employees working in this building when Zombosis hit.

While they were not members of the military, they had guns in their possession. Aside from the assault rifle, which Zack kept close, Pixonov had a shotgun resting on his shoulder.

Two guns and no extra ammunition — it's a good thing cricket bats don't need to reload.

Dan wanted to ask about the weapons straight away — how did they get them? But he was sure that their hosts were expecting an overview of their survival story. He felt that swapping the incredible tales of how they made it this far without becoming infected was the best way to ease the tension between the groups.

"We're from the university," he began his story, "and we held out in the mall for a while. We met some guy from the army named Captain Stone and he told us that the military was here. He said they would have sent someone for us, but they never came, so we decided to move out ourselves. Where's the military?"

A significantly abridged version of their story, but it was good enough. Zack motioned for everyone to have a seat around the table.

"Our security division is partially comprised of the army, so I think we know the same Captain Stone you mentioned. They went out under orders when the summit's security was breached. Actually, it's a long story..." Zack explained as he leaned back in his chair.

ACT 2
DESPERATION

Survivor Group Infernal

Life is the greatest gift that can ever be given
Even when drowned in sorrow and pain
Life is an experience like no other
Even if to love only once and never again
Or smile a few times and cry even more
It is worth the short time that it lasts
That is why we fight to survive

~Do not forget the past but remember that it is gone and
cannot be changed~

10

THE SUMMIT

[Day 1]

~Death is the only cure-all~

THE DAY STARTED JUST like any other. I put on my white-collar slave uniform and signed in to my job like I did every damn day. By midday, I stood on the roof of the tallest building on the island. The sun was cooking me in my clothes, and the dry, warm wind threatened to blow me down. I stood a short distance from the edge, but I hadn't come up here for the view. I was prepared to see what flying felt like, or so I thought.

You know how people say suicide is the easy way out? The truth is, it's never easy. It takes a shit-ton of courage to take that leap into the unknown.

I wasn't that brave — not today.

Picture a man with no friends or family, who spends his daylight hours at a dead-end job, staring at a flickering computer screen. The fluorescent light over his tiny cubicle flickers too, and the rattling air conditioning always breaks down. His nights are spent in a tiny apartment, where he is constantly terrorized by blood-sucking mosquitoes, hungry cockroaches and the occasional rat. He just barely retains his sanity with a daily bottle of rum. That man is me, sadly.

I straightened my tie and went back down to my cubicle. Back to the daily grind — updating files, sorting documents, and writing procedures that no one really gave a shit about. I had a miserable realization — as much as I hated my job, it was the most important thing in my life.

I barely got the chance to settle in my hard, uncomfortable chair when my boss called me into her office. I had already prepared an angry speech for my abusive overlord and this was my time to use it.

I stepped into a dimly lit room filled with a noxious mixture of scented candles and incense. There were stacks of papers and books haphazardly laid out and a broad wooden desk, which I swear was hiding a witch's cauldron.

"Sit down, Zack," commanded the boss, gesturing to an empty chair in front of her desk.

I did as I was instructed, gripping the handles of a chair even less comfortable than my own. We were on the twelfth floor of the tallest building in the city. Outside was a man risking his life to clean the boss's windows. In that moment, I wished I was in his place.

In an equally uncomfortable seat to my left was Oscar. He avoided eye contact and didn't say a single word. I wondered why he was there but knew it couldn't be good. That lazy snitch's greatest skill was getting other people to do his work for him.

"You're rubbing me the wrong way, Zack," said the slave-master, while adjusting a plaque on her desk with the words "THE BOSS" etched into it.

Mrs. Hefflebottom — the worst person I have ever met.

She was a stout woman whose short stature evenly matched her temper. Her saggy face was barely human, and more closely resembled an old, angry bulldog.

A yellow telephone rang out loudly. RING... RIN— She grabbed something that looked like a ripe banana and verbally abused it.

"John! Why were you late?"

The voice on the other end of the banana phone squeaked like a mouse — I couldn't make out what John was saying.

"I don't care if your brother died, John. I expect you to do your job! I have an unhappy client!"

The banana squeaked again.

"You know what, John? I've had enough of your excuses and selfish demands for time off. YOU'RE FIRED!"

She slammed down the telephone so hard that it smashed to pieces.

"Where was I? Ah, yes. Zack, your colleague over here informed me that you called him, and I quote, 'a lazy piece of shit'," she screeched, her already prominent underbite protruding even more.

Oscar, that polo-shirt-wearing asshat!

"I had instructed that you work with Oscar to complete the assigned project," she continued, slobbering like a dog. "To keep this short, you either need to work as a team or find yourself another job. Do I make myself clear, Zack?"

"Yes, Mrs. Hefflebottom."

Back at my desk, I kept replaying what had just happened in my mind. I could have said so many things.

As angry as I was with Hefflebottom and Oscar, it was my own head I wanted to knock off with a solid punch.

If there's one thing I hate, it's a parasite. There's always an asshole that will take advantage of generosity without giving anything back.

I forced myself to complete the mundane tasks with the human parasite named Oscar. That lazy bastard had disappeared just as he did whenever there was work to be done.

The entire staff was working for the international summit that was to be held in the city. Leaders from all over the world gathered to discuss political bullshit. Months of preparation came down to these three days.

The city was the main port on the island. There were always ships docked in the harbour, right alongside the towering skyscrapers on the waterfront. A seawall formed a barrier between the eternally black, still waters of the harbour, and the cobblestone walkways of the waterfront. The shiny new skyscrapers, that seemed to sprout up every month, did a good job of distracting from all the grime and crime of the city.

The entire waterfront had been completely sealed off from public access because of the summit. No one was allowed in or out without authorization. It was like being trapped in a prison with no walls. It wasn't too bad though. All the summit workers had to stay on the nearby cruise ship for the week. It was far better than that vermin-infested cesspool of an apartment I lived in.

It was the first official day of the summit and the building was much emptier than usual. While there were normally hundreds of workers in the tower at once, that day, only one floor was occupied. It was nice not having to wait fifteen minutes just to get on the elevator.

For weeks, we had been working on extended shifts with no overtime pay. I thought that the extra work would have diverted my body to positive things and my mind to positive thoughts. It just made me more depressed. At least on this day, the long shifts were over, and I could return to the ship to get some ice cream.

Almost everything on the ship's menu tasted the same. The squid tasted the same as the chicken, and the vegetables were indistinguishable from each other; but that ice cream was the greatest of all time. The sweet vanilla upon a waffle cone was undeniably the best thing in my life. It was the one brilliant light that lit up my dreary, dark world. I had to have more.

To be clear, this story is more about my quest for magical ice cream than surviving the zombie apocalypse.

***

That evening, I stood with my friend, Jill, and four other co-workers awaiting the arrival of a shuttle, which normally took us directly to the ship. Night had only just begun, and the lights in the courtyard and from the buildings lit up the place. The fountain's lights stole my attention as it changed colours as often as patterns. My world was black and white, but that fountain was like a luminous rainbow at night-time.

"You know we can just walk, right?" I said to my colleagues.

"I am not walking that far in these heels!" snapped Jill.

Jill owned an unquantifiable number of stiletto shoes and was never seen without a pair on her feet. She had grown so adept at wearing them that she could balance her entire bodyweight on a single heel while standing on an empty can of soda. However, no amount of skill could protect her from blistered feet.

"Did you have the ice cream on the ship? I need to get back before they close up the stall." I folded my arms and paced.

"Ice cream? What kinda loser eats ice cream when there's unlimited rum and a pussy buffet on that ship?" said Oscar, his mouth dribbling.

Pixonov laughed scandalously.

"Since when were you a cannibal, Oscar?" Ash threw the insult at Oscar with a kind smile on his face.

Pixonov laughed even louder, this time pointing at Oscar.

"Wha—?"

Oscar was too dumb to feel insulted. He whipped his tongue in the air as he continued fantasizing about satiating his thirst.

The lights from the cruise ship brightened the dark sky. It leaned against the dock like a monstrous leviathan from the ocean. From the outside, the vessel looked like a terrifying, old, wooden pirate ship. Giant cannons pointed in our direction and could have bombarded us if they were more than decorative dummies. Giant masts pointed skyward, rivalling the height of the waterfront towers, and black, tattered, holographic sails fluttered in the wind. They were the finest Halloween decorations in all the seas, I reckoned.

"Ladies and gentlemen, I can no longer wait to eat, so I will be walking to the ship now... doodles di do," said a man known as Mr. Puffs, in a lazy, nasal tone.

Jill and her friends had created the nickname because of the fellow's enormous puffy potbelly. It was very mean of them, though they never spoke his rude nickname while in his presence. However, Mr. Puffs was quite proud of his seemingly pregnant paunch. He usually used his belly to rest his plate on when dining and sometimes, like a drum.

He walked off toward the ship, alone, rubbing the large mound, which appeared to be ripping apart his plaid shirt. He was a fair distance away when he fell victim to the infection. That was the first time any of us saw a real-life zombie.

Just as Mr. Puffs was about to walk around the corner and out of sight, a man collided with him and they both tipped over. I hadn't even noticed the guy at all. He must have been running pretty fast to knock Mr. Puffs off his feet. Cries sliced the silence of the open air.

At first, I didn't suspect at all that the guy was a zombie. I mean, a robber was far more likely than a zombie. I thought the guy was mugging Mr. Puffs, so I was about to hurry over to assist. But then the cries multiplied into a terrifying din. Shadows reached out to the fallen victim and the predator.

Everyone around me froze. Mr. Puffs was being brutally murdered before our eyes by a man who wielded no weapon. Teeth penetrated flesh and blood gushed freely. The chorus of cries grew louder as the sources of the shadows drew closer.

In that instant, zombies swarmed into my mind. Fear gripped me, and while I wanted to help, I knew I couldn't. My legs froze, holding me in place, and it was as if an invisible force had wrapped its fingers around my throat, so I couldn't utter a word. When I looked back, Jill was already inside the building and the others rushed for the door. My legs became energized again, and I dashed toward the building, entering just as a group of zombies arrived.

People don't act that savagely, not even the wickedest in the world. But the sickest, yes — sick with an infection I previously thought only possible in works of fiction.

The wait for the elevator was nerve-racking. Oscar hid behind a plant whose leaves trembled as much as he did. When the doors finally slid open, everyone piled in and pressed the button which forced the door to close prematurely. It was awkward having five fingers pressed on a button designed for one.

The doors inched shut and everyone stood still, index fingers still attached to the button. In those few seconds, I imagined zombies running inside the elevator to greet us with hugs and toothed kisses. The doors closed and reopened on our floor with two seconds of smooth saxophone jazz. I usually heard the entire elevator song on busy days — after the hundredth repeat, it just became an annoying reminder of my enslavement.

I was the last to step out of the elevator. My heart pounded so hard, I felt like it was about to burst out of my chest and tear through my shirt. My fingers were cold and shaking and the tips were numb.

Everyone was absolutely terrified. Jill was crying and her tears smudged her eyeliner — black streams flowed down her cheeks. Oscar's pink pantaloons had become magenta at the crotch. They were all talking to each other, but everything was just inaudible, muffled noise to me.

I shook my head and broke from my daze to realize that we were all at the corner table in the office. From there, we could see down below, to the spot where Mr. Puffs had been killed. Was Mr. Puffs dead?

Though we were fairly high up, the figure of Mr. Puffs was unmistakable. He stood up from the very spot he had been attacked and wobbled around a bit. His attackers were still in the vicinity but were dispersed. No one attacked him again as he stood.

"He's alive! He's okay!" cried Jill.

Pixonov, who was standing next to her, thrust his hips about in what I interpreted to be some sort of celebratory dance.

"He can't be alive," I said. "This doesn't make sense..."

"He's standing, which means he's okay. I think we should go help him," said Oscar, while applying lip balm to his pouted, pink lips.

Oscar was the embodiment of narcissism. His self-adoration was so great that he thought of himself, not only as everyone's physical superior but also as being on the highest intellectual plane in all of humanity.

He admired himself in his pocket mirror. His puckered lips matched the colour of his polo shirt and pants. He had no intention of going to help Mr. Puffs, but by feigning an interest to do so, he managed to interest Pixonov in a rescue mission.

"Wait!" I commanded, stopping Pixonov, who was already heading back to the elevator. "Ash, do you have your binoculars?"

I knew he had them. He used his binoculars every day at work. There was no shortage of interesting things to spy from this vantage point.

Ash nodded and took a few giant steps with his long legs to his desk and back. He held the black binoculars up to his eyes and stared down through the window at Mr. Puffs.

"It's kinda shadowy, I can't really see what... OH MY GOD!" Ash stumbled backward, only just avoiding falling over completely. "He definitely can't be alive!"

I grabbed the binoculars and had a look for myself. It took me a few seconds to focus on the target, but I could see what had shocked Ash. Mr. Puff's belly wasn't quite as puffy anymore — a large hole in the middle dripped blood and guts. He could have used his own intestines as a jump rope, if he could skip at all. It was the most disgusting thing I had ever seen, yet he stood there, seemingly alive.

I passed on the binoculars to someone else just as quickly as Ash had.

Jill was the only one who didn't dare look. Oscar still gave her a very vivid description of the horrific image; her face went pale and she looked nauseous.

"How can he still be alive with a giant hole in his belly? What is he, a zombie now?" she asked in a quavering, high-pitched voice.

"What's a zombie?" asked Oscar.

That was the first time I'd ever heard of a person who didn't know what a zombie was. A definition of zombie then ran through my head — a dead human returning to life to consume living brains. The more I thought about it, the less sense it made. Zombies couldn't exist in real life. But a man with a huge hole in his torso couldn't possibly stand up.

"Should we call an ambulance?" asked Pixonov.

Even after working with this guy for months, I remained convinced that his accent was fake. He sounded and looked like a cheap knockoff foreign bodybuilder.

I reached into the right pocket of my trousers, retrieved my phone and dialled the emergency response number. The call failed, as did my repeated attempts. None of our phones were capable of making the call, or any sort of communication, for that matter.

"The networks must be flooded, or maybe there is some kind of hardware failure," said Ash, as he continued to spy downward through his binoculars.

"So, what do we do now?" asked Oscar, dancing on the spot in panic.

"We'll just have to wait here for a while," I said. "This is a very important area right now, so someone should come to clean up this mess soon."

"I just want to go back to the ship, get drunk and party," said Oscar. "If Mr. Puffs dies or goes to the hospital or whatever, I'll get our room all to myself. I never really liked him anyway. Did I ever tell you that he leaves his underwear all over his bed?"

11

HELLFIRE

[Day 1]
~In death there are no regrets~

WITH NO COMMUNICATION, ALL we could do was wait. One hour had passed since the Mr. Puffs incident and everyone was quiet. I could see in Jill's eyes the worry she carried for her boyfriend, who had ditched work early to relax on the ship.

Jill was like a beautiful banana in a world filled with hungry gorillas. Her skin was flawless, and she was sweet on the inside, too. There was never a shortage of lustful men in pursuit of female fruit.

The zombies below were all gone, including Mr. Puffs. I preferred to know where they were. I ensured that all the doors on the floor were locked, just in case they took the elevator up.

On the roadway below, no vehicles moved, but it had been this way ever since the summit roadblock. The faint wailing of sirens whirred inside the city, hidden behind the buildings. Somewhere out there were cops dealing with those zombies. We all kept a lookout for any sign of help.

The only things visible from my seat were lights from the buildings and silvery clouds floating below a hidden moon. If I were on top of the building, like I had been earlier in the day, I might have been able to make out tiny living and undead dots in the city.

The mountain behind the city was also adorned with lights. At the far end of the town, was a large building shaped like a nautilus spiral. The opening ceremony for the summit was held there. The building's bright, blue glow stood out among the city's white and yellow lights.

It was deathly quiet inside the office and times like these are when the darkness would seep into my entire being and corrupt my thoughts. Even with my colleagues around me, I felt very much alone, and just like always, I thought about death.

I'm not afraid of death but I find the process of dying to be terrifying. I strongly suspect that disembowelment by zombie is not the best way to go. I'd rather endure life, for now, if only to get some ice cream.

"Did anybody notice the security guards downstairs?" I asked to distract myself from my poisoned thoughts.

Everyone stared at me and simply shook their heads. There was normally a small contingent of security officers who stayed on the ground floor.

"Do you think they abandoned us?" asked Jill, tearfully.

"They never abandon their posts," I continued. "They may be part of the zombie mob."

"I never liked them. Hated them, in fact," said Oscar.

"If no one knows we're here, we may end up spending the night in the office," I said.

"I can't survive all night without eating anything! I'm starving!" complained Oscar.

"How can you eat after what just happened?" asked Jill, her voice unsteady.

"Because unlike *someone*, I am not a self-starving stick!" replied Oscar.

Yeah, Jill was pretty skinny, but I wouldn't say *too* skinny. She actually ate like a ravenous beast, but only when she was sure no one was looking.

Everyone was under a lot of stress and we needed to get along for however long we were stuck together. That didn't mean we had to like each other. Oscar was still an irritating idiot.

"You can check the fridge in the kitchen," suggested Ash, trying to break the tension.

I never put anything in the fridge, and I wasn't prepared to eat food of unknown origin or age. I knew we had some crackers and bottled water in the storage room — Hefflebottom had Oscar and I pack and retrieve everything. Of course, Oscar always disappeared, and I was left doing all the manual labour on top of my regular duties. I grabbed the keys from Hefflebottom's office and followed everyone to the kitchen.

"Oh, hell no! I forgot about the TV!" exclaimed Ash with a smile, as he turned on the black box at the front of the kitchen.

It had also slipped my mind that we had a TV in the kitchen. With what we had just seen, and the apparent chaos in the city, there was bound to be a news report on it. Ash switched the channel to the local news and a live broadcast was in progress.

"We're here in downtown where rioting has been taking place since earlier this afternoon," said a female reporter. *"The*

cause is still unconfirmed and everyone in the city is advised to stay indoors. The army has been called in to assist the—"

There was a loud thud and the camera shook wildly. As it fell, so did the reporter, her head splitting open on the concrete. Her shrill scream was cut off as the broadcast shifted to the studio.

"We seem to be having some technical difficulties but do standby as we—" the reporter in the studio began talking but stopped in mid-sentence as his co-anchor's head dropped onto the desk like a free-falling coconut.

The crew rushed in to help her as the reporter continued, *"She's okay, just fainted but fear not, the news shall continue!"*

After just a couple seconds, she rose up, but she was different from before. Blood dripped from her red lips down to her pointy chin. Her eyes were nothing more than tiny dots surrounded by white tissue. She snarled, turned to her left and bit her co-host on his neck.

"AHHHHH! GET THIS BITCH OFF ME!" cried the news presenter in agony as he struggled to get free.

The news presenter vocalized his pain in a tremendous tenor voice, with the vibrato of a professional opera singer. The channel suddenly signed off. Everyone in the kitchen stared at the TV with their jaws dropped.

"There's no food in here!" exclaimed Oscar as he slammed the fridge door shut.

Everyone ignored him, unable to tear their eyes away from the coloured vertical bars on the screen. For a minute more, we all kept watching, waiting for the news report to continue, but it never did.

"Check the international news," I suggested.

Sure enough, it was on every channel. Rioting on our little island would have been inconsequential if not for the summit. This was big news.

Ash settled on one channel as the non-zombified reporters read the story.

"We have received unconfirmed reports that the Queen has been hurt at the summit earlier today. The severity of her injury is not known, and the state of the delegates was not disclosed. Some are suggesting a terrorist attack in the small island nation. For now, this is just speculation and we remain hopeful that the issue will be resolved shortly."

Everyone continued watching the news, but I spaced out. I was trying to visualize the many ways in which the Queen could be killed by zombies.

"I guess the maids cleaned the fridge today, so I'll just go check the storeroom for some crackers," I said calmly, after returning to reality.

Everyone was still focused on the TV, with the exception of Oscar who kept rubbing his belly and staring at the closed refrigerator door, so I quietly got up and left. Thankfully, Oscar didn't come with me.

The storeroom wasn't very far from the kitchen and I didn't feel particularly nervous opening it. It was not like I expected a zombie to jump out as I opened the door, but I still stayed clear until I turned on the light.

Did I call this a room? It felt more like a cupboard. I took one step inside and couldn't move any further. Metal shelves pressed against the walls were packed to capacity with office stationery — pens, inks and paper mostly. Why would they store crackers in a room like this? That was a question that could only be answered by Lord

Hefflebottom — I had no influence over snack storage protocol.

I narrowed my eyes at the cases of bottled water stacked precariously next to an open electrical panel — Oscar's handiwork. Next to the electrocution hazard, a large brown chest rested upon the crackers, which I suspected were squashed into powdered form.

The chest was made of solid wood, with a golden trim. It called to my curiosity, and I was unable to resist. I opened the lid and yellow light poured out.

I'd always been a forgetful person, so I self-diagnosed myself with amnesia, with the possibility of a brain tumour. To further substantiate my diagnosis was the fact that I had completely forgotten about the TV in the kitchen and also the walkie-talkies in this treasure chest. If only I forgot my problems as easily.

I grabbed a walkie-talkie and held it up in the air in triumph. A short victory song played in my head.

I held the device before me and inspected it — a rectangular plastic box with a rubberized grip and an antenna on top. I had used one before, but could I remember how? What were all the dials, buttons and switches for? I returned to the others with crackers in hand and the black radio transceiver in my pocket.

Only Oscar noticed me when I entered the kitchen — he quickly grabbed the crackers and tore open a packet.

"Guys, look what I found," I said.

"Oh, hell no! I forgot about the walkie-talkies too!" exclaimed Ash.

I didn't know Ash personally, but I knew he was a really intelligent guy, an unmatched wizard with computers, and a former hacker (allegedly) best known for his infiltration of project White Cell. If this guy forgot about the TV and the walkie-talkies, then maybe I was too hasty with my asinine brain tumour assumption.

"I know the transport division is using them during the summit, which means we can call for rescue." I took a seat, resting the walkie-talkie on the table as if it were made of fragile glass.

"Do you know how to use it?" asked Jill.

"I used it once before, so I should be able to do it again, I hope."

I was the only one in the group who had used the walkie-talkie before, during the summit's trial run. I hadn't been paying much attention when they were training us on how to use it, but all I had to do at the time was push a button and talk. I hoped that the settings hadn't been changed.

"Hello, is anybody there? Over," I spoke into the device as I pressed the button on the side.

I released the button and waited for a response. The room was quiet except for Oscar's crunching.

"That was some professional radio talk there by—" As I spoke, my sentence was interrupted by a voice that came from the walkie-talkie.

"This is Hellfire 1, send your message."

"Hey, this is Zack. A few of us are trapped at work and we need some help, over."

"How many of you are there? Over."

"There are five of us. Over."

"Roger. Stay put and we'll get you. And for any further transmissions, your call sign is Hellfire 9, over."

"Okay, sure... over."

"I'll radio you when we're near. When I give you the all-clear to leave, you'll need to get out of the building and into the vehicle immediately. Over and out."

Jill and Ash cheered, Pixonov grunted, and Oscar continued crunching crackers.

I placed the walkie-talkie down on the table and walked across the room to the window. As I stared down, I could see the dark water of the ocean crashing against the waterfront's retaining wall. The adjacent twin tower blocked the view of the city. Both towers had just recently been built, and only our tower was occupied.

I stared at the pier where the water taxi docked every day. Every morning I used to watch it reach late, making the passengers frantically rush to their respective jobs. I imagined it docking and zombies walking out slowly and awkwardly, with stiff limbs. I always thought zombies were slow and even so, they were terrifying, but fast zombies were just shit-your-pants scary.

"So what kind of codename is Hellfire anyway?" asked Oscar, who was bored after eating all the crackers.

"The summit is the hotspot for activity these days. Hot as hell," said Ash with a chuckle.

"I agree with the hell part," added Jill.

I just stared down at the fountain on the waterfront below; it was even larger than the one in the courtyard. This fountain had a holographic great white shark, that synchronized its leaps and dashes with the fountain's water streams. On the hour, a giant kraken was programmed to appear and do battle with the shark. The kraken's size was randomly generated and sometimes the shark swallowed it whole. Other times, the sea monster wrapped its tentacles around the ferocious fish and picked it apart with its beak. People always gathered to witness the spectacle and sometimes they placed bets on the winner.

The time went by slowly as we waited for a voice to come from the radio. I went through the evacuation plan in my head: receive the call, rush to the elevator and get into the vehicle. It was a simple plan but accounting for the variables was difficult. All I could do was hope for no zombies and a quick escape.

I kept looking at the shark, which swam in circles around the fountain, and as the water formed a little black whirlpool, my mind was sucked into a vortex darker than the night-time ocean. On the outside, I might have looked calm, composed and maybe even happy, but my smiling face was a mask that hid hopelessness beneath.

I had a lot of time to think about my condition and on careful analysis, the root cause of my problems has always been crippling loneliness. The obvious solution is pretty simple — get some friends who share common interests, reconcile my familial relationships, and start a family of my own. Sounds nice in my head, but I wouldn't know where to begin. I'm a lost soul on the chaotic sea of despair, with a boat that has no rudder.

"When is this guy going to call back?" asked Jill through gritted teeth, bringing me back to reality.

As if responding to her, a voice came from the walkie-talkie.

"Hellfire 9, come in, over."

"You just spoke the magic words, girl!" said Ash with a grin.

I rushed to the walkie-talkie and answered, "This is Hellfire 9. Are you ready for us? Over."

"Get downstairs in two minutes. The rendezvous point will be the courtyard by the fountain, over."

"Roger that, we're on our way now."

No one wasted time in hurrying to the elevator. Oscar led the way, and I made up the end of the queue. The elevator door opened as soon as the call button was pressed — it was the same one we had come up in. I entered last, and the ground floor button was already glowing. On a normal day, the elevator would stop on every floor on the way down. But today was a day as far from normal as it could be. The elevator glided down quickly and quietly, and we were on our way outside again.

12

DEAD AIR

[Day 1]

~Prayers may save your soul but not your body~

THROUGH THE GLASS WINDOWS on the ground floor, I saw two vehicles parked outside. We headed straight to the door and exited the building. The night air was chilly, and I shivered as I glanced across to the spot where Mr. Puffs had been attacked.

It was dark but I could still discern a black puddle that stained the ground where he had been bleeding. He was nowhere to be seen, and his attackers were absent as well. I didn't want to get a closer look at him anyway — seeing him through the binoculars was bad enough.

Other than our group, no other human, living or zombie, was in the open. We hurried over to the nearer vehicle, which had stopped behind the other. The doors of the black car in front flew open and three men emerged. All three of them wore army uniforms and the two who flanked the sides cradled assault rifles in their arms.

"We need to move quickly," said the man whom I had been speaking with over the walkie-talkie.

His name was Captain Stone and he carried his military rank as if it were his first name. He worked on the same floor as me and while we were familiar with each other, we weren't exactly friends. I only really saw him whenever he came to see his girlfriend, who sat in the cubicle opposite mine.

"Is Chelsea with you?" asked Captain Stone.

"No, she left earlier today," I replied. "A couple hours before we did."

I guess he couldn't discuss any personal matters over the walkie-talkie, and the regular communication lines were unusable. Since Chelsea wasn't staying on the ship with us, she had left long before the Mr. Puffs incident.

Captain Stone then pulled out a flashlight and asked, "Has anyone been bitten by the infected?"

It took me a couple seconds to figure out that by infected, he meant zombie. "Oh no, no one. Can't say the same for Mr. Puffs though."

He flashed the light in my face, focusing the beam on my eyes. The intense brightness immediately caused me to tear up. He did the same for everyone else.

"Okay, let's move," he said as he went back to the driver's seat of the car.

Jill and I took the two available seats in the car while Ash, Pixonov and Oscar went in the black SUV. There were exactly five available seats between both vehicles. With his death, Mr. Puffs had made an unwitting sacrifice for the benefit of the team.

As soon as the doors closed, the vehicles sped off. We drove around the fountain and headed to the highway. The traffic lights in the area were still working but we didn't stop for any red signals.

As we drove past the city, the wail of sirens mixed with what sounded like screams. My seat had an unsightly ocean view — the port's dark water was uninviting. Our vehicles zipped along an empty roadway but between the nearby buildings, scores of people ran about. I tried my best to see what was happening; at our speed, it was a blur.

We stopped at the lighthouse at the edge of the city. This was the border of the area that had been blocked off for the summit. There was a heavy military and police presence here. Dozens of heavy-assault-weapon-wielding soldiers in thick armour stood guard as a posse of police officers directed civilian vehicles onto the highway.

The traffic out of the city reminded me of rush hour — usually no less than two hours of sedentary stress. It looked like we weren't going anywhere soon.

Captain Stone rolled down his window and spoke to someone on the outside, "Five soldiers and five of our staff on board. We have orders to head to the airport."

"Okay, this way, Captain Stone," said the soldier as he saluted.

He directed our vehicles across the intersection and onto the lane that normally allowed traffic into the city. The civilians angrily protested as we made our way onto the clear lane of the highway. A police officer on a motorcycle escorted us, a soundless spinning blue light trailing behind him like a fairy.

"You mentioned something about someone encountering an infected," said Captain Stone.

"Uh, yeah, Mr. Puffs was attacked a few hours ago. We've never seen anything like it before. No one can survive having their guts ripped out like that!" I explained.

"It's an infection they're calling Zombosis. They have no cure for it except for the one I discovered."

"You found a cure?" Jill's excitement broke through her fear.

"A bullet to the brain."

Jill's mouth opened ever so slightly, speechless; I hadn't immediately noticed, but so had mine. That was not the best cure for anything. I could see his point though. It was not unheard of to euthanize an animal on its way to a certain, long, painful death. If these zombies were people on a course not much different from such animals, then surely a bullet was a humane end.

Our vehicles kept moving steadily on our broad, traffic-free roadway, while cars lined up on the other side of the highway. People were walking between the vehicles. There was probably an accident, which occurred quite frequently.

Not only did accidents stop the flow of traffic in one lane, but they reduced the speed of the vehicles in all the others when curious drivers slowed down to observe but never help; this phenomenon was locally known as maccoing, performed by maccoes.

We didn't slow down and the policeman astride the motorcycle in front of us kept his head pointing straight ahead.

For the time, I forgot my problems.

"Why are we going to the airport?" I enquired.

"When things started getting out of control, the summit's delegates were rushed to the airport. We're going to rendezvous with them over there," replied Captain Stone.

"Are we flying out of the country with them?" asked Jill.

"All flights are grounded. Not even the delegates are

out yet, but they will be ready to leave as soon as we get clearance," said Captain Stone. "Don't worry, the airport is like a fort now, so you'll be safe there."

We approached a large intersection where highways converged. The incomplete concrete overpass loomed overhead. If it had been completed on time, the traffic probably wouldn't have been as backed up as it was.

There were people all over, like ants from a disturbed colony. They scuttled between cars and crawled on the overpass. Some shoved and fought each other. From inside the car, the muffled sound of a hundred frightened voices broadcasted fear.

The traffic wasn't as bad here and many cars headed north for the hospital. At the very peak of the mountain was Hope Hospital. The roads to the top were narrow and winding and, ironically, caused the deaths of many seeking medical care. The entire mountain was rumoured to be haunted by the restless souls of sick patients, angry doctors, and dead babies. Hopeless Hospital was surely in a more hellish state than usual. No doubt the wards had already become flooded with the zombie infestation.

From this intersection, cars moved in all directions, so we switched across to the regular lane and flowed with the traffic. Our police escort created a path between the vehicles so that we could slip through quickly.

We moved to our destination steadily, without so much as a single delay. Jill usually slept during car rides, but her eyes were wide open. Perhaps the invasion of zombies had something to do with that.

We came to another intersection of roads, this one at the university campus. All the students trying to leave were blocked by a girl who had crashed her brand-new car into a pickup truck. The front of her car was completely wrecked, and she stood there crying a river of tears. Meanwhile, the driver of the pickup truck, a short slim girl who looked too young to even possess a driver's license, laughed maniacally. The pickup truck barely had a scratch on it.

A shabby man with disproportionally large forearms ran with a limp between the cars trapped in the traffic. He banged on the windows with such force that the glass shattered. We picked up the pace and I couldn't see what happened next. I think it was safe to assume that the zombies weren't just in the city, but on the campus and possibly even throughout the entire island already.

"Isn't the police officer going to help them?" asked Jill.

"He has his orders. Our forces are split between the airport and the summit site right now, and the delegates are the highest priority. We can't dilute forces to deal with petty incidents," answered Stone.

Things at the university must have been an absolute nightmare. Thousands of students on one campus with no help from the police. Still, it couldn't have been worse than the hospital, where there were zombies *and* ghosts.

Our path snaked around abandoned cars and people roaming the roadway like lost animals.

We passed a large building on our left; the bright lights revealed an empty compound. The mall was already closed for the day, but I wondered if the zombies had made it inside. If I had the choice, I'd much rather die there than at Hopeless Hospital.

A few more traffic lights and turns later, we found ourselves at a military checkpoint. The airport was just ahead — all we had to do now was get past the military blockade.

Getting in was easier than I expected. Captain Stone didn't have to do much other than state his presence and we were allowed to drive onto the compound. We were the last to enter though, and all civilian vehicles were turned away.

The entire airport was very well lit. But even under the radiant lights, most of the cars in the parking lot were indistinguishable from each other — they were the brand-new vehicles bought by our government to impress the world, at a hefty cost to hardworking taxpayers like myself. We added our vehicles somewhere between all the mechanical clones.

The airport terminal glowed brightly, and a solid beam of lavender light formed a pillar from the glass roof up to the clouds above. The central part of the terminal looked like a pink crystal heart lodged in concrete. The lavender beacon came directly from the heart and guided planes to the airport.

The night air felt uncomfortably warm as we walked briskly toward the beacon. On the way, several soldiers who were on guard saluted Captain Stone.

Inside, it was much cooler, brighter and not at all pink. Dozens of people were scattered about, some of whom were co-workers. The heart was made up of hundreds of hexagonal glass panes, which were completely transparent from the inside of the structure, held in place by a steel frame. Beyond the glass ceiling, the stars sparkled, only partially blocked by small clouds.

"This is where I leave you guys. I expect you will be

spending the night here, so make yourselves comfortable," said Captain Stone as he walked off, followed by his soldiers.

Oscar jumped onto a nearby couch and spread his legs across the cushions. The woman who had been sitting there stared at the bottom of his shoes, got up and walked off. Apparently, his mother had not taught him any manners.

"How are we supposed to spend the night here?" asked Jill, with a tone of rising frustration in her voice.

The spoilt, pampered princess was not used to spending the night anywhere without three full suitcases. I decided to go for a walk when she began complaining about hair frizz and her need for a warm bath and a soft bed.

I took small, slow steps at first, then faster, large steps when I realized that no one noticed me sneaking away. Honestly, I felt disappointed that not even Jill cared to enquire about my departure. I don't think anyone even noticed me missing. The further I walked, the more my mind became contaminated by terrible thoughts.

Certainly, there must be a causal relationship between loneliness and depression. However, I was alone before the outbreak, and still will be after the zombie dust settles. I can't be lonelier than zero, right?

I tried to focus on the sights and sounds in the airport to get my mind into the light. There was a lot of murmuring echoing in the large hall and I attempted to decipher some of it. I paid close attention to those who I walked past and picked up pieces of conversations.

"I need a king-sized bed to sleep in!"
"We were authorized to use live rounds."
"...had to run for my life!"

"Did you hear the Queen was bitten?"

When I got back to the group, Oscar, Pixonov and Jill were sharing the couch. They were still talking to each other, but I was too far away to hear what the discussion was about. I took a seat nearby and rested my eyes.

13

TWILIGHT DRAGON

[Day 2]

~Sometimes, seemingly perfect things show their flaws
and begin to fall apart~

*I DON'T REMEMBER FALLING asleep. The last thing I recall is
a group of people talking about insurance, checks and the stock
market — seems like the right type of conversation to fall asleep
to. I definitely remember waking up.*

I awoke to waves of sound that shook my eardrums as
much as the building I was in. Somewhere in the sky,
hidden behind all the steel and concrete, there was a colossal
metallic dragon that cried out as it fell to the earth below.
Or so I thought, as I quickly returned to the world of the
waking and sober.

The thunderous noise grew louder still as the dragon
crash-landed. The building shook violently, and the lights
flickered rapidly before shutting off. The auditorium was
coated with the faint light that poured in from the skylight
above.

Was it an earthquake or an explosion? I was sure that
the building was seconds away from folding under the

strain and collapsing onto everyone within it. The noise was replaced by a deafening ringing in my ears as the room filled with dust and cries almost as terrifying as the dying dragon.

Everyone was alert and in panic. Even after the sound had ceased, the screams and cries continued. People ran about madly — some ran to the exit, while others ran aimlessly. There was one man who ran in circles. The rain of dust made it impossible for me to locate my group. Were they among the runners or those huddled together in the corners?

I needed to get out of that suffocating dust but had lost all sense of direction. Completely disoriented, I walked forward with one hand along the wall and the other in front of me. My face was exposed to the floating debris as I manoeuvred as best as I could with the limited visibility.

A faint light cut through the shower of airborne particulates. My eyes and lungs were polluted with particles as I headed toward the light. I emerged in an open, paved area and didn't stop until the air was clean and I could finally breathe again.

I stood upon a huge spread of asphalt and concrete with white lines painted all over. I had managed to get all the way to the landing zone. Planes sat in the distance, stationary and empty.

As I looked back, I saw the back end of an airplane protruding from the side of the building. The smouldering wreck had penetrated the external wall and caused the structure to collapse partially.

The heart terminal was broken. Most of the glass panes had shattered on impact and a large crack ran down the middle of the heart. The lavender beacon was no more.

Not too many people can say they survived an airplane crash. I'm sure even fewer can say they survived having one crash into them.

I was mesmerized by the giant dancing flames that burned like the sun, fighting away the dark. Not too far off to my right, something else stood, keeping the flames company. It was not another human but a brown beast. The dog's ears stood up straight, like concave dishes funnelling sound waves from far off in the distance.

He turned his head to face me and we stared into each other's eyes. I was pretty sure he was checking to see if I was infected, just the same as I was doing for him. He took a few cautious steps closer and stopped. I got down to one knee and motioned for him to come closer.

"Here boy..."

He crept nearer until I was just able to pat him on the head. There was a black collar around his neck with a silver name tag dangling.

"Bingo?"

He gave a little nod of his head at the sound of his name.

"Smart dog."

I was the only person who had come through to this side. The runway was empty, and the fading night was lit up by the growing flames. The sky in the east glowed as the sun rose. The twilight crash was eerily beautiful. As the sun's rays broke over the horizon, the military personnel swarmed onto the scene.

***

Half an hour and one exploding plane later, I finally met up with the others, with Bingo in tow. No one seemed to notice the dog; I don't think they even noticed me. The building had been completely evacuated and the flames put out. Black smoke still floated off in the air as if a volcano had just erupted.

Everyone was busy fabricating seemingly implausible theories about what could have caused the plane to crash. The one that garnered the most terrified looks was that the infection had already been on the plane. If this were true, then even getting off the island did not mean getting to safety.

The sun was now fully visible and cast shadows behind the scattered groups of people. The military was mobilizing around the perimeter — the sound of the crash or maybe the heat could have attracted a horde of zombies. I knew we wouldn't be able to stay there for much longer.

It wasn't long before the sound of gunfire cracked the silence of the early morning.

Jill covered her mouth and spoke between her fingers, "What are they shooting at?"

No one answered, because the only response to her question was exactly what she didn't want to hear.

"I think we should find Stone and ask him what the hell is going on," I suggested.

Stone had brought us to that place and he was our best way out. We moved to the perimeter fence where several infantrymen were stationed. Soldiers were also perched on top of scaffolding behind the fence, firing shots at distant zombies. There was no large horde yet, and the only zombies I saw were being picked off one by one.

"Stone, when are you getting us outta here, man?" Oscar asked the officer who had been overseeing the approach of the infected.

"All civilians are to remain in the compound until an all-clear is given," replied Captain Stone firmly. "Anyone outside this fence can be shot if they attempt to enter, so you are all still safe."

"The airport's perimeter is too large to hold the infection back. If they're attracted to the plane, then there's no stopping them," I argued.

"Prep the helicopter for take-off," Stone commanded a soldier, who saluted and ran off.

"What? You're leaving? Take us with you... please..." begged Jill, palms together, fingertips firmly heavenward.

"I have orders to investigate the potential point of origin for the infection. I don't think that is where you want to be," said Stone as he walked off toward the helicopter.

We happened to be in the right place at the right time because just as the captain turned his back and took no more than two steps, the infected horde made its appearance.

"Oh my God, how many of them do you think there are?" shouted one of the snipers with a clear note of fear in his voice.

"There must be... OVER NINE THOUSAAAAAAND!" screamed the other soldier.

"What? Nine thousand?! That can't be right!"

In the distance, zombies approached the fence with great speed. The bullets barely seemed to affect their numbers. It was like watching an approaching tsunami and being unable to do anything at all to stop it. The flood of death collided with the perimeter fence with tremendous force.

"GET TO THE CHOPPER!" Captain Stone commanded us.

We wasted no time in hurrying to the extraction vehicle. The infected had already broken through the fence and were spreading very quickly. The perimeter soldiers were smothered in seconds. Everyone within the compound retreated from the fence but had nowhere to go.

Oscar hopped into the helicopter first, followed by Pixonov, Jill and Ash. I entered last and sat between Jill and the open door. Bingo barked at the approaching zombies and at the civilians who were desperately trying to reach the helicopter.

"Bingo!" I bellowed to my new friend.

The intelligent beast responded right away and leaped into the helicopter, just as it began to take off. He lay low at my feet and continued barking.

A few civilians managed to get close to the helicopter, but it was just a tad too high to reach. Zombies either scared them off or devoured them.

Captain Stone was still on the ground, picking off zombies with precise shots to their heads. As the helicopter flew over him, he climbed a zombie like a ladder. With one boot on the zombie's shoulder and the other on its head, he jumped. The zombie's neck broke and Stone rose vertically, grabbing onto the landing gear. With acrobatic ease, he muscled himself up into the chopper and looked down to see the spot he had been standing get swarmed with undead.

As the helicopter flew higher, the entire compound came into view. The fence had been ruptured in several areas, and zombies ran into the compound freely.

All defences in the airport were quickly taken out by the massive number of infected. It appeared as if we were the only ones who had escaped.

The wind pulled at my clothes as if egging me to skydive. It took me back to my time on top of the building. I still wasn't ready to jump.

"What are our orders, captain?" asked the pilot, his head protected by an oversized helmet and eyes hidden behind bug-like glasses.

"We continue with the mission," he replied as he surveyed the ground below.

"And the civilians?"

"We have no choice but to take them with us for now. Once we scout the area, we'll head back to headquarters. They should be safe there."

Was *anywhere* safe?

"So where is the point of origin?" I asked, as soon as Captain Stone had finished outlining their plan.

"We believe it's somewhere on the university campus. We should be there in a minute."

Only four soldiers sat with us in the helicopter, including Captain Stone. I couldn't have been the only one concerned about being overwhelmed by zombies after landing.

Since everyone was deathly silent, I proposed another question, "What if the zombies are attracted to noise? Wouldn't the helicopter attract them straight to us?"

"From what we have seen, the infected have a pattern of forming large mobs — what we call 'mobbing'. It takes them a while after hearing a sound before they mobilize. That should give us a few minutes," explained Captain Stone.

He sounded so confident in his words as if they were fact and not merely speculation. He showed no sign of fear at all — it was inspiring. After his amazing display of zombie-slaying abilities at the airport, his confidence was certainly justified.

No more than five minutes had passed before the helicopter slowed down and began descending. I imagined being raided by zombies as soon as we landed. My stomach rumbled as fear slowly increased again, and only then did I realize I hadn't eaten at all. I remembered the vanilla ice cream and my longing for it returned.

"What do you expect to find here, exactly?" I asked my final question as we descended.

"Hopefully, there are survivors who have some useful information. I doubt we'll find anyone, but we'll still do a quick scout and be on our way."

The helicopter had set down upon the flat roof of the university's library pyramid. We were well above ground level and no zombies were around. Stone and two of the soldiers exited while the pilot remained seated, ready to take off at a moment's notice.

The pilot turned off the engine, and I realized how loud it had been. Stone and his soldiers steadily climbed down the sides of the pyramid.

I hopped out of the helicopter with Bingo at my side and looked down at the university's courtyard where the three soldiers carefully treaded. The place was quiet and calm — maybe a bit too calm. I just wanted Captain Stone to complete his mission quickly so we could leave. But really, leave and go where? Even if we weren't in the middle of the zombie apocalypse, I had nowhere better to be.

For a moment, I almost missed the old days of studying and exams. Seven years had passed since I first graduated from the university. After two degrees and several shitty jobs, nostalgia was inarguably unjustified.

My life was a collection of misfortunes, some comical, others tragic. Somehow, perhaps because of perfect timing, I wasn't among the first people to become zombified. I tried to keep a positive outlook, but I feared that things would take a sudden nosedive into zombie hell.

Bingo and I kept a close watch over the courtyard. In all my wasted years at the university, I had never seen it so empty. It was creepy, but far better than having it full of zombies. I shuddered as I recalled how the zombies had just swarmed the airport.

Suddenly, there was snarling, growling and screaming. Bingo and I spun around to see the pilot chasing Oscar around the rooftop of the building, while the others scattered and cried out in terror.

I didn't expect one of the survivors to zombify without direct contact with the infected. Was the infection airborne? If that were the case, surely we were all infected.

The pilot chased Oscar in circles and didn't change his target to anyone else. While Oscar grew weaker, his attacker was relentless; Oscar couldn't run forever. Paralyzed by fear, no one tried to help.

"AHHHHHH! HELP... ME!" Oscar bellowed, as his lungs and legs tired.

Bingo growled at the zombie but didn't bark. Everyone stood in position as if weighed down by lead feet. I had to do something because if Oscar became infected, we would have had to deal with two zombies on the roof. I surveyed the area and identified my options.

My first option was to push the zombie off the pyramid. However, there was the risk of getting bitten.

Option two was to fly the helicopter, but the risk of crashing was far too great. Then I saw the assault rifle that had been left behind by the zombified soldier. Option three was the most viable.

I dashed for the helicopter, picked up a gun for the first time in my life, aimed as best I could, and pulled the trigger just as the zombie pinned Oscar to the floor. Nothing happened except for the cry of pain as Oscar's blood flowed from the fresh bite wound on his neck. I flicked a switch near the trigger and tried again, and this time the zombie stumbled back and fell over the edge. The gun's recoil was intense.

The mangled corpse twitched on the ground after having crashed into the steps below. The zombie struggled to stand, even with bullet holes in his torso, broken bones and torn skin.

I'm sure Stone could have taken out the zombie pilot with a single bullet to the head. Headshots are much more difficult than they seem, especially with trembling, sweaty hands.

Everyone then turned their focus to Oscar who lay on the floor, spewing blood from his wound and mouth. We carefully encircled him as he cried out, clutching his laceration. I was the one with the gun, and the only one capable of stopping his infection. But putting a bullet through someone's brain was not that easy, even as much as I despised him.

"He is going to turn into one of them," said Ash, "so you know what you need to do, Zack..."

"No, no, no..." cried Oscar as he struggled to his feet, the gurgling blood obscuring his words. "Give... give me... that gun!"

With one hand holding his bloodied neck and the other reaching forward, Oscar tried to grab the weapon that I held onto firmly. He moved slowly and stumbled forward, barely keeping his balance. With a burst of energy, he lunged at me, and his hand only just missed as I evaded.

He sang a note of terror as he flew straight over the edge of the building. His body fell halfway down the pyramid's steps. He twitched and moaned just like the zombie pilot.

"What if he isn't infected?" whimpered Jill, her face covered in leaking, black eyeliner.

"Who wants to find out?" I asked.

"Pixie?" Ash had his arms folded in his signature pose as he looked down below.

Pixonov looked down at his best friend, Oscar, and turned his back on him. He hung his head like a sad tortoise standing on hind legs.

"Hell— come—" a voice spoke over the radio in the helicopter. The words became clearer as the ringing in my ears finally subsided. *"Hellfire 9, come in, over."*

Jill was the first to rush over and answer, "Captain Stone? This is Jill. The pilot is dead... and the zombies... Oscar fell over..."

"Calm down and explain what happened, over."

"The pilot was infected, and he killed Oscar. They're both off the roof now, but now we don't have a pilot, over," explained Ash in a considerably calmer tone, as he took the radio away from the weeping Jill.

"Roger that. We'll have to regroup and rendezvous back on the roof. Just hold on until we get there. Over and out."

Bingo barked a single time and attracted everyone's attention.

"I think the soldiers should hurry," said Pixonov, the man of very few words.

From the far buildings on the campus, zombies shuffled out into the daylight. The moans grew louder as more zombies constantly poured into the open. They were unquestionably infected, but they walked slowly with stiff limbs, instead of quickly like those we had seen before. But fast or slow didn't really matter at that point, since we were trapped on the roof, unwittingly besieged.

"Are they infected? Why are they moving so slowly?" Ash still had his arms folded.

"Slow, fast, who cares? Just shoot them!" demanded Pixonov.

"There are at least thirty of them already. Ash, report the situation to Stone," I said, peering through the rifle's scope.

As he spoke over the radio to the soldiers, the sound dissolved as I drowned in thought.

There are so many ways to die — poison, suffocation, blood loss, chemical overdose. I would never have guessed that Zombosis would jump to the top of that list. The thing that really worries me about the zombies is whether they are really dead. Are they people trapped in undying bodies with the insatiable desire for human flesh? If that is the case, then infection is far worse than death.

"Zack! Zack!"

I snapped back to reality. "Yeah, Ash, what did Stone say?"

"We need to get out of sight!"

I retreated to the helicopter, along with the other survivors.

14

TRAPPED

[Day 2]

~Perspective determines good and evil~

THE ZOMBIES SLOWLY SURROUNDED the building. Our only consolation was the fact that they were no longer the sprinting kind, filled with bloodlust and energy. These zombies were much slower — like stiff corpses struggling against rigor mortis. But if they managed to get to the roof, their numbers would have definitely made up for their speed handicap.

Hours passed and their numbers grew. Everyone remained in the helicopter, hiding from the blistering sun above and the supposedly ice-cold undead below.

"Hellfire 9, come in, over."

I picked up the radio immediately. "Captain Stone, where are you guys? Over."

"We've located some survivors and are going to attempt to extract them, over."

"How long is that going to take? Over."

"We're working on a plan to clear out the infected. I will update you on the ETA later, over."

"The zombies are surrounding the building!" Jill grabbed the radio. "The longer you wait, the harder it's going to be for us to get out of here!"

"Just hold tight until I give you a time. We're keeping an eye on the situation, so don't worry. Over and out."

Captain Stone's words weren't reassuring. Jill was right — the longer we waited, the more our chances of escape diminished.

"Didn't he tell us he was going to do a quick scout?" said Jill.

"I'd rather be waiting here than back at the airport," said Ash, wiping beads of perspiration off his forehead.

Ash always wore a suit and tie, and refused to remove any part of it, even as it became drenched with sweat.

"What if the other survivors are surrounded by zombies like we are? It will be impossible to get them out!" argued Jill, as if we had the power to command the captain to return immediately.

"If that's the case, then there is no way *we* can escape," I said, causing Jill to gasp. "Stone will get us out."

Why weren't the zombies climbing the pyramid to get to us? Maybe they had heard the noise but didn't see us on the roof, or perhaps the walker zombies couldn't climb the pyramid's steps. Surely if some runners had seen us on the roof, they would have been upon us in seconds.

As time passed, my faith in Captain Stone shrank. If he died, then we had no way of escape. But just like at the airport, it seemed as if he was the only one who could save us.

The helicopter was controlled by two flight sticks and an unintuitive jumble of gauges, switches, and buttons, all presented on a digital screen. I wasn't yet desperate enough to risk crashing, but the temptation was mounting.

I laid back in the cabin and tried to get in a comfortable position. I closed my eyes a bit, resting them from the bright glare of the sun. The grunts and groans of the undead rose from below, just like it had been for hours.

With nothing to keep me occupied, the dark thoughts returned. My mind was slowly decaying as death grew like a necrotic infection. However, my body still clung instinctively to life. This disparity left me alive, but my tether to this existence was but a brittle thread.

Humanity desperately hopes for immortality of body and soul, but anything of the sort would be damnation to me. I find the thought of nonexistence to be most comforting.

Bingo clawed at my arm. He growled and my muscles tensed. At first, I thought that Stone had made it up to the roof quickly and quietly. But it was not the captain or a soldier at all. Oscar stood silent at the edge of the roof. The blood was dry and the flow had ceased.

I fumbled for the gun as the zombie charged, snarling and baring his red teeth. It all happened so quickly. I took aim and squeezed the trigger.

BANG! My first shot missed.

Oscar manoeuvred much quicker than the walkers below. He reached inside the helicopter and grabbed Jill's ankle before I could fire again.

RATATAT! A burst of bullets pierced his chest. The zombie loosened his grip on Jill.

RATATAT! One more punctured his forehead, ending his savage attack.

The gunfire echoed throughout the courtyard and the

zombies stirred, trying to pinpoint the source. Still, they didn't attack.

Everyone was terrified, panicked and screaming — Jill most of all. I kicked the unmoving corpse out of the helicopter and fell back onto the seat. My shoulders and neck were terribly tense, and my breathing raced with my heartbeat.

Pixonov ripped off his tight dress shirt and covered his dead friend. Tears trickled down to his chin and dripped onto his swollen pectoral muscles.

"H-how was he so fast?" asked Ash when his breath allowed him.

That was a good question — he never moved that fast when he was alive. My brain was returning to clear thought again.

"Maybe when they turn, they start off fast — runners," I began explaining my theory. "Those walkers below probably turned when the infection first spread, so their bodies are stiff like corpses."

"Hellfire 9, come in, over."

"Oh, hey Stone, what's up?" I responded in a calm manner, atypical of someone who had just been attacked by a zombie.

"Are the infected on the roof? Over."

"Zombie Oscar managed to get back to the roof but he's dead now. I mean, dead dead. How come you haven't fired a single shot yet? Over."

"We're not using bullets unless absolutely necessary. Have you noticed the zombies in the courtyard below you are slower than the ones before? Over."

"Yeah, I was thinking that they eventually slow down, over."

"Exactly. We're going to use that to our advantage to get these survivors out. Timing is everything so just be patient. We'll be out of here before sundown. Over and out."

"Sundown?!" cried Pixonov as soon as Captain Stone signed out.

"Well, it's better than never," said Ash.

Jill was still crying, huddled in a corner of the helicopter. I awkwardly put my arm around her shoulder, and Bingo rested his head on her lap. As the day got cooler and the sun fell lower, she regained her composure and seemed much more stable.

***

It was close to sunset when Stone contacted us again. Finally, it was time to leave. The captain's mission, which I thought was going to take only a few minutes, had actually taken most of the daylight hours.

"Hellfire 9, come in, over."

"I was beginning to think you had forgotten about us, over," I answered.

"I can't forget about the helicopter. Speaking of which, I need you to prep it for us. We need to take off as soon as we make it to the roof. Our ETA is five minutes, over."

"Roger that, send instructions, over."

"Just remember that the noise from the helicopter might attract more infected. First, we'll draw them to us with some decoys, and once the courtyard is clear, start the chopper."

He gave us the instructions on prepping the helicopter for take-off. The plan was in motion and the next five minutes were the most important of the day. Gunfire rang out in the distance and the zombie walkers slowly forced their bodies in the direction of the disturbance.

We waited until the undead were far off before prepping the helicopter. As the blades began turning, a loud beeping noise chirped in the distance, followed by an explosion. Captain Stone and his men sprinted across the empty courtyard.

They scrambled up the sides of the pyramid, each step more laboured than the last as their lungs struggled to supply their muscles with oxygen. By the time they got into the helicopter, the ground below was swamped with infected runners.

The zombies numbered in the hundreds, coming from all directions, like cockroaches emerging from the dark spaces of a seemingly clean kitchen.

The runners didn't tire as they climbed the building. The steps of the pyramid became covered by the rising flood of infected. Just before the zombie deluge inundated the structure, our helicopter took off. The landing gear was just beyond the reach of the clawing hands as we climbed steadily upward.

Suddenly, the entire helicopter tilted before Captain Stone stabilized it. A lanky, basketballer zombie the height of a lamppost had made a slam dunk on the landing gear and held on firmly.

Pixonov painted the zombie's head and hands with a coat of fluorescent-orange vomit. The blinded zombie tried to pull himself up, but his lubricated hands slipped. The infected fell all the way back down into a zombie mosh pit.

Pixonov's nausea seemed contagious because sickness roiled in my stomach. I hadn't eaten anything all day anyway, so all I could vomit was air. Whatever Pixonov had thrown up, I didn't want to know.

"I hope you weren't too close to that corpse," said Stone while in control of the helicopter.

"Who, Oscar? We kept him at the far end of the roof. We didn't throw him off because we thought that might have attracted more zombies," I explained.

"It's fine as long as none of you came in contact with the crawlers."

"Crawlers? You mean the walking zombies?" asked Ash.

"Crawlers are little bugs that crawl out of the corpses and spread the infection. Make sure none are on you or in the chopper," said Stone, still focused on piloting the helicopter.

"How do you know about crawlers?" I asked, curious as to whether the government had information on Zombosis.

"We were informed of the mechanism of infection. It's caused by a parasite called the HNP. The bite is the primary means by which it spreads, but crawlers can also become a major problem. Flesh of the infected is also contaminated, even after their bodies cease to function."

"What do the crawlers look like?" asked Ash.

"Individually, they're almost invisible to the naked eye, but in a group, they look like a puddle of moving blood."

Everyone searched frantically for bloody patches in the helicopter. Bingo began sniffing around.

The zombies massed below. From our aerial point of view, it was clear just how coordinated their mobs were. They were all closing in on one target on the ground — a canary-yellow SUV speeding toward the campus' exit.

Then out of nowhere came a reptilian beast as large as the SUV, ploughing through the zombies. The huge crocodile cleared a path through the horde, on its way to the university's pond. The few zombies that managed to hold on to the monster were unable to penetrate its armoured hide with their teeth.

With its powerful hind legs, the croc jumped into the air like a dragon in flight and dove into the pond, splashing water all around. The zombies on its back became tangled in the swamp-like plants and the others that were chasing did not follow any further. As suddenly as it had appeared, the croc disappeared beneath the pond's murky waters.

The vehicle knocked over the "No Parking or Driving on the Grass" sign, left skid marks on the lawn, scattered two garbage bins and flew over every speedbump as it avoided the mobs that were flanking and chasing.

As soon as they made it out of the perimeter fence, Captain Stone pressed a button and a bright light cut through the darkening sky. A massive explosion caused a nearby building to collapse partially and sent flaming zombie parts flying in all directions.

"Let's clear these kids a path to the mall, shall we?" said Stone as he guided the helicopter over the SUV.

"The mall? Why the mall of all places?" asked Ash.

"Kids these days think the mall is the best place for them to weather the so-called zombie apocalypse. They probably teach that in Zombie Survival 101," said Stone with a smirk.

"That must be a new course," I added.

The SUV drifted onto the highway and raced against the setting sun behind it. They definitely weren't going to make it to the mall before dark but at least there were no infected along the roadway, except, of course, for the zombie marathon which trailed behind them.

"Why not just bring them with us?" asked Jill.

"We didn't get close enough to tell if any of them were infected. They were surrounded by crawlers for a long time. We can't risk spreading the infection," explained Stone as if he had been expecting that question.

I wondered what he would have done if *we* were infected by the crawlers. Would he have hesitated to place a bullet in our brains? Would he have left us behind on the rooftop?

Bingo sat quietly between Jill and me. Ash leaned back in his seat with folded arms, and Pixonov clutched his undulating abs. Stone and I were the only ones tracking the vehicle below.

The sun had set completely before they reached the mall, as I expected, but they weren't far off. In the distance, lights beamed from the large building. As they approached the mall's compound, the darkness stirred and bent and extended. A zombie horde ran out into the light, chasing the yellow vehicle.

The rattle of gunfire overpowered that of the helicopter's blades. The large bullets glowed in the dark as they travelled from the chopper's gun, cutting down the swarm of infected. The weapon's aim was dead on, and the zombies disintegrated and fell to pieces.

We descended slowly, and the helicopter hovered just above the ground. The bullets continued slicing through the darkness and infected flesh. For a while, I was worried that the bullets would be depleted before the zombies were. But Stone never ran out of ammo and the machine gun kept firing until the night stood still.

The SUV had made it onto the mall's compound, no longer being chased by the infected. The vehicle stopped by the mall's entrance and three persons emerged.

When the infected had all been mowed down, Stone set us down in the parking lot. It was evident that everyone felt extremely uneasy as the engine powered down and the blades stopped rotating — Jill's fingers tightened on her knees, Ash's fingers wiggled behind the knot of his tie, and Pixonov's calloused palms held down whatever was causing his belly to roll. We had just encountered a huge horde of zombies and used loud gunfire to put them down. Was it really a good idea to land there and then?

Captain Stone and one of the soldiers exited the helicopter, while the remaining soldier took the pilot's seat, ready to take off as soon as the instruction was given. We waited in the helicopter while Stone went inside the mall.

"Did you see other survivors in there?" I asked.

My words seemed to fall on deaf ears since no one answered. There was just eerie silence and darkness. I stared into the black night, trying to see if zombies were approaching. It felt strange to be surrounded by death when it was usually trapped in my mind. It was as if death had escaped from within me and manifested itself in physical form.

I thought about what Stone had said about the survivors staying in the mall. It really didn't seem like such a bad idea to me, provided that we had some guns and proper fortifications. But I certainly wasn't going to hop off a military helicopter to join a bunch of people who were probably incompetent, or assholes, or a combination of both.

It was only a few minutes later that Captain Stone and his soldier re-entered the helicopter and we were taking off. I inhaled deeply as we ascended above the mall, relieved to be in the air again. Even from this height, no more zombies were seen.

Stone remained as stoic as I'd ever seen him. Everyone was dishevelled in some way, but Stone's posture was impeccable, his armoured uniform immaculate, and his attitude nonchalant.

"Are we leaving them there?" asked Jill.

"They should be able to hold out there for a while," Captain Stone answered quickly, as he was no longer behind the flight controls. "The other group of survivors in the mall had already set up some barricades."

Knowing that there were others who had managed to avoid infection was consoling. I closed my eyes and imagined life after Zombosis. I pictured returning to my boring life and shitty job.

The helicopter flew above the highway as we headed back into the Hellfire. We were to be dropped off at the military headquarters while Stone continued with his missions.

"On the bright side," Ash shared what he had been thinking about, "at least things can't get any worse."

I cringed at his words. I knew only too well that no matter how bad things were, they could always get worse.

15

CRASH COURSE

[Day 2-3]

~After suffering is when you can really appreciate the most mediocre of things~

ON DAY ONE OF the infection, we had sped away from the city. Now we were heading back. Was the helicopter any safer than a car? Sure, we were high above the reach of any zombies below, but if anyone zombified inside the flying contraption, we would have certainly been doomed. In any case, we couldn't fly forever.

Beneath us was the highway, where every vehicle had been abandoned. There was no animal life on the cursed earth below, or in the starlit sky above.

The skyscrapers grew larger as we approached the city, their lights shining brilliantly. A wishful thinker might have seen this as the bright light at the end of a dark tunnel.

Everyone has difficult times — their dark tunnels. Ice cream is my only light. I don't know how my story will end, but my life has been a journey I would never choose to relive.

The helicopter neared the waterfront towers. Everyone slept except for the soldiers, Bingo and me. Ash still had his arms folded and Jill rested her head upon Pixonov's thick shoulder.

The adventure was over, and we were safe. The end.

*

*

*

Of course not. Like I said before — it could always get worse. There was just no escape from the infection. Without warning, the pilot changed and lunged at the soldier next to him.

There was a struggle and the helicopter spun out of control.

You know those dreams you have where you're falling and then you wake up in a bed? Well, everyone woke up, but they were actually falling.

I held on tightly to Bingo and his body trembled.

Stone kicked the zombie back and fired a burst of shots, while the helicopter spun wildly. Everything became a dark blur and the screams were completely obscured by the sound of crumpling metal.

I tumbled out of the flaming wreck. My brain felt scrambled and I was disoriented. Nothing but a loud ringing filled my ears. Was this what it would have felt like if I had jumped from the top of the tower?

I stumbled away to a safe distance and looked back at the wreckage as the others crawled out to safety as well. The helicopter's wings had been plucked and flames danced around the deformed shell. Jill, Ash and Pixonov had safely made it out but no soldier exited. Fuel leaked out of the shattered aircraft, and the flames grew.

My vision blurred and my head wasn't completely clear, but I knew that the helicopter was a ticking time bomb. I stood up and shuffled toward Jill. Suddenly, the flying machine exploded, picking me up off my feet.

While sailing through the air, I thought about all the zombies that would be attracted to the noise. More importantly, the bright burning ball reminded me of a perfect scoop of vanilla ice cream.

Odd, I know.

As soon as my body fell upon the hard asphalt, I stood up. No pain or numbness troubled me. If there was one thing to be thankful for, it was my body's resistance to physical harm. I'd never so much as fractured a bone or had an incessant infection. Mental durability was another matter.

Pixonov was already standing, flexing his biceps. Ash hadn't even been thrown back by the explosion — he just stood there with folded arms. Jill was not accustomed to falling, and her skin had never been broken before. She had cuts and bruises all over her body, especially on her hands, knees and elbows.

Bingo was gone, as were the soldiers. There was no way any of them survived the explosion. I cared more for animals than humans, but the loss of Bingo hadn't quite registered in my groggy mind.

"We need to get in the building," I called to the others over the crackling flames.

My voice felt as weak as my muscles, and I choked on the billowing smoke.

I didn't think we would end up here again.

I suppose it's just part of cyclical nature. Just as the seasons change and repeat each year, or life leads to death and rebirth, the past always returns to us in some unexpected way.

We were back where we started, but this time we had to do things differently.

The dawn always comes as long as you're there to see it; bad times don't last if you persevere. At least that's what I tell myself.

We crossed the courtyard and entered the same building we had left at the beginning of the infection. We packed inside the elevator and everyone pressed the same button simultaneously — this time, there was one less finger. I remembered Oscar and pictured his zombie form standing in front of the elevator as the doors closed. I pulled away and gasped.

Only when I saw my reflection in the shiny metal door did I realize that I had an assault rifle strapped over my shoulder. I wasn't sure if it was the same one I had used to destroy Oscar and the zombie pilot — my memory felt hazy. The other weapons had to be in or around the helicopter, if they weren't completely destroyed in the explosion.

The elevator ride felt like déjà vu, only this time Oscar was missing. I disliked Oscar, but I didn't hate him enough to want him dead. I wanted to go to sleep and forget everything.

"Work sweet work," said Ash sarcastically as he took his usual seat at the corner table.

My body felt heavy, weak, tired. My mind was in a worse state. What kept me going? I dropped onto a chair.

"What if zombies got into the building when we weren't here?" asked Jill with a trembling voice.

It would have been disastrous if zombies did somehow manage to get all the way up here. But with an empty building, they wouldn't have the need.

"They wouldn't be able to make it through the security locks," I explained while flashing my keycard, "unless, of course, the zombies are intelligent."

"Smart zombies?" Jill shuddered.

"Smart zombies are just regular people," I replied.

Truthfully, I'm a smart zombie. Sometimes I feel like humans are the slaves of a hive mind — something that unifies and controls us. We're convinced that we need to work to get the things we need. Really, we're working for the good of the rich, while being fed just enough scraps to stay alive. It's sad that I have to go on like this until my body becomes too old to be useful.

"So, let me get this straight. All the walkie-talkies were destroyed in the helicopter, all the soldiers are dead, and we have one gun," said Pixonov, just when I was thinking about how quiet he had been all along.

After a brief pause, I responded, "Well, we have more walkie-talkies in the storeroom but no one to contact with them. Other than that, you pretty much summed it up."

"So, what do we do now?" asked Ash.

"I have a plan," I said. "Tomorrow we'll head out and try to recover any weapons that may have survived the crash. Then we'll try to get something to eat and attempt to contact the army again."

I hadn't eaten in so long, but I didn't really feel very hungry. But food was a top priority since we couldn't keep going for much longer like this. The problem was finding food suitable for consumption without becoming food ourselves.

Putting my mind at ease was far more difficult than ignoring my hunger. My hands shook and restlessness tormented me all night. I tried again to make calls using the phones but had no success.

Bingo's loss troubled me deeply. He had been with us all this time and now he was just gone. His company had comforted me more than any of the other survivors.

Though I only knew him for a short time, his absence made me feel incomplete.

***

I awoke as soon as the first rays of the morning sun penetrated the windowpanes. I couldn't recall when I had fallen asleep or for how long, but my mind and body appreciated the rest. I looked down on the city as it gradually grew brighter. It was empty and quiet — much different from the way we had left it on the day of the first encounter.

My stomach grumbled angrily, and I immediately remembered the plan for the day. I needed to get something to eat right away and the calmness of the early morning led me to believe that the zombies were all gone. It was as if the city had laid out a trap by giving me a false sense of security.

The others all awoke shortly after. I wondered if our reeking bodies could somehow trick zombies into thinking we were one of their own. Aside from a hearty breakfast, we all needed a bath.

"Plan?" Pixonov mustered one word.

"Eat," I gave a fair response.

I could tell they were all reluctant to leave the building, but we had no choice. I walked to the elevator and pressed the call button. I was the only one with a weapon, so they all stood close behind me.

"How about we wait here for a rescue?" suggested Jill, her finger on her pale lips.

"We already did that," I responded. "We can either die of starvation or from zombification."

"I think I would rather deal with the starvation," she said. "Becoming a zombie looks painful. I wonder if they can feel."

212

"The streets are clear so we should scout around anyway." I realized my previous statement involved a poor choice of words. "If you want, you can wait here until I get back."

The elevator doors opened, and I alone stepped inside. Ash held the door open just as it was about to close and entered as well.

"I'll stay with Jill," said Pixonov.

I didn't like the idea of splitting up, but I couldn't force Jill to go with me and face the potential horrors on the ground below.

The elevator descended and the doors slid open. The entire ground floor was empty, and the sunlight slowly filled up the space. Ash blew a sigh of relief as we headed out of the building. We approached the crashed helicopter.

"Do you think the zombies are mobbing right now?" asked Ash, noticing that everywhere seemed completely abandoned.

"The crash didn't attract any zombies last night, which probably means there are none around," I answered. "I hope."

We had seen this unsettling quiet before and, with good reason, I dreaded that a zombie horde would attack. Even a slow horde could be the end of us if we got trapped in a building without supplies.

The helicopter lay crumpled, blackened and broken upon the cracked asphalt. All of its contents, including the passengers, had either been burnt to an unrecognizable crisp or flung far away.

"I guess any guns in there were torched," I said, shifting my view away from the black ashes. "We should just get some food and head back. We may be able to get some canned stuff in the store across the road."

"What about the cruise ship?" asked Ash.

I remembered the ice cream and immediately craved its sweetness. It was so close now, and I was tempted to risk my life for it. In my head, it called my name, whispering things, promising eternal bliss.

"It's way too easy to get trapped on board if the zombies happen to be there." I had to resist the ice cream... for now.

"What if no one on board was infected? Entry to the ship is restricted, so it might be possible."

The cruise ship would have been a good place to hold out for a while, but going in there was risky, especially with only one weapon. But if we weren't rescued soon, we would have to take the risk anyway.

"Let's camp in the office for today and wait for a rescue. If it doesn't come, then we'll have to risk it," I said.

"Weapon over here!" Ash hurried to pick up a gun that lay in the middle of the empty road. "Nice."

Ash now had a battered shotgun, blackened and scratched all over, with a strap that had been severed and burnt.

A shotgun is certainly one of the best weapons for obliterating the entire head of a zombie with a single shot.

We crossed the road and entered the silent city. We were careful not to make any noise that could attract a horde of hungry zombies. They might have been hiding in the buildings that surrounded us, so every step deeper into the concrete jungle was one closer to an ambush.

The city had never been this dead since its inception.

The thousands of busy workers had vanished. Every vehicle was abandoned, and pollution had dropped to zero. There was no noise or fumes from horribly inefficient internal combustion engines. If left like this for a while longer, nature would surely reclaim what humanity had taken and attempt to heal what was destroyed. Was Zombosis nature's immune response to the human disease?

The working-class slaves, business owners and corporate elite were all equal now. They either hid together for survival or were zombie buddies.

Nothing in life brings people closer to each other than shared adversity.

I surveyed the dead city. The nearest supermarket was nine blocks away — too far. Instead, we entered a nearby pharmacy.

The door chimed as I pushed it open. The windows had been shattered and the store appeared partially looted.

"We can just grab some of these for now," I said, as I picked up the biscuits and snacks from the shelves and shoved them into a paper bag.

"Pills here!" shouted Ash delightfully. "Grabbin' some pills!"

Ash was rather happy to get a bottle of painkillers. He stuffed them into his bag, along with some bottled water, a manicure set, toothbrushes and toothpaste.

"Let's head back," I said, as soon as our bags were filled to capacity.

There was a noise by the exit — we were not alone. My heartrate spiked and I placed my trembling finger on the trigger. I turned around slowly and took aim with the gun, as did Ash.

Once again, there was a jolt to my heart, but it was not fear that I felt. Bingo had survived, and he ran in to greet us! He pounced on me and attempted to lick my face.

This is how the dead should return to life!

"I hate to break up your happy reunion, but I think we should leave before we get any more surprises," said Ash, already at the exit.

As quickly as we came in, we hurriedly left. Bingo trotted next to me, and my movement was closer to skipping than walking.

We knew Bingo wasn't infected because he showed no signs. *I* knew he wasn't infected because I just didn't want him to be.

"If Bingo survived, do you think the soldiers did, too?" asked Ash.

"I'm sure they would have come looking for us if they did."

"Maybe there are other survivors in these buildings," said Ash, looking at all the tall skyscrapers.

"I think whatever happened while we were away must have strangled all the life from the city."

We passed an empty, red streetcar, which was normally packed with more passengers than seats. Then we passed a subway station that led to the grimy underground transit tunnels, where the air was always stale and smelled like grease and metal.

We made it all the way back to our building without encountering a single zombie. Things seemed to be getting better and I thought that perhaps the zombie apocalypse had reached an abrupt end. Surely, Bingo's return was a good sign.

16

ZOMBIE ZEN

[Day 3]
~Consistent actions materialize dreams~

WARM SWEATY BODIES PRESSED against each other. Not even the cool air pumped into the club could dispel the heat generated by hundreds of patrons. The place was packed and cutting through the crowd was like swimming through a lake of viscous honey.

The darkness retreated and returned as the strobe lights flashed on the dance floor crowd. Everyone rocked to the trance-inducing tunes that surrounded them. I drifted through the shifting sea of bodies covered in a black robe, my face hidden by a hood.

Everyone was dressed in costume for the annual Halloween party. I moved between a group of French maids. There were so many of them, surely some must have been hired to clean up the club.

I passed a table upon which a schoolgirl, a witch and a she-devil were dancing, and couldn't help but ogle at them. That schoolgirl would have definitely been suspended for wearing a uniform that looked like it belonged on someone five years younger and considerably smaller. The witch was no different from the schoolgirl, except she went to a school of witchcraft; she would have surely been suspended just the same. I didn't pay much attention to the she-devil — the red tail was just a bit too disturbing.

Thirst came upon me, but the girls were using the bar counter as a dancefloor. If anything, the girls made me thirstier.

I headed for the stairs and squeezed my way up against vampires, maids and the occasional nurse. From the balcony, I could see the dance floor below, totally packed and squirming in time with the music.

On the stage, a group of people competed with dance for the most original costume. Needless to say, none of them were vampires or maids. An ear-piercing scream came from beside me as a maid girl cheered the contestants.

The first contestant dressed as a hooker with fishnet stockings. The second was a dominatrix clad in a tight leather corset, wielding a whip. Apparently, it was a contest for the most sexualized costume, rather than the most original. The third girl to go on stage was draped only with a towel. Unlike the other girls, who did their best to display their twerking abilities, towel girl just stood there, staring at the crowd.

The dominatrix, still keeping in character, approached towel girl, posed seductively, and ripped the towel off. Everyone gasped as the girl's bare breasts jiggled in sync with her exposed intestines! With the revelation that she was actually a zombie, the crowd burst into cheers and applause.

However, she was not merely dressed as a zombie to

win a contest. She pounced on the dominatrix and bit her on the neck. Blood spewed out as the victim was mauled. Red droplets rained down upon those on the dance floor below.

Still convinced that it was an act, the crowd cheered on the apparent performance. The other contestants ran off the stage and the zombie jumped on someone in the crowd. Only then did the panic truly begin. The cheers turned to screams and everyone in the overcrowded club tried to rush outside simultaneously.

It was a free-for-all scramble to the exit, excluding those who were too drunk to move anywhere on their own. Friends were forgotten in fear. Relationships ended faster than a blindside breakup.

The dominatrix had already turned into a zombie and was on the attack. The number of zombies in the room rose exponentially, as more people became infected.

I rushed to the rooftop, where the air was cool and the screams below were muffled. The sky glowed silvery blue with the light from the full moon. The city was bright but very still at this time of night.

Gurgling of blood, gnashing of teeth and wailing voices — the infection had spread to the roof without the need for a human carrier. Real blood splattered on the vampire costumes; real bones and flesh were exposed in those dressed as zombies. Sadly, the pseudo-nurses were not qualified to patch the wounds.

Even on the rooftop, the zombies outnumbered the living. I was forced all the way to the edge. I looked over the short wall behind me to see zombies spilling out into the street below — jumping was not an option.

The rooftop zombies marched toward me, but before the vicious undead could feast on my brains, my mind awakened. I immediately realized that this was merely a dream — a nightmare. None of this was real. This was a world where I was in full control. My only limits were my imagination and my suffocating subconscious.

Time froze as I engaged in mental combat with myself. Like a warrior stabbing the heart of a seasoned soldier twice his size and three times as skilful, I managed an unexpectedly quick victory.

I reshaped the dreamworld to insert a mounted minigun and used it to tear the zombies to shreds as they charged. The hooker, dominatrix and towel-zombie were disintegrated somewhere in the biomass.

The bullets cleaved through the horde as I rotated the cannon to spread the damage. Bones, muscles, fat and jewellery were ripped apart as easily as the skimpy dresses and lingerie worn as costumes.

And then, climbing from the side of the building came a giant beast — a monstrous infected man three times my size. His bulging muscles had torn off his shirt and his pale, dead skin looked as solid as concrete.

He charged toward me, the bullets from the minigun doing nothing to slow his approach. The regular zombies were tossed aside by the bounding behemoth. The hulking creature roared with a deep, echoing voice as he knocked the gun aside like a toy.

Another swing of the giant arm would have been all that was necessary to knock me down to my certain death. But just when the giant's hammer-like arm came crashing down, the world faded to blackness.

***

I woke from one nightmare into another. It took a moment for me to readjust to reality. The undead plague was most certainly real, but tank-like zombies were likely conjured by my subconscious.

Bingo sat by my side, looking at me with a tilted head and pointed ears. His saliva was on my cheek.

I sat up, patted Bingo on his head, and checked the time — it was already mid-afternoon. It would be dark again in a few hours.

Since our return to the city, we hadn't encountered any other person or zombie. Even the vultures from the not-too-distant festering landfill had disappeared. Nothing moved other than the fountains and holograms. There was just quiet and emptiness.

Loneliness pulsed through my core, corrupting my mind, weakening my body — an invisible affliction. I frowned. Bingo scratched my arm and pushed his head toward me. I stroked his fur. We both smiled.

At 5:00 pm that afternoon, we held a meeting to discuss a long-term survival plan. The sunlight was already beginning to fade when everyone sat around the table.

"Good evening, everyone," I opened the meeting.

Jill replied with a small smile and her own, "Good evening."

"Alrighty then, let's get straight to business. Since we haven't had any communication with any other survivors or military personnel, I think we need to find a place where we can hold out for as long as we need to. Somewhere that is safer and has some food."

As I said that, I remembered the mall where the other

survivors were supposed to be holding out. Maybe we should have remained there with them.

"Why can't we just stay here?" asked Jill.

"I really don't feel safe being trapped in this building," said Ash, arms folded as usual. "If the zombies somehow get up here, then we're dead."

"Exactly," I agreed.

"But we have guns," said Pixonov.

"Yeah, but there are more zombies than bullets," I said.

"Shall we go to the cruise ship now?" asked Ash.

"I checked the deck with the binoculars and didn't see any zombies there," I explained. "That could mean that the ship is empty, or they are all below deck. It's risky but I think the ocean is our safest bet."

"I think it might be safer for us to stay here," suggested Pixonov, still shirtless but, somehow, less imposing, as if some air had escaped his overinflated muscles.

"I agree. It's a huge risk to go to the ship," Jill supported Pixie.

"So, two of you want to stay here, and Ash and I want to go to the ship," I said.

I was sure Pixonov had no intention of ever going into the city to scavenge for food; his plan was to wait until rescued. The risks of resource hunting fell entirely on Ash and me. With the stores having been looted, supplies were surely low, making the task more difficult and dangerous.

"I guess we'll have to stay for now then, but if anyone else comes in and breaks our tie, then we will be going to the ship tomorrow morning," I said.

"Yeah, like someone is just going to walk up to the building tonight," laughed Pixonov.

The cruise ship plan was very risky, but I just had a feeling it would work out.

I could imagine sleeping with some peace of mind knowing that the ship was completely infection-free and beyond the reach of the zombies. Plus, I would be able to get some ice cream.

ACT 3
HOPE

Infernal Nightmare

Shape your own future
Walk your own path
Defeat your demons
Have no regrets

~Failure can be a tough shell to crack but success lies
beneath~

17

ESCAPE

[Day 3-4]

~Hate pushes you, love holds you~

ZACK UNCOILED FROM HIS comfortable position in the executive chair. To his right, sprawled like a brawny octopus, Pixonov snored and dribbled. To his left, Ash sat upright, arms folded. Jill stood by the window, staring at the city's lights from the twelfth floor of the waterfront tower.

"With our stories combined, we'd make an interesting adventure," said Dan to Zack, "but the ending hasn't been written yet."

"None of it has been written yet, but I'll be sure to mention you in my future bestselling book," retorted Zack.

Augie, who was seated to Dan's right, clapped both palms on his round cheeks, squashing his smile. Pixonov snorted like a great, thick pig, jumped in his seat, and pretended he had been awake all along.

"I really hope I live to read it," said Augie, anticipating a new addition to his vast collection of everything zombie.

"You fight zombies with a cricket bat?" asked Pixonov

with a chuckle, cradling the shotgun in his arms.

"Guns are scarce. At least I never run out of ammo."

Pixonov had obviously lifted the firearm from Ash's possession and was pretending to be a brave hero. He didn't know the first thing about gunfighting. It was extremely rare for citizens on the island to possess guns. Most people never handled such high-powered weapons; some never even saw a real gun.

"I think you made the right decision coming here since Stone is no longer among the living. You would have been waiting, even now, for your rescue," said Zack, bringing the fingertips of both hands together.

Dan was a bit unnerved when he learned of the death of a soldier who was so well-armed and seemed so competent. He pushed his glasses up the bridge of his nose with a single finger.

"How long will it be 'til the army returns here?" asked Kelly, seated to Dan's left with her legs crossed at the knees.

"I don't think they'll be back soon enough," said Zack. "We can't wait for them here anyway."

"I'm sure I can come up with another plan of escape," said Augie proudly, feeling important.

"I already have a plan," said Zack, "but it's admittedly tricky and fraught with danger."

"As long as you don't ask us to hunt down every last zombie on the island, then we're listening," said Zoe, standing behind Dan's chair and leaning over the top.

"That's Plan B."

"Well, let's hear Plan A then," said Augie, resting his elbows on the table and listening intently, head still held in his hands.

"It's simple, really. We head to the cruise ship."

There was a moment of silence, as everyone expected to hear the rest of Zack's plan.

"That's it?" Augie sneered at the lack of details and planning. "I get the feeling you didn't think this through."

"I hope your nefarious ice cream is not leading us to our deaths," said Kelly.

"A cruise ship can work as long as there are no zombies aboard," said Augie, who had already started computing the logistics of the plan in his head.

"We don't have much choice anyway," Ash added, adjusting his tie. "We just don't have the supplies to support everyone here."

"And what if there are zombies on board?" asked Dan.

"We send them to hell!" said Pixonov in a thunderous tone.

Zack raised an eyebrow at Pixonov's display of faux bravery. Pixonov flexed his muscles and pouted his lips in the direction of Zoe, who rolled her eyes and clung to Dan.

"With what fockin' army? There are more zombies out there than fockin' bullets!" screamed Rock, with his voice raised to a pitch that Pixonov's vocal cords could never match.

Rock had been practicing his martial arts while everyone was seated. His body was at its physical peak and he could snap bones with ease. But Rock was only willing to fight air, not zombies.

"Listen, just give it some thought and get back to me in an hour. Whether you help me or not, I'm going on that ship in the morning." Zack stepped away from the table, leaving everyone with a lot to think about.

Bingo the dog, who had been hiding under the table, trotted by Zack's side, wagging his tail. The lean mutt was barely taller than Zack's knees and didn't appear to be a match for anything larger than a child-sized zombie.

The groups scattered and did as Zack had suggested. Deciding whether to stay or risk the trip to the ship was a simple binary decision complicated by undetermined hazards and probabilities.

Kelly, Rock, Omar, and Zoe all had their eyes fixed on Dan, waiting on his opinion. When he saw this, he shifted his own view to Augie, whom he was sure had already calculated the likelihood of success.

"A cruise ship has food, water, power and is a means of escaping the infection and getting help," Augie spoke his thoughts aloud.

"Don't you normally stay put and await rescue in times like these?" said Kelly.

"Yeah, if your plane crashed and you aren't surrounded by flesh-eating zombies, bitch!" exclaimed Rock.

Dan shot Rock a menacing look but didn't have to jump to Kelly's defence.

"You're the bitch, you big-eyed bobolee!" She put her fist near Rock's chin and squared up with him as if posing for a pre-fight poster.

Through the window behind the two fighters, the city and mountains were visible. The lights were still on, but nothing stirred in the town.

"What if we lose power here too?" asked Kelly, unclenching her fists.

"The ship should still have power, as long as it doesn't malfunction," guessed Dan.

"Score one for the oceanic cruise!" squealed Zoe excitedly, grabbing onto Dan's arm.

"The only problem is that there may be a horde of zombies waiting for our brains as soon as we enter that ship." Augie clutched his head with both hands dramatically.

"But if not, then we're protected from the infected, have enough supplies for a long time and there must be a radio or something we can use to send out an SOS," chimed in Omar.

"We're going on a cruise, bitches!" said Rock so loudly that Zack and his group heard.

They had settled on the plan but the thought that they'd be mobilizing at dawn made everyone nervous. And although Dan never liked leaving things to chance, he had to trust that Zack knew what he was doing. Dan knew very little about the ship, the dock and the other survivors, and that made it difficult to predict the plan's viability.

"Omar and I have already broken the rule that the fattest guys die first," Augie spoke to Dan as the short meeting ended. "We also have the distinct strategic advantage of being able to survive the longest without food. I'm really afraid that the next one to get dead would either be the nerd or the guy with the fewest lines."

They glanced across at Omar, who was twiddling his fingers and staring blankly into the space before him as if daydreaming about playing a video game.

"You're also a silent nerd, Dan. It's gonna be you or Omar next! You need to talk more," said Augie with a smug look.

Augie was certainly the nerdiest nerd in all the land —

the self-proclaimed Nerd King. However awkward and inept he was, he was still a king, and an incredibly arrogant one at that. He routinely bragged about his collections and insulted other nerds so that he could retain his throne. However, a more accurate title for him would have been the Nerd Jester.

Augie had everything a nerd could possibly want: a custom-built gaming computer, a TV the size of a cinema screen, a zombie apocalypse survival story, and even a girlfriend, who was, oddly enough, not nerdy at all. He had to live so that his stuffed dolly collection could grow.

"If we do this, we'll be going all in," said Dan. "We probably won't have any chance of turning back."

"I think a cruise is a fantastic idea," said Augie. "Maybe next time we can find a place on a nice beach."

"If the ship leaves the dock, there'll be no guarantee of a return to land anytime soon. That means leaving everything and everyone behind," Dan lectured his group.

Everyone remained quiet and sombre. After running from death for days, they had either acknowledged the possibility that everyone they knew was dead or ignored the subject altogether.

Tears trickled down Kelly's cheek, but she didn't utter a sound. She smiled and grabbed onto Dan, wiping her tears on his shirt.

Zoe puffed up her cheeks and her chest. She tried to cry as well, but couldn't; instead, her entire head turned red. She whistled and awkwardly walked away when Dan's eyes caught her antics.

Omar tried to wirelessly connect his mind into his video game world, where the great dragon, Vakashtas, had returned and was ravaging the land with his fire breath. Omar's online guild desperately needed his leadership to once again vanquish the evil monster. Truthfully, they hoped to obtain the rare tooth fragment, craft the legendary Staff of Vakashtas, wielded only by Omar, and defeat him in battle.

Augie sat on a toilet, back hunched and knees to his chin, fantasizing about being reunited with Cacti and the rest of the stuffed animal kingdom. Just like he thought of himself as the leader among his friends and king of all nerds, he had autocratically appointed Cacti as the Cactus King, ruler of his stuffed toy collection. His greatest worry was having his plushies shredded by zombies. Aside from his collection hobby, Augie enjoyed pooping as much as he could, and he left this particular toilet clogged to the brim with poop.

Rock kept himself busy by practicing lightning-fast kicks and powerful punches. He made high-pitched shrieks with each strike and while he hit with enough force to break a hole in a concrete wall, he never broke a sweat. His physical form was practically invincible, but his mind was made of glass, already cracked from the pressure. He listened to some classical music to ease the stress away.

A fantasy played through Dan's head about having a happy ending with Kelly. It clouded his mind about the possibility of other things. He did take some notice of Zoe's odd behaviour but didn't give it much thought. In his mind, he was living a romantic zombie comedy and Kelly was his co-star and love interest. He knew his time was running out if he wanted to win her over, but the bridesmaid debacle still made his head spin.

The survivors talked, brooded, exercised, and milled around until settling down for a few hours of sleep before departure time. The floor fell silent after Augie spent two hours creating a smelly gas bomb in the toilet.

***

The midnight hour passed, and Dan lay on the floor near his friends. He thought about everything that had happened over the days since the infection spread. No longer did it feel surreal. He accepted the changed world he was in. Nothing would be the same as before.

Everyone who had survived not only managed to avoid being infected but also successfully defeated the mental fatigue that could have caused madness. They had proved that they deserved to live. Natural selection, long nullified by science and medicine, had once again filtered out the least resilient Homo sapiens.

Zack stood near the window, staring down at the haunting ship. It was merely a black silhouette with white light leaking out the portholes. Atop the mainmast, flapping in the wind, was a black flag with a glowing white skull and crossbones.

"Do you expect this plan to work?" asked Dan, as he stood beside Zack.

"It has to," Zack replied. "We have no other choice now."

"There's always another choice."

"We can jump into the ocean if things go bad."

"I'll take my chances on the ship." Dan shuddered at the thought of sinking in the deep waters of the port, with the undead above and the muddy earth below.

They remained quiet for a while, staring at the ship,

the city and the mountains. Bingo, who always kept within range of Zack, had a single ear raised and pointed in their direction.

"Did you really kill zombies with that gun?" Dan asked, pointing at the assault rifle with the tip of his cricket bat.

Images of Oscar and the zombie soldier flashed in Zack's mind. "Yes. Did you really kill zombies with a cricket bat?"

"This isn't just a cricket bat anymore. I call her Zasha, the zombie masher." Dan brandished the bat like a sword.

Zack looked at Zasha and doubted her zombie-mashing achievements and abilities.

"So, what exactly do you plan to do once we get on the ship?" asked Dan, returning Zasha to her scabbard.

"As long as it's empty, we can stay on board for a while. There's a lot of food stocked there for thousands of passengers and we can set course for another island or the mainland if necessary."

"I take it that you know how to operate a cruise ship."

"We wouldn't need to. Once we get inside, it'll be like a fortress." Zack didn't want to admit that he knew nothing about ships.

"I hope you're not leading us on a suicide mission," said Dan as he returned to the others.

Everyone was quiet and still, except Augie who was snoring loudly and cactus walking. Dan laid down next to them and tried to force himself to sleep, despite feeling restless and a little bit worried about the morning.

***

Dan's eyes opened at daybreak, precisely when the first

segment of the sun peeked over the horizon. His body awakened as the sun fully emerged for its daily duties. However, the darkness stayed as if it were still night-time.

Zack was talking to his group just distantly enough that he couldn't be heard clearly. Everyone from Dan's group was already awake and doing the same.

"I hope you had a good rest, Dan," said Zoe as Dan joined the group.

"Good enough."

He felt a bit disoriented, having entered in the middle of all the planning. This morning reminded Dan of the days of school field trips — the anticipation of the unknown. There was an air of excitement, rather than apprehension.

He looked over at Kelly, who stood opposite him. As usual, he overlooked her flaws and was foolishly enthralled by what he thought was perfection. He convinced himself to make a move today.

"We have a little less daylight than expected but it shouldn't be much of a problem," said Augie, who had been boring everyone with his zombie predictions and assumptions before Dan joined them.

Through the office window behind Zack and his team, the overcast sky was as obvious as a flying whale. Heavy cloud cover had rolled in overnight and the sky was black and the ocean choppy. It looked like a hurricane was about to strike within the hour.

Rain had not yet begun to fall but the first burst of crackling thunder shook them. The tumultuous sound was like the starter's pistol in a race, as everyone began mobilizing for departure.

"Okay, we need to head out right now before we get

caught in a storm," said Zack, with a note of urgency in his voice. "Just follow my lead to the ship."

By the time they made it down to the front of the building, rain had begun to drizzle. Zack led the way with a brisk jog, using his hand to shield his eyes from the splatter of raindrops.

18

BLOOD STORM

[Day 4]
~Love can make you as stupid as a zombie~

NO ONE HAD EXPECTED the weather to change so suddenly. Dan may have liked dark, rainy weather, but only when he could keep himself dry. He never packed an umbrella, even in the rainy season, and preferred to watch the rain fall than get caught in it. He definitely did not want to get wet and fall ill now.

The unified group of ten marched on undaunted, the rain soaking their clothes and flattening their hair. The buildings partially sheltered them from the developing icy winds that pelted water droplets all over.

The droplets steadily grew larger and heavier and everyone had gotten soaked despite not travelling very far. They took temporary shelter under the eaves of a boxy brick building on the port. Bingo took the opportunity to shake some water off his fur. The roaring downpour and distant rolling thunder were enough to mask the noise from an impending attack. They kept their eyes on the misty rain and anywhere else a sneak attack could possibly originate from.

Visibility through the veil of rain was low as the shower peaked in intensity. The wind picked up, causing the water droplets to dance about before stinging faces and kissing the earth.

Dan's glasses offered his eyes no protection from the wild, biting raindrops. He disliked getting his lenses wet in the rain, but this time it was unavoidable. He glanced over the rims whenever he felt like the visibility through the foggy plastic was too low.

The shower rapidly intensified into a hurricane-like storm, with flashes of lightning and the cracking of thunder happening more frequently as they waited. As far as they could see, clouds blanketed the island and far off into the ocean as well. There was not a sliver of light in the sky except for when it was rent by the strike of a lightning bolt.

"This weather is getting worse by the second," said Zack. "We should just press on to the ship."

There was no opposition. They marched back into the icy rain. Re-entering the stinging bombardment of falling water felt even worse than before. Dan somehow felt colder and shivered as the fierce rain splattered upon his skin and stole his body's warmth.

"The ship is just through this building!" Zack shouted over the tempest.

They entered a short building that separated the inland area from the sea and docked ships. The carpeted floor became drenched as the water rolled off their bodies. A slippery tiled floor would have certainly been worse. A broken limb during the zombie apocalypse was guaranteed sustained torture and, most likely, a grisly death.

No time was wasted in catching breath or getting dry.

They just hurried through the building, making sure to avoid the metal detectors, which were still on and very much functional.

"Don't get too close to the metal scan-AHHHH!" Augie made an about-turn and bolted.

Zombies attacked and the group scattered. Fortunately, there were only four, but even though they were slow, the room was small enough for them to be a significant threat.

"Don't shoot them!" Dan shouted at Pixonov, who was taking aim.

Zack was the only other survivor who had a gun. He held his weapon at the ready, aiming down the sights at the zombies in front of him — three were dressed in baggy coveralls, each tight at the waist, and one wore denim overalls with a straw hat.

Dan and Augie bludgeoned the one nearest to them until it collapsed with a fractured skull and a pulverized brain. Jill cried out at the brutal sight and ran behind everyone else. She pressed her back against the wall and covered her teary eyes.

The Infernal group didn't go anywhere near the melee range of the infected. The Nightmare group, on the other hand, proved themselves as being very capable of vanquishing the undead with close-quarters combat. They pummelled yet another one as it lurched forward. The slow, clumsy zombies seemed to have no chance of even touching a single survivor.

It certainly seemed that way until the window behind them shattered and a pair of nasty, gnarled arms poked through. Jill's bloodcurdling scream was cut short as a zombie tightened its hands around her pale, narrow neck. Her voice was completely silenced as she gargled her own blood.

"Shit! They're trying to turn her into a fockin' Jill sandwich!" shouted Rock as he prepared to run in the opposite direction.

The zombie bit down and ripped out the flesh from Jill's neck, spreading the infection to yet another host. It continued to chew on her face and no amount of struggling helped her break free.

"JILL! NOOOOO!" cried Pixonov, running to assist while pulling the trigger of his shotgun.

The slugs caught the zombie in the arms and head, forcing it to loosen its grip. It fell over the window and its body hung halfway into the room. Broken glass cut through its dead flesh and impaled it in place.

But with Pixonov's wild dash and assault, Jill had also been hit by several slugs. Her body slumped to the floor like an unstrung marionette, bleeding from her neck and the punctures in her torso.

The amateur gunman dropped his weapon and fell to his knees in tears when he realized what he had done. His crying added to the sound of the security alarm, which he had triggered.

The Nightmare group, preoccupied with the stiff walking corpses, didn't see exactly what had happened. But Zack, Ash and Bingo stood transfixed by Jill's bloodied body, which lay face-first on the floor.

Pixonov wept as he crawled over to his lifeless friend. He swallowed all the words of regret which he mumbled incoherently.

"Get up, Pixie! We need to go right now!" commanded Ash.

But Pixonov didn't move. He held Jill's limp body up against his — tears mixed with blood. Zack picked up the weapon that Pixonov had dropped and handed it to an overenthusiastic Augie.

Augie's eyes shimmered when he accepted the weapon as if it were an ancient holy relic. To him, the gun glowed with a divine brightness and a chorus of angels sang in celebration. His attack damage increased tenfold; the threat of collateral damage increased just as much since Augie consistently fought with his eyes closed.

"I think you should tell your friend to let—" Augie wasn't able to finish his sentence in time.

Jill had already risen as a zombie and Pixonov's head was bleeding all over. His cries of sorrow had changed into howls of anguish. Though he was a muscular man, Pixonov's muscles were like fluffy clouds. He put up no resistance against his attacker.

Jill threw Pixonov to the side like a contorted puppet and lunged at Zack. Her trajectory changed mid-air as she was blasted away by high-powered gunfire — a lucky shot by a closed-eyed Augie. Jill's head exploded like a watermelon in the mouth of a hungry alligator, and her red body stuck to the wall like a flattened mosquito. The sight was truly sickening.

"Oh shit! Oh shit!" Zack dropped to his knees, with wide-open eyes.

Zack would have sacrificed himself to save her if he could. To him, it wasn't fair that such a young, beautiful girl with great potential died a horrible death, while he was allowed to live.

"He's going to turn too..." said Dan, pointing at the wounded Pixonov with Zasha. "I don't believe in killing anyone before they zombify, so we can either wait for him to turn and then kill him or just go now and leave him behind."

"Let's go." Zack hopped to his feet and ran back out into the rain.

They left the bloodied Pixonov behind in the building. He hadn't spoken a single audible word since causing Jill's death. The HNP had entered his body through the bites on his head. There was no way for him to resist the infection.

The survivors, eight of them now, were all back in the rain, but its intensity had lessened. The visibility was better, and the roar of the rain had subsided. They could see the cruise ship docked like a huge hotel in the sea to their left.

They were very wary that all the noise and commotion would have alerted more infected, so there was no dawdling. The rain quickly washed away the trail of blood they had left behind when rushing to the ship.

"Shit!" Zack yelled, stopping suddenly. "This is the entrance, but the bridge isn't here!"

Regret welled up in Dan. Another risk, another failure. He sulked over trusting Zack.

"We're dead," said Omar lazily, with his eyes droopy.

"No, this is a good thing," Zack remained positive. "It means that no zombies got on board. We just need to find a way in."

"How do you sneak onto a cruise ship?" asked Zoe.

"Rope, hook and some sexy muscular physique, bitch!" said Rock, flexing his muscles.

"I don't suppose you have any of those in your

backpack, Augie?" said Dan.

"Everything except the last one," Augie replied with a frown.

If Dan hadn't seen him pull a bolt cutter from that backpack before, he might have been surprised. Augie pulled out a neatly tied grappling hook from his zombie apocalypse survival kit.

"Hand it over to the expert!" Rock took the rope. "Observe, nerds!"

With a single toss, Rock managed to secure the hook somewhere on the deck. All eyebrows raised — everyone was immensely impressed.

"Just a little something I learned while training in ninjutsu," he said.

"I was hoping we wouldn't need to use that rope at all," said Augie, pulling his head back so his chin doubled and flitting his eyes around, looking to see who else was worried. "Did I mention that the nerds always die?"

"So you never climbed anything as a kid, you fat sissy bitch?"

Rock may have mastered three forms of martial arts, but he had learned no discipline or respect. Rock, the Rude Ninja, assassinated the Nerd King's ego.

"I'ma go first, bitches!" Rock climbed up the rope with ease. "Kill the fat ones first!"

Everyone looked toward the direction in which Rock had prattled his insults. Zombie Pixonov was charging at them at full speed. Zack fired at the zombie, surprised by the rapidly approaching threat, but a pierced torso did nothing to slow Pixonov.

Augie stepped in front of Dan's raised cricket bat.

With a loud bang, Pixonov's head vaporized before Augie's smoking gun barrel.

"Headshot!" shouted Augie, punching the air in triumphant celebration.

"Zoe, you're next," said Dan.

Every part of Zoe's body blushed. She was transported into a daydream with Dan. They were in a field of white lilies atop a lush, green mountain. Zoe was draped in a white wedding dress, while Dan wore a handsome black suit. They ran toward each other with open arms, and when they met, Dan lifted her up by the waist and spun her around. After one full rotation, Dan rested her upon the lilies and put the weight of his body upon her. He leaned in closer, his sweet lips approaching Zoe's parched, dry ones. "Yes, kiss me!" was her last thought before the fleeting creation of her mind dissolved.

"Zoe, you're next to climb the rope!" said Dan.

"Good thing I'm not wearing a skirt," Zoe blushed again before grabbing onto the rope and climbing, "or a wedding dress..."

Despite not being a professional athlete, Zoe was ridiculously fit. She made the rope climb look easy.

The climb was manageable but precarious. There was no safety harness and no one to catch anyone should they fall. This task was not as easy as Rock made it seem.

"Can you imagine how much worse things could have been if we were sick or something?" asked Dan, worrying about catching cold from the now drizzling rain.

"I feel like I have diarrhoea," said Augie, his knees buckling. "I could poop my pantaloons any moment now."

"Hey listen, bitches!" Rock shouted from the ship.

"We'll open the door from the inside so that the fat asses can get on board too!"

"It'll only take a minute, guys," said Zoe, before following Rock and disappearing from the sight of those below.

"They don't even know the layout of the ship. It'll take more than a minute," said Zack.

Augie and Omar, who were very unlikely to have successfully climbed the rope, were particularly relieved. All they had to do was wait for the door by which they stood to open, and they would be home free.

"How are you gentlemen?" a familiar voice called to them. "That ship belongs to us now!"

From the building through which they had just passed, emerged a man. The beads of precipitation hid him in a haze, but when he stepped under the bright lights of the port, his identity was clear.

"Captain Stone?!" said Zack, eyes wide in shock. "You were most certainly dead!"

Bingo growled and barked with absolute ferocity.

"You are on your way to destruction!" The captain's voice boomed in stark contrast to his usual cool demeanour.

"Say what?" asked Zack.

"You have no chance to survive. Don't waste your time!" Captain Stone grinned.

"Surviving the helicopter crash. Speaking strangely. Bloody evil smile. The dog doesn't trust him. He has to be infected, but how is he able to speak?" Dan's mumbling went unheard under the downpour.

Captain Stone was still dressed in his army uniform, just as he was when the helicopter had crashed. Though he was unarmed as he slowly approached the survivors, he exuded a threatening aura, and his grin was blood red.

"Can you get us to a safe house?" asked Ash, his voice cracking.

"I have an army with me, and you can join us if you like. In fact, I insist."

"Where's our transport, Stone?" Dan shouted over the spattering raindrops.

"Well it's about damn time that the army came to the rescue!" said Omar, gleefully skipping over to the soldier.

"Omar, wait!" Dan tried to warn his friend.

Alas, his words were too late. Stone had already sunk his teeth into Omar's head and tossed him aside. His speed was incredible and his strength, unnatural. He acted like an infected but with his intelligence retained.

Zack and Augie opened fire on Stone, but his agility was so high that he evaded every shot.

"Are you telling me that he can dodge bullets?!" exclaimed Augie while squeezing his trigger.

While alive, Captain Stone was a formidable soldier; when enhanced by the neural parasite, he was much more — he was a super soldier. But his mind had given in to the insatiable desire to spread the infection.

He dashed around and dodged every shot as he got closer to his prey. He was just within reach of Augie when a slug from the shotgun's spray pierced his leg. He stopped moving, not because of the wound that had been inflicted on him, but by his own volition. He grabbed onto the shotgun and twisted his undead lips into a bloody, sinister smile.

"Dodge this!" declared Zack.

In the time Captain Stone took to target Augie, Zack had gotten him in his sights. The zombie fell onto the wet ground with a thud as Zack opened fire.

A door on the ship flew open, but it wasn't the one by which they had been waiting; this one was further away.

"Over here!" shouted Zoe, peering out of the open door. "I suggest that you hurry!"

Omar's zombified body began twitching as it struggled to stand. The survivors ran to the open door as if it were the end of this nightmare. But Omar was only the beginning of their problems — the horde had finally responded to all the noise.

Zombies closed in from behind Stone and Omar. At the very back of the sea of the dead were the slow walkers, while the front waves were comprised of the extremely quick runners. The terrifying cries and moans from the undead army infused the survivors with fear.

So this was the army Stone had just mentioned.

Many of the approaching infected fell on the damp port and were trampled; however, this did nothing to significantly affect their numbers.

The survivors had almost reached the door and Augie was the furthest behind. He most likely would have been second to last if Omar were still with them. The zombie Omar was much faster than the living one though, and he was catching up.

"This is normally... the part... when... someone—" Augie was short of breath as he ran faster than he had ever done in his life. Then he completed his sentence with actions instead of words, falling and rolling like a barrel.

By the time Dan realized that Augie had tripped, he

was already at the door. He was about to run to his friend's aid but Augie somehow managed to preserve his momentum while tumbling and rolling and had gotten back to his feet. It was funny, really, but the approaching zombie horde completely neutralized any comedic effect.

Augie fired his weapon blindly behind him, just missing Omar, who had gotten very close, but hitting the horde, which wasn't too far off either. The last shot caught Omar in the leg and dropped him.

Everyone was already inside the ship and cleared the entrance for Augie. He charged in like a freight train (the horn was practically audible) and crashed into the wall at the far side of the room. The door was sealed immediately.

"YATAAA!" Augie celebrated his successful escape with two fists raised in the air.

Augie then fell onto his back like a stiff tree that had just been cut down. He breathed heavily, desperately trying to absorb all the oxygen in the room.

There was pounding on the door as the infected attempted to get in. But the lock was secure, and they were safe.

Augie stood up, clutched his side and hunched over in pain. "That's enough exercise... for the rest... of my life..."

"I can't believe the plan actually worked," said Dan, delightfully surprised.

"Well, yes and no," said Zoe gloomily. "The zombies outside can't get in, but there are already zombies on board."

Bingo tilted his head and raised his ears.

19

NIGHTMARE PRINCESS

[Day 4]

~Do not attempt to reason with fools and the brain-dead~

DAN THOUGHT ABOUT HOW things could have been had they not left the building; he probably would have been sitting idly, burdened by boredom and anxiety. Instead, he was soaking wet in a ship full of zombies, but the benefit was momentary distraction from his usual exhausting amorous musings.

"At least they're the slow kind," said Zoe with a shrug.

"How many do you think there are?" asked Dan.

"From what we saw, it isn't packed, but they are scattered all over."

"Then we'll have to check the entire ship," said Augie.

"And dump the corpses somewhere distant so that the crawlers don't pose a problem," added Dan.

Slow zombies were definitely easier to deal with than the runners, but eradicating hundreds was a monumental task. Dan also knew very well that the infection could be spread even without noticing it, via the crawlers. If the infectious bugs were already scuttling about the ship, then the survivors had just walked themselves into a trap.

"The sooner we can do this, the better," said Rock. "I would like to actually sleep tonight without worrying about waking up with a bloody bald spot! Nam sayin'?"

Another survivor, Omar, had been lost to the plague. Only seven survivors remained, and the resilient dog, Bingo.

No time was taken to grieve the dead. They focused on their next mission — get all the zombies off the ship. Zack saw it as a prerequisite for completing his true quest — get all the ice cream on the ship.

"We'll be lucky to clear the ship by nightfall," said Dan.

"Don't be so negative," said Kelly. "Now that we know there are zombies on board, let's clean out the lowest levels first and work our way up to the deck."

"How 'bout we clear the deck first, so that way we can always run up if we have an emergency and get in a lifeboat or something," said Augie.

"Shall we vote on it?" proposed Zack. "I am with the deck crew."

"Fat bitch or skinny bitch? I can't believe I'm saying this, but I'm with the nerd," said Rock.

"I'm with Kelly," Dan's answer prioritized love over logic.

Dan wholly supported Augie's idea and thought everyone else did as well. He'd backed Kelly just to strengthen their bond, while fully expecting to lose the vote.

"I'm with Dan," said Zoe, immediately after Dan had voted.

Dan's muscles tensed and his jaws tightened.

"Deck," voted Ash.

Kelly sighed in defeat but gave Dan a small smile as thanks for his support.

Dan returned a fake smile, lips together and chest puffed as if holding his breath. His rigid, upright frame relaxed when Kelly turned away.

"Let's get to it!" said Zoe, grabbing Dan and pulling him to the stairway.

On the deck, the sharp wind whistled, and the rain felt like tiny bullets on their skin. The black clouds still completely blanketed the sky. The storm was sure to get worse throughout the day. In the distance, lightning flickered, and thunder rolled loudly.

They walked cautiously on the wet deck. The raindrops pricked the surface of the pools and turned the hot tub into a cold tub. Over the edge of the ship's starboard side, the sea churned, angry and rough, though not nearly enough to cause such a large ship to sink; on the port side shambled a horde of zombies so numerous that everyone chose to avert their eyes.

The infected were the most wretched form of human existence possible. The more time that passed during the infection, the more they degraded into something demonic. The acrid stench alone was enough to give away the presence of the rotting, walker zombies.

The survivors approached some of the foul-smelling demons on the far side of the deck. The zombies shuffled angrily but slowly toward the healthy humans. Their bodies were covered in boils and sores. The pulsating skin swellings looked like they were about to burst, sending neon-yellow pus all over.

One zombie in particular had skin that was deeply cracked all around its mouth. Its face looked like an arid landscape where the sun had dried up all the moisture and parched the soil. The platforms and pits on its face glistened with the moisture of its own secretions; not even the rain could wash off the disgusting, filthy oils. A large chunk was missing from its torso, exposing the ribcage, lungs, spine and the zombies that stood behind.

The sight was nauseating but transfixing. Dan couldn't look away or ignore the horrendous sight. The distance wasn't enough to disperse the repugnant scent. Dan involuntarily imagined that the zombie would taste like rotting, maggot-filled meat mixed with spoilt eggs, if his tongue ever pressed against the cold, dead skin.

He wanted to knock the zombie off the ship, never to be seen again, but at the same time, he didn't want his bat coated with pus. Everyone stayed a step back, allowing Dan to have the first hit on the infected. As the zombie got into range, Dan sliced through the air with his weapon and hit the zombie directly on its temple, sending it flying off the ship.

Every boil exploded with a POP, ejecting the warm phosphorescent pus mixed with septic blood. The stiff corpse crashed into the sea of undead on the port below. Fortunately, the blood and pus rained on the zombies below and not on the survivors.

The other survivors went to work immediately, following Dan's lead by knocking the zombies clear off the ship. These infected were dispatched fairly easily, most likely because they were just waiting to be tipped over the edge. There was no gunfire; their shots were being saved for whenever the need arose. There was no extra ammunition on the ship and melee weapons were only effective against small groups of walkers.

Bingo served as the scout, sniffing out the undead. He pointed and growled at the zombies, but never got into range.

The survivors passed the largest pool on the ship. The once clear water had been fouled by blood.

"I checked the ship's deck just before we departed and saw not a single zombie," said Zack, feeling excessively guilty about his floundering plan.

"They must have emerged when we came aboard, somewhat noisily," suggested Dan.

"I just hope none are hiding in here," said Augie.

They passed through a door that led to a narrow hallway. Crimson wallpaper covered the walls, but the bloodstains were still visible. It looked like a twisted work of art by an angry painter.

From here, the cheap cabins stretched to the end of the ship. Straight down the hall on both sides, all the doors appeared to be open.

While the outside of the vessel was made to look like an old pirate ship, the inside was shiny and new. Metallic surfaces were made of either gold or silver and were polished to perfection. Orbs of light hovered in the air, casting away all shadows while making the metal sparkle.

Bingo shook the water off his body, splashing the already soaking wet survivors. Their footsteps echoed in the empty hallway, and the pearl-white tiled floor ingeniously absorbed the rainwater that drained off their bodies.

"The doors are normally all locked," said Zack, barely louder than a whisper. "Just be careful in the bathrooms, they can hide in there."

"Speaking of toilets, I need to drop a ten-ton turd in one," said Augie.

Every time they entered one of the small rooms, their hearts raced faster. Only one person was able to enter at a time and the confined space made it difficult to move around or swing a weapon.

Most of the rooms they had entered on this floor were empty. But one room was particularly interesting, especially to Augie, who was very much excited, rather than scared.

"OBLIGATORY NAKED ZOMBIES!" squealed Augie with a wide grin. "GHE-HEHEHE!"

Two completely naked female zombies stood in the cramped cabin. Their pale bodies showed the effects of zombification, although it was not difficult to mistake them for mildly malnourished living women. The blonde was presumably in her twenties, with a petite body and perky, small breasts. The brunette was probably in her thirties, with breasts so large that they caused her to misbalance.

"GHE-HEHEHE!"

Augie took a bit too much pleasure in killing these zombies. He smiled and giggled the entire time as he beat them mercilessly with random objects. The nude zombies were, in fact, more dangerous than the average walker, because their innocent appearance and uncommon beauty among the undead elicited feelings of sympathy from the other survivors. Augie had immunity to the zombies' manipulating halos.

At the end of the hall was another zombie. This one was fully clothed in a maid's uniform. One lone zombie stood no chance.

"Alright, this card should open all the doors," stated Zack as he took a small rectangular object from the maid's battered corpse.

"Is that a master key?" asked Augie, trying to calm himself down from the hyperactive mood he was in.

"The ship has a similar access card system to ours," said tech master Ash, looking down at the maid. "She likely needed access to all rooms, so this should be her master keycard."

"All of the doors are open anyway, bitches!" said Rock.

"I'm pretty sure there's at least one door that is locked, Rock," said Zoe. "And it'll probably be the best suite."

"Who wants to hold on to this?" asked Zack, holding out the master keycard between his fingers.

Augie and Kelly stared at each other for a moment, like gunslingers preparing for a shootout. Augie's eye twitched, and Kelly took a deep breath. Their arms shot forward like speeding bullets, both aimed at the same target. Kelly managed to just barely swipe the card first, leaving Augie spinning round like a tornado.

"Look at me!" commanded Kelly, pointing at her eyes while staring into Augie's dizzy eyes. "I'm the Master of Unlocking now!"

Kelly did indeed open every locked door on the ship while Augie sulked.

The next location on their list was the night club, which was at the back end of the ship. It may not have been night-time but that didn't stop the zombies from wining to the music.

There was no natural lighting and the floating orbs were replaced by a single large orb in the centre of the room. The centre orb projected strobe lights of various colours and holograms of beautiful women scantily clad in colourful costumes. The computer-generated ghosts danced provocatively, gyrating their hips, twerking their perfectly round behinds and bouncing their bewitching boobies, which appeared to be on the verge of bursting out of their minuscule brassieres.

There were nine zombies in here, but the room was large enough for the survivors to dance around the slow-moving targets. The one in the red jacket was the most difficult to take down – his movements were jerky and unpredictable.

By separating the infected, they were able to take their time in dispatching the undead threat. It was almost too easy.

The survivors were becoming overconfident. The red jacket zombie had gotten extremely close to biting Augie when he and Dan posed for a picture. Despite the obvious danger, Zoe insisted on getting a picture with Dan and the red jacket zombie as well.

Deeper down in the bowels of the ship there were even more zombies, but they weren't all clustered together in a horde. They mostly just stood there, bumping into the walls and furniture. The survivors quickly annihilated them.

By now, killing zombies had become somewhat routine to them. Not everyone fully adjusted to slaughtering the undead, but Augie seemed very comfortable with it now. His strategy was the same for each encounter. Firstly, he would rush ahead with great confidence to get the first hit in. Then he would allow everyone else to maim the target, before rushing in at the final moment to get the last hit and claim the kill.

***

They had spent the entire morning carefully scouring the ship for any stray zombies. The excitement had died down considerably. Destroying the infected wasn't as scary as it was initially — it had actually become a bit boring. Everyone was tired, even those who hadn't lifted a weapon; just walking around the ship was a workout.

By late afternoon, they finally sat down on the deck to eat. The sky was still dark and cloudy, but the rains had abated. The floor was wet from the recent downpour.

Food was abundant but with no living chef available, they had to prepare it on their own. Everything tasted delicious to the starving survivors. There were taters, steak, squid, veggies, pizza and juices from seven exotic fruits.

"Crusty, burnt food never tasted so good!" declared Dan, chewing on a slice of the squid.

Kelly puffed up her cheeks. Though she had no experience in cooking, she had attempted to prepare calamari.

"Try the pizza, Dan!" Zoe cut a large slice of the pizza she had made and replaced Kelly's squid. Zoe indiscreetly fed the squid to Bingo, who after having one bite, decided that he was not a fan of seafood.

The pizza was certainly more delicious than the squid. Dan devoured it while Zoe sat and watched, her eyes once again becoming pink pulsating hearts.

"Now try the steak! I know you need lots of protein!" said Zoe, pushing a huge slab of beef onto Dan's plate.

"I'm kinda full now..." said Dan, rubbing his belly. "I ate half of your pizza..."

"Eat it!"

"Okay!" Dan immediately stuffed his face with steak.

"How is it?"

"It's really good actually." Dan's stomach stretched to accommodate the delicious meat.

Zoe clapped her hands when Dan had finished his meal. She wanted nothing more than to offer her lips as Dan's dessert but held back for the moment.

"Ah yes, this is the life," said Augie, leaning back on his chair while taking a swig of passion fruit juice. "Killin' zombies and a free stay on a cruise ship. What more can I ask for?"

"Now that we're all safe and fed," said Zack, gobbling down the remainder of his chunky vegetables and guzzling a glass of water, "I need to get my ice cream."

Dan nodded while Ash, Augie, Kelly, and Zoe carried on eating, drinking, laughing, and talking. Zack strode off.

Bingo followed him closely. His mouth salivated upon a giant drumstick held tightly between his jaws. The meat and bone formed a large club-like weapon. If they encountered any zombies, Bingo was well equipped to join the fray.

"How many zombies did we kill today?" asked Dan. "I lost count."

"Forty-two," answered Augie.

"It could have been a lot worse. At least we can relax now," said Kelly.

"I needed a vacation anyway," said Ash, sipping a martini at the bar.

"Where's Rock?" asked Dan, realizing that he hadn't heard any insulting comments in this conversation.

"He found out that he's allergic to seafood," said Zoe. "Or maybe the squid wasn't cooked right."

"He must be destroying a toilet with human excrement," said Augie. "Wait, where do the toilets on cruise ships keep all their poop?"

***

Nestled at the very heart of the ship was a cosy tavern called The Pirate's Cove, where they served alcohol, ice cream and chicken wings. Wax candles cast yellow light upon the completely wooden interior. Mounted upon the walls were cutlasses, pistols and pictures of legendary pirates.

The windows were actually electronic screens that displayed 3D images of a cove with beautiful blue waters and a white, sandy shore. Sometimes, in this virtual dimension, a pirate ship would set anchor in deep waters and the buccaneers would come ashore in dinghies. The mermaids, who often came to bask on the rocks, would lure the pirates with the mystical power of breasts and drown them one by one. However, if the pirates spotted them first, an all-out battle ensued. The mischievous mermaids were usually safe in the water and rarely suffered any casualties.

Zack sat upon a stool at the bar. He looked out the window at the mermaid who kept her lower body hidden in the water while she beckoned an unsuspecting, young pirate.

Bingo hopped up onto a stool and wriggled his body until he was comfortably seated. He continued stripping the meat off the bone, savouring every bite.

"I'll have one ice cream, please," said Zack to the bartender. "Cone, no sprinkles."

The bartender was a beautiful female robot named Luna, almost indistinguishable from a human. Her attire was not unlike the typical pirate, except for a very tight corset around her waist. A brown tricorn hat adorned her head and knotted dreadlocks draped the sides of her bronze face. Between her exposed cleavage was a single black pearl, attached to a cord around her neck.

"Coming right up, mate," she responded in her usual flirtatious manner.

She handed Zack an edible cone with a swirl of white ice cream on top. "Here ya go, love. One ice cream cone, no sprinkles."

He held the waffle cone between his fingers and turned it slowly to admire its beauty. After overcoming great adversity, he had exactly what he wanted most. Or did he? While he was somewhat satisfied, his achievement felt anticlimactic. However, there was not much pleasure to be gained from gazing upon the frozen cream until it melted into sauce.

The ice cream was by far the most delicious thing served in The Pirate's Cove. The icy treat had the magical power of dispelling stress and replacing it with vivid imagination.

Zack's eyelids drooped as he began consuming his favourite snack. His arduous quest was finally complete. His worries faded and his mind became clear and focused.

The robot bartender set her eyes on one of the digital windows, and he did the same.

The mermaids and pirates were battling once again, but the most unusual thing had happened: the mermaid and pirate he had seen earlier were not engaged in battle. Instead, they embraced each other.

"They've fallen in love," said the bartender, clasping her hands together and placing them where her heart would be, if she were human.

"Love..." Zack muttered to himself.

The clarity of mind brought about by the ice cream made Zack realize that the biggest void in his life, which sucked the joy out of everything else, was love.

If love could save a dastardly pirate, surely it could do the same for Zack's depressed soul. He had seen the love that Zoe held for Dan. He needed love like that, yet here he was, spending time with a machine and virtual images. If love would not find him, he would try his best to give it.

"Thanks for the ice cream, Luna," said Zack, as he stood up and exited the tavern.

"You're welcome, love," replied the robot. "Take care!"

With a smile, he popped the last piece of the ice cream cone into his mouth and walked off with an uncharacteristic spring in his step. He certainly wasn't magically freed from the darkness within, but a seed of bright hope had been planted in his soul.

On his way back, Zack thought about how he could improve himself and help others. Of highest priority was dealing with the zombie menace. After that, he planned to help those in need — surely after the eradication of Zombosis, there'd be people struggling with their mental health who'd just like someone to talk to, animals in need of love like Bingo, and hungry bellies of all kinds to feed.

He had no doubt that love and happiness would find him. Something told him that everything was going to be alright. For the first time in as long as he could remember, Zack felt genuine joy and excitement for the future.

***

When Zack finally returned to the others, it was obvious that their zombie problem had not been properly taken care of. Bingo began barking madly, dropping the bone, which had been stripped bare.

Rock was fully zombified and on the attack. Everyone scrambled between the tables and slid chairs around to block the quick zombie. Rock was more likely suffering from parasites in his brain than an allergic reaction to squid.

Dan, who still kept his weapon with him at all times, was closing in on the infected Rock. Augie had gotten far away and didn't seem as brave as he was earlier.

Ash clocked the zombie on the jaw with a solid straight right punch. Out from the straw nest hat on Rock's afro emerged two tiny canaries. The birds flew in circles around the zombie's head and chirped like little yellow alarms.

"Sorry, but it turns out that your afro is going to be a bloody mess after all!" Dan shouted at the zombie.

Zombie Rock threw himself into the air, grabbed onto Ash's arm and clamped down with his jaws. Before Dan could get to them, the struggle had already sent both Ash and Rock over the edge, down to the infected port below.

Ash's neck snapped on impact and the zombies tore him apart. Rock's bones were also broken, and his body was trampled by the mass of undead.

The survivors stood frozen in shock, staring at each other with round, dewy eyes. They had just lost two of their people at a time when they genuinely felt safe. Everyone searched their memories for clues about Rock's infection but remained baffled. They'd all be suspected carriers until the mystery was solved.

Perspiration dripped down Augie's forehead as he breathed heavily. He reached inside his backpack, pulled out an asthma inhaler, and delivered its medicinal contents to his lungs.

Everyone kept a fair physical distance from each other. They didn't want to take the chance of having an unexpected zombie biting their skulls. But there were no more zombies around.

"H-how did R-Rock get infected?" Augie panted.

"He could have been bitten earlier," said Zack, his eyes still wide.

The sun sank low on the horizon. The survivors felt like death would creep up on them the moment the last rays of the sun were hidden.

"Rock's afro looked perfect," said Kelly, "and I didn't see any bite marks or blood."

"If there are crawlers on board, then we might be focked," said Dan, taking over the role as the potty mouth.

20

NEMESIS

[Day 4]

~A war cannot be won by one man unless he faces an army of cowards~

"MAYBE IT WAS SOMETHING he ate," suggested Zoe, stroking the straight, dark hair of her ponytail, which hung over her right shoulder. "Definitely not the pizza or steak. Probably the squid."

"If the infection could be spread by food, then we would all be undead," said Augie.

"I hope there are no crawlers on this ship," fretted Kelly. "We have nowhere to go now."

"Even if there were, I don't think they would infect us all. Like I said before, I think they're selective, so let's just hope none of us are selected," said Dan.

"If you feel like you're turning into a zombie, just jump off the ship please," said Zack.

"Well, if no one else plans on turning into a zombie right now, I suggest we head inside before nightfall," said Dan.

Rain began drizzling again. The remaining survivors

followed Dan back down into the ship. Zack brought up the rear.

Everyone was solemn and quiet. Zack could tell that they weren't handling the recent zombifications well.

"I thought the ship was safe now. For sure, for sure, it was safe," Augie mumbled.

They had just lost more survivors and even though Dan was still alive, he felt dead inside. Kelly no longer haunted his mind and his hopefulness had diminished almost to non-existence.

Zack was, ironically, the most positive among them. Dark thoughts possessed him no longer. His posture was strong and confident, and his face, relaxed.

Surrendering was easy, but none of the survivors had given up. Even as death stalked them as closely as their own shadows, they carried on.

They stood in the art gallery just off the ship's atrium. Several works of art hung within the small area — a painting of a red steam train, a wolf howling at a silvery moon, and a large white owl perched atop a tree's branch at night-time. There were even a few sculptures here as well. No holograms or machines — only paint, canvas, wood and stone. Bingo took the opportunity to urinate on a sculpted fire hydrant.

"So now what?" asked Zoe.

It was a good question, for this was as far as they intended to get.

"This might be one of those movies where everyone dies in the end," said Augie.

Augie was obviously getting panicky and hyper-stressed. Droplets of sweat covered his face.

"We just survive," said Zack.

"We need a hero!" shouted Augie. "A superhero!"

"Have you lost it? You should know better than anyone else what happens to the person who goes mad in zombie movies," said Dan.

Augie nervously gulped down a bolus of mucus and saliva.

The storm was gaining strength again. The fierce thunder was audible even from deep inside the ship. Heavy rain beat down on the round brass portholes, but it was almost invisible without sunlight.

The darkness of another unsettling night amplified the fear of death. All the survivors could do was hope that the infection wasn't on board with them — ignoring Rock's mysterious infection was the first step in comforting themselves.

"I need a nice long, warm shower to get my mind off everything," said Zoe.

"Do you want to be the shower scene victim?" asked Augie rhetorically.

"This isn't a movie!"

"Isn't it?!"

"You're insane!"

"We should all stay in the same room," suggested Zack.

"No room can hold all of us," said Kelly. "Besides, we girls could use some privacy now that we're safe."

"Did you not witness what just happened? Two people died when we thought we were safe!" argued Zack.

"We can each stay in adjacent rooms. That way, we would be close enough to help each other, and if anyone zombifies unexpectedly, they won't have anyone to kill," said Dan.

Everyone agreed with Dan and they found themselves five clean rooms, all within close proximity to each other. Bingo bunked with Zack.

***

That night the storm was as intense as ever. The survivors didn't dare go back on the deck, although they did search for any stray zombies they may have missed. They encountered neither zombies nor crawlers.

On the port side of the ship, the survivors could see the city lit up just as it had been the night before, and every time there was a flash of lightning, the massive horde of zombies could be seen shuffling below. So they chose to stay in the rooms with an ocean view, not that a tumultuous sea was the best view, but it was certainly better than an army of the walking dead.

The ship had power, food and water, which could keep them alive for some time – days at worst, but much longer with sustained energy. They were safe as long as none of the zombies got on board – impossible from the outside since the doors were sealed shut. The very recent deaths of Ash and Rock still bothered the survivors though. The origin of the infection on the ship remained an unnerving mystery.

Before the night's much-needed rest came dinner. They'd decided to make it fancy and dress up to unwind.

Everyone was excited about their first warm shower in days. The ladies each took no less than thirty minutes in the bathroom, half an hour more for applying makeup, and another thirty minutes to change into clean clothes. In one third of the time, the men had showered, shaved, and gotten dressed.

Kelly was able to find a nice black dress in one of Jill's

suitcases. Zoe wore a tight, red strapless dress she was sure would attract Dan's attention.

Makeup, hair, dresses, and nail polish were all normal parts of Kelly's routine but completely alien to Zoe, whose usual boyish style was in striking contrast.

Zack's clothes were a perfect fit for Dan, who searched for the most casual wear instead of the pressed shirts and ties; he wore a pair of faded black jeans, an off-white t-shirt and a fitted black blazer. Bingo happily wore a black bowtie around his neck, matching Zack's.

Augie didn't care what he wore. He was just relieved to have finally released the contents of his bowels into the porcelain toilet. For a while, he was nervous that it wouldn't flush, but it did. Then he became worried about clogging the pipes and overloading the waste tanks.

The survivors had decided to have dinner in the restaurant below deck. Unlike the deck's buffet restaurant where they had their earlier meal, this one was, under normal circumstances, much fancier, having three pairs of knives and forks, and waiters dressed like penguins. Of course, the waiters were understandably unavailable.

Everyone helped cook something, which they did mostly in silence. Eating as well was mostly quiet, except for the clanging of cutlery and crockery.

Dan was seated next to Kelly, around a circular table with an ivory tablecloth. On the opposite side was Zoe, who kept her eyes focused on Dan and sometimes on Kelly, just to make sure there was no physical contact.

"I wonder if this crab is real," said Dan, holding up a piece of meat that was impaled on his fork.

"If it tastes like crab, then that is good enough," said

Augie, stuffing his mouth with an entire potato.

"Anything will taste great after having your first shower in days," said Zoe.

"Not to mention starving for days," added Kelly.

"At least with the five of us, there's plenty to go around for a long time," said Zack.

A moment of awkward silence followed Zack's words. He was the only human survivor from the Infernal group. Everyone had lost friends, but Zack had no one.

"Augie, how do you plan to clean your braces?" asked Dan, staring at the potato-covered metal frame that forced Augie's teeth straight. "Actually, how do you plan to remove them if there are no dentists around?"

Augie began to eat faster. He swallowed his food without chewing, and had a nervous smile plastered across his face. "Ghe-he..."

Kelly jabbed her elbow into Dan's ribs as punishment for scaring an already shaken Augie.

Zoe jumped to her feet, ran around the table and grabbed Dan's arm. "Let's dance!"

"But there's no music," said Dan as he was lifted off his seat.

"We don't need it."

"I can't dance."

"It's easy. Just loosen up and do what feels right."

Zoe put her arms around Dan's shoulders, and he held on to her waist. They brought their bodies close together and began slow dancing. Zoe kept her eyes focused on Dan's before resting her head upon his chest.

Dan was no dancer, but this moment with Zoe was special. He forgot about the others, who were staring intently, even Kelly, who didn't seem to care.

Zoe then picked her head up, blew Dan a kiss and turned around. She bent over and jammed her buttocks into Dan's crotch. Her waist gyrated as she dropped her booty low to the ground, and then came back up, pressing hard against Dan's pelvis.

Everyone's jaws dropped simultaneously in response to Zoe's raunchy dance moves. Dan's part in the dance involved standing firmly in place, despite his partner's furious attempts to have their bodies merge.

The dance changed to yoga, with Zoe showing off her downward-facing dog pose, then transitioned seamlessly into the much more sexual wheelbarrow position.

Zoe's hands were planted on the ground and her legs around Dan's hips when a suspicious sound disturbed their dinner party. Everyone froze and listened – the sound was coming from the ship's atrium.

"Do you hear that?" whispered Dan.

"Footsteps!" said Kelly so quietly almost no one heard.

"I didn't know this ship was haunted!" squeaked Augie, biting his fingernails. "Zombies are okay but ghosts aren't my thing!"

"It sounds like only one zombie and it's coming this way. Get ready!" Zack leaped from his chair and grabbed his gun, which he had laid on the adjacent table.

Zoe reluctantly ended her mating ritual dance. Everyone stood up and faced the wide-open door that led to the ship's heart. Before they had the chance to say another word, the source of the footsteps was revealed.

"C-Captain Stone?!" choked Zoe.

His body bore no obvious wounds to suggest that he'd

been shot. The only clues were the blackened scars on his tattered bulletproof vest.

Bingo immediately began barking and growling as ferociously as he could. His fur stood on end and his body appeared to double in size.

"Oh shit! He's the last boss!" squealed Augie as he opened fire on the zombie soldier.

Just as he had done before, Stone displayed amazing agility, avoiding the slugs being fired by the amateur marksman. He hurled a table at the survivors, scattering them all except for Augie who was struck down.

Zack aimed his weapon at the zombie, trying to get a clear shot, but more tables had begun flying about. It was hard to keep track of Stone in all the chaos. When Zack finally had the target in his sights, a large object blocked his view — Stone had hurled Augie across the room, toward him.

Augie crashed into Zack with tremendous force, knocking the wind out of them both. Augie tumbled in the air and crushed a table to smithereens.

Stone stood over Zack and grabbed the assault rifle. A burst of bullets ejected with a fiery flash and punched a hole in the ceiling.

"Not this time," said Stone, as he tossed the gun to the furthest point in the room.

Bingo grabbed onto Stone's boot and pulled with all his might. His eyes glimmered yellow with fury and his teeth and claws seemed to have lengthened for combat.

The captain fell flat on his face, breaking his nose. He rolled onto his back and used his other leg to kick the attacking animal. Bingo sailed through the air with a whimper, the captain's boot still trapped in his jaws.

The zombie soldier stood up; the missing boot disturbed his perfect balance. He grabbed Zack's shirt and lifted him off the floor. His blood-red teeth were exposed as he snarled in preparation to bite into Zack's skull. But just in time, the familiar cricket bat came crashing down on the head of the zombie. Stone released his grip on Zack and stumbled on the spot. Another cranial strike came from the side. The zombie dropped to one knee.

The third strike didn't connect — Stone had wrapped his cold fingers around the bat, holding it just inches away from his skull. He flung it away, sending Dan crashing into a distant table.

The zombie was once again interrupted when he tried to infect Zack. Chairs had become missiles, which bombarded Captain Stone. He turned to face Zoe and Kelly, who both screamed and ran. Zoe's scream was particularly eardrum-shattering.

Stone left Zack on the floor and chased the two girls. With his speed, it would have only taken a couple seconds to reach either one of them. But it only took half that time for Dan to knock him down with a burst of bullets from Zack's gun.

Dan ran close to the zombie, who was already getting back to his feet. He aimed at Stone's head and pulled the trigger — nothing.

"You only had one shot!" Stone laughed as he stood up to face Dan. "You missed your chance!"

He grabbed Dan by the neck and growled as he motioned to bite into the cranium of his victim. This time, it was Zack who saved Dan, not a moment too soon — he grabbed both legs and tackled the zombie to the floor.

However, Stone still sank his teeth into living flesh. He had bitten Zack on the arm with bone-crushing force. Zack cried, grasping his wound from which blood flowed freely.

"Hahahahaha!" laughed zombie Stone, feasting on the pain of his victim. "HAHAHAHAHA!"

"Haul your MOTHERCUNT!" shouted Dan as he jumped into the air with his bat raised.

The wooden weapon splintered as it collided with Stone's head. The accursed soldier dropped to one knee but immediately stood up again. Dan continued pounding on the stone-hard head until the zombie finally fell prone, absolutely motionless.

"Zack's been bitten!" cried Zoe as she rushed to his side.

"Where's Augie?" asked Dan, noting that Augie had barely been in the action.

Augie hadn't moved from the spot Stone had put him. His body lay motionless in a nest of wooden fragments and tablecloths. Dan dashed to his friend's side.

A broken table leg had impaled Augie straight through his torso. Dan fell to his knees, his breathing heavy. After all the zombies, blood and guts, he never expected Augie to die — at least not this way.

"I can't... believe that... I have to die the... lame death..." Augie choked over the blood issuing from his mouth. "At least... I survived long enough for... my dramatic last words..."

"And you didn't even get infected," said Dan, bitterly.

"Ghe-he..." Augie chuckled and spat blood. "Indeed..."

His eyes closed slowly, and his body went limp. Augie was the master survivor, but now he was dead. If it weren't for Augie, Dan would have probably died on the first day of the infection. In fact, everyone from the Nightmare group may not have made it as far as they did. Augie died a hero's death.

"I can't stay here," said Zack, through clenched teeth.

He got to his feet and began walking slowly out of the room. A limping Bingo clambered to his side.

"Where will you go?" asked Zoe.

"It doesn't matter as long as I'm not on the ship."

"Those things will tear you apart! You can't go down there while you're still alive."

"NONE OF YOU ARE LEAVING!" the zombie had gotten back to his feet.

He made to attack Dan first, but his head immediately exploded as a spray of slugs cleaved his bone, flesh and neural tissue.

"Bag yourself up, man..." muttered Augie with his final breath, "you dead."

And those were the last words of the zombie expert Augie. He would have been proud.

The permanent reality of every death and loss possessed Dan, and he was overcome with fear. His entire body trembled, and his accelerated breathing couldn't satiate his need for air. Panic paralyzed him and hope abandoned him.

The room dimmed and Dan's heart pounded, each beat like the boom of a great bass drum. With every beat, the blackness thickened.

Fortunately, Dan's condition was not contagious.

Kelly's hand touched his right shoulder, and Zoe's grabbed his left. He wasn't alone. Dan accepted that reality was irreversibly changed, but there was still hope for happiness. Colours gradually returned like a creeping sunrise.

Everyone remained still until they were sure that the zombie boss had been truly defeated, and Dan's courage returned like water filling an empty vessel. Zack shuffled out of the room, grasping his wound, which bled profusely.

The girls grabbed the ankles of the captain and dragged him up to the deck. Their cheeks were stained with running black mascara.

By the time they arrived on the ship's deck, Zack was already pale and panting. The rain was still pouring, and the night was as cold and dark as ever. They threw the zombie into the horde below.

"Now I guess it's my turn," said Zack, his voice hoarse. "Writing our story is up to you now, Dan."

Dan nodded but didn't know what to say.

"Finally, I can be in peace," said Zack, clasping his hands and closing his eyes.

He felt the infection taking over. His vision became blurry, his body numb, and all sounds distorted into incomprehensible noise. He had to jump, or the others would be in danger.

He thought back to day one of the infection, when he couldn't jump off the building. He was glad that he didn't. He had already fulfilled his wish to help others.

However, he expected more. He was so sure that his quality of life was going to skyrocket. Alas, his positive thoughts weren't enough to forge blessings. Perhaps his next life would be better.

With no regrets, Zack leaped off the ship and fell into the darkness below.

Bingo howled for the loss of his friend and cried for the hours that followed.

And so, everyone from the Infernal group was dead and gone, except, of course, Bingo.

21

CLEAR SKIES

[Day 5-7]

~Only after the turmoil has passed do you think the suffering was worth it~

AT DAWN ON THE fifth day after the Zombosis outbreak was Augie's funeral. It was an unofficial ceremony dedicated to all who had been lost. The sky was blue and remarkably bright as the sun rose slowly. The only traces of rainclouds wafted away in the cool morning breeze. There was little evidence to prove that a terrible tropical storm had ravaged the port only a few hours earlier.

Neither Zoe nor Kelly knew Augie well enough to say a few final words about him. Dan was mostly silent as well. He still found it difficult to accept that beneath the white sheet on the ship's deck was Augie's dead body.

Augie's contribution to their survival was invaluable. His contribution to Dan's life as a friend was worth just as much. The biggest zombie fan in the world could not have hoped for a better farewell — experiencing the zombie apocalypse, killing the zombie boss, and dying without even being infected.

"Thank you, Augie, for everything," he finally said, "for without you none of us would have gotten this far. You were a good friend, and I will be sure to tell the world of how you helped us survive the zombie apocalypse."

Dan pulled the white sheet away, looked at his friend's lifeless face for a moment, then averted his eyes. He squatted and placed his forearms under Augie's back and knees. His legs shook as he lifted the heavy load. With slow, laboured steps, he carried Augie to the edge of the upper deck.

Kelly and Zoe helped Dan lift and roll Augie over the railing into the ocean, which was now calm and blue.

"May his soul rest in peace, along with all the others taken by the infection," said Kelly with a bowed head.

The place seemed so serene. The rising sun shimmered in the sea and made the world feel like it was a better place. Even the horde of undead on the port had vanished.

Their goal now was just to survive until rescue arrived. They never saw the infected enter deep bodies of water, so naturally, a ship was the safest place they could be.

The mystery of how Stone had gotten on board was solved that day and Dan cut the rope that Rock had attached to the ship. He would have felt better if the ship wasn't so close to land, but piloting the vessel ran far too great a risk of damaging it to the point where they needed to abandon it and return to the cursed land.

Nowhere on the ship did they find any crawlers, stragglers or stowaways. Now that the zombie nightmare was at an end, Dan could enjoy the company of his fellow survivors.

Zoe always kept very close to Dan, successfully wooing

him with charm and persistence. She made her feelings for him very clear, and by the night of the fifth day, their bodies merged just as she had craved.

"Doe!" blurted out Zoe while lying in bed.

"What?" Dan responded.

"Our couple name. 'D' from 'Dan' and 'oe' from 'Zoe'! It's perfect!" Zoe squealed and kicked her legs in the air.

Dan truly did fall for Zoe. He respected Kelly's desire to get married, but he wasn't going to be a bridesmaid – he never even asked about it again. Perhaps if he had tried to steal Kelly's heart before Zoe confessed her love for him, things could have turned out differently.

Kelly didn't make it apparent that Doe affected her to any degree. She didn't think of Dan the same way he thought about her. Kelly wanted nothing more than to have her old life back. She promised herself that she would appreciate it more.

Days passed without event and everyone's spirits had risen, especially Dan's. Not a single zombie had been spotted all the while, giving the impression that they were no longer an issue. But they knew better than to wander out into the city.

The survivors passed the time by retelling the story of their survival, while Dan documented everything, as Zack had requested.

Zoe also documented her own events. She recorded when she first met Dan and everything they did since then. She also planned their future together, including being wed within five years and having three children within nine years; she even knew all of their names.

***

It was the evening of the seventh day. The sky was orange and there were a few wisps of clouds moving slowly in the gentle breeze. It felt just like what a tropical island cruise sunset should be like. Zoe had mixed Dan a martini with a green olive on a skewer.

Zoe had never consumed alcohol before the cruise and was drunk after a single shot. Kelly, on the other hand, had a rum barrel in her belly.

"You know, it's strange that it was only a few days ago we were cracking zombie skulls," said Dan, glancing down at his battle-worn cricket bat. "Now we're talking about babies."

He lay on a lounge chair on the deck, absorbing the late afternoon rays with his exposed chest. Kelly sat beside him and Zoe was at the nearby bar. Both girls were also tanning their bodies with the cool sunlight.

"You should be grateful for the peace," shouted Zoe before taking a shot of something she had mixed.

"It's been an entire week," said Kelly. "I wonder when we'll be rescued."

"I'm happy right where we are," said Zoe, drunkenly running to Dan and planting a kiss on his lips.

She dropped her body upon his and the kissing intensified. Kelly rolled her eyes and looked away.

For all they knew, they could have been the last people on the planet. A grim thought, but in this moment, things weren't so bad.

"I haven't seen a zombie in days," said Dan, finally coming up for air.

"Don't tell me you're missing them now, Dan," said Kelly. "They're like cockroaches."

"Except they can't survive if you cut off their heads," added Zoe.

Zoe pulled a lounge chair close to Dan's and lay upon it, never once breaking the contact her hand had with his. She was in an absolutely blissful state. Nothing that happened in the past mattered while she was with him. In her mind, fireworks were set off every time they kissed, and heart-shaped balloons drifted off toward a double rainbow whenever they touched.

"It's been so long. I just wish I knew how my family is doing." Kelly looked up longingly at the sky as if it could grant her wish.

Dan couldn't predict life beyond the present. All that there was now, was Zoe. She had so suddenly moved into his heart and evicted Kelly. His affection for her grew consistently until she became all that mattered. Now more than ever, Dan feared the zombie curse that could separate them.

From the ship's deck, they had a full view of the city and mountains. While the ship still ran on power reserves, the island was silent, and the nights were pitch-black.

The sun turned into a red ball and slowly descended as night-time drew closer.

Bingo spent most of his time sitting in the spot where Zack had jumped. Perhaps he hoped that Zack would return. He hadn't made a sound in days, so it was peculiar when he suddenly began barking at the sky.

Then there was a noise like no other they had ever heard before — an explosive crack followed by strange whirring. A squadron of flying machines zipped across the sky before breaking formation and going off in different directions.

"The flare gun!" shouted Dan.

Kelly kept the ship's emergency flare with her just as Dan did his bat. They had been waiting for the ideal time to use it — there was no better time than now.

Kelly aimed in the air and fired without delay. A red flare burst in the sky above like a giant firework, and left a red trail as it slowly fell.

"They must be here to recon," said Dan. "There's no way they would miss the flare."

The island's military had no machinery as advanced as those aircraft, which meant that outland aid was inbound.

"At least they decided not to nuke us," said Zoe, waving her arms to grab the attention of the potential rescuers.

The trio embraced each other, overjoyed that things were steadily improving. Soon they would be rescued, and Kelly could be reunited with her husband-to-be. Doe would be able to live the life planned in its entirety by Zoe, which included Bingo as the family dog.

"The nightmare is finally over," said Dan.

Epilogue

At this point, you have two choices: you can stop reading and believe that the story ended happily for Dan, Zoe, Kelly and Bingo. Believe that they were rescued, and Kelly was reunited with her family and eventually got married. That Dan and Zoe lived a long, happy life together with three kids and Bingo. That everything on the island returned to normal.

Or you can keep reading and discover the extended ending.

*

The aircraft were not there to rescue anyone. They were there to put an end to the threat. The infection had grown out of control and could have easily spread to the mainland.

The world leaders who attended the summit were all dead. In fear of having the infection spread to other countries, a drastic decision was made — eradicate with the power of Shivastra.

Shivastra was a powerful cannon that orbited the planet, originally designed to obliterate extra-terrestrial threats. Morality always prevented its use as a weapon of mass destruction. Zombosis was the ideal excuse for testing its maximum destructive power.

For the first time, Shivastra was fired at full power toward the earth. A beam of concentrated energy scorched the heart of the island, destroying almost everything. Only the coasts were spared destruction.

The island became a desert wasteland. The population, which had been over a million people, was reduced to mere hundreds.

Zombosis was successfully eradicated, but there was immediate political backlash. Rescue operations were launched by every country capable of sending aid, each racing to claim first credit.

All survivors were rounded up and evacuated. Dan, Zoe, Kelly and Bingo were taken to a facility in the far north. Everyone was thoroughly screened for any trace of infection.

After two months of being kept for safety and research, the survivors were formally released and integrated into a new world. Aside from the climate, their new home was similar to their lost one, even better in many ways.

Buildings and people were taller and wider as if the air made them grow larger. Roads were broader and smoother and connected large cities. There were more vehicles but less traffic. The people were beautiful, strong and diverse. There wasn't much to complain about but the freezing cold winter, from which there was no escape.

The trio spent some time in a large city but eventually parted ways.

Kelly was fortunate enough to have been reunited with her fiancé. They got married and had two beautiful children — one boy and one girl.

Zoe met with her first love and fell for him as quickly as she did with Dan. As Dan's love for her grew, her love for him diminished. Zoe disappeared one day, leaving behind a note. Lazily scrawled on a badly torn piece of paper, she wrote that she was in love with another and that it was best that Dan move on.

Dan was heartbroken but Bingo kept him company until he met a wonderful woman and fell in love again. After years of consistency, he finally completed and published his written account of the Zombosis adventure. He married and raised his own family, which included two more dogs to keep Bingo company.

The official account of the events stated that a highly contagious disease killed most of the island's population, and the spread was stopped by a weapon of world peace. The existence of the walking dead was downplayed and even denied.

Zombosis became a popular story and urban legend.

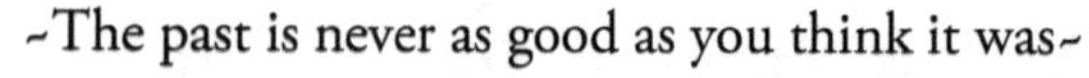
~The past is never as good as you think it was~

APPENDIX

TITLE: A STUDY OF THE HUMAN NEURAL PARASITE

Introduction

The Human Neural Parasite (HNP) is an internal arthropodan parasite, which is capable of infecting multiple species. While humans can serve as viable hosts, they are not the primary hosts of the parasite.

The HNP was originally discovered in a rodent species found in a tropical rainforest habitat. It shares a mutualistic relationship with its primary host and intraspecies transmission is achieved via non-fatal bites. There is no natural cross-species transmission while in its normal host.

The HNP was manually transferred to another rodent host. Within this new host, the HNP became parasitic. In all tests, every host species other than the primary lost conscious brain functions. The parasites forced their new hosts to bite and infect every other animal to complete their natural reproductive cycle. Unlike with the primary host, infections were not confined to a single species.

The HNP is capable of infecting any host with a complex nervous system that is controlled by a brain. However, only *Homo sapiens* provide a suitable host environment that can sustain the parasite for extended periods of time. Other infected species display aggressive behaviour but die after a twenty-four-hour period. All infected are infectious.

The HNP grants its original host increased physical strength by pushing bodily functions to the maximum. The same is seen in humans, where all muscle fibres are activated, making them stronger, faster and without any apparent fatigue.

A unique ability granted to humans when infected is possible biological immortality. While the host may be subject to decay over time, it is capable of regenerating to the point where tissues do not completely diminish. The host will, therefore, exist indefinitely, as long as it periodically consumes flesh to facilitate regeneration.

The major downside to human infection is brain destruction. The HNP destroys brain tissues so that the host loses all conscious abilities and is considered brain-dead. The parasite then has full motor control over the host's body. Its only purpose at this point is to attack other animals for two reasons: 1. To reproduce by spreading to a new host (infected hosts are sterile) 2. As a food source for regeneration.

*

Mechanism

The primary means of transmission of the parasite between hosts is via bites. Any region of the body can be targeted as long as tissues are penetrated; the head and neck are most often selected. Once the skin is breached, the parasites contained in the infected host's saliva (which appears blood red due to contamination by parasites) enter the body of the new host.

By following the nervous system, the HNP (juvenile stage) relocates from the site of infection to the host's brain. The length of this process can vary, depending on where the victim is bitten. A neck bite can result in zombification within minutes, while a foot infection can take up to an hour.

Upon reaching the brain, the HNP develops into a cocoon form and metamorphoses into its adult stage. This pupal stage is the shortest of any known organism, estimated to be under a minute for a full transformation. The emerging adult exists in a sedentary body form and secretes chemicals that cause selective destruction of the brain.

The HNP then assumes control of the host's body, being able to control movement and use all senses as a normal human would. The rate at which the host loses control depends on the number of juveniles that enter the body and make it to the brain.

It is important to note that while the host's memories are removed from the brain, muscle memory is retained. This means that the body would still be able to perform actions that it used repeatedly throughout life.

Once the parasite assumes control, the adults reproduce sexually, producing eggs. In the human host, these eggs follow two paths. In the first path, the eggs hatch into juveniles that reside in the host's saliva.

The juveniles are also referred to as "crawlers" when they become mobile and search for a new host to infect. They only do this if their host's body no longer functions. They crawl in search of a new host and can penetrate skin to infect their victim. Because of their small individual size, crawlers can easily avoid detection, although a large number would be conspicuous.

The second path of the egg targets the host's muscles. Tissues are infected by a stage of the parasite that takes the form of a cyst. These cysts survive as long as they are encased within muscular tissue. The most efficient way to destroy the cysts is by burning the infected tissue.

The purpose of the cyst is to infect any animal that consumes the infected flesh. The tough outer layer protects it from destruction by gastric fluids, including acid. In the intestines, the parasite emerges in the juvenile stage to make its way to the brain. However, the path is not as simple as pathway one (bite infection) and the parasite can become disoriented, causing it to stay in juvenile form and eventually die without affecting the host. If a large number of cysts are consumed, the odds of a successful infection are significantly higher.

*

Sign and Symptoms

The onset of the infection is quite rapid. Zombification ranges from minutes to an hour. When the HNP settles in the brain, the host loses control within a span of seconds or minutes, depending on the severity of the infestation. Memories fade and the senses dull, most notably vision. Headaches and nausea are also common just before brain death. Once these symptoms are being exhibited, zombification is close to completion.

The zombified host is easy to identify, especially as time

passes. The initial stage symptoms include dilated pupils and faded irises (which become as white as the sclera), extremely aggressive animalistic behaviour, and a "bleeding" mouth (the appearance of the juveniles/crawlers).

During the initial phase, zombies have extreme strength and speed. They also have a heightened sense of awareness for uninfected potential hosts. They select targets if faced with multiple potential host choices. The primary criterion for this selection is host vulnerability – that is, targeting the weak, easily infected individuals.

The zombies use ambush tactics to spread the infection, especially during the later stages of Zombosis. They form large groups (hordes) in a process termed "mobbing" to gain the advantage of numbers. They may remain hidden until prey presents itself.

The zombies have an extremely strong urge to bite and infect other hosts, and normally leave the body mostly intact. But they must also feed on tissues periodically to maintain their optimum state. If a zombie does not feed for a twenty-four-hour period, its body slows down considerably, and it can only move about with slow, jerky movements. In such a state, zombies depend on overwhelming numbers or surprise attacks to capture prey. After a feeding frenzy, these "walkers" are reenergized and become "runners" once again. Note that although walkers move slowly, their strength is in no way impaired.

The infected remain mostly silent until a potential victim is detected. Runners snarl and screech when chasing their victim, while walkers groan. The noise is both an instrument of fear and a way of communicating that prey is nearby.

Zombies that are several days old (late phase) exhibit signs of decomposition such as foul stench and rotting bodies. In addition to reenergizing the muscles, feeding also facilitates bodily regeneration but never to a pre-zombified state.

Handling of corpses when death is due to Zombosis
The head must be severed from the body of the animated corpse, or its brain must be crushed/ scrambled.

- Impervious gloves and clothing must be worn when handling cadavers.

- All orifices are to be packed with cotton soaked in a biocide.

- Bodies are to be wrapped in plastic or impervious fabric.

- Any leakage of bodily fluids must be cleaned up and the area cleansed with a biocide.

- Bodies must be cremated as soon as possible.

GLOSSARY

Crawlers — The juvenile life stage of the HNP, which leave a non-functional host in search of a new one. They are red in colour and virtually invisible to the naked eye unless in great numbers. They are infectious and can penetrate human skin.

Horde — A large group of zombies.

Human Neural Parasite (HNP) — The parasite that causes Zombosis (i.e. the causative agent).

Mobbing — The act of zombies forming a large group/horde.

Runners — Humans become runners when first infected and are capable of running very quickly. Vocalizations are normally high-pitched and loud.

Walkers — Zombies that have not consumed any flesh within twenty-four hours become slower and can no longer run. They use lower pitched, quieter noises than runners.

Zombie — A human that is brain-dead and fully under the control of the HNP. A zombified animal carries a hyphenated name: zombie-cat; zombie-dog, etc.

Zombification — The process of being infected and

becoming a zombie.

Zombify — To turn into a zombie.

Zombosis — The condition that describes the state of a zombie.